A Force of Nature

A Tryst of Fate Series Novel—Book 2

KARA LIANE

Cover design by Francessca's PR & Designs. Cover images by DepositPhotos.com.

Edited by Mountains Wanted Indie Author Services.

Author logo designed by the author through Canva.com.

Clipart chapter images by Pixabay.com.

ISBN-13: 978-0-578-20079-8

Disclaimer: This book is intended for an adult audience. This work of fiction contains strong language and explicit sexual scenes, with mature content, that may not be appropriate for anyone under the age of eighteen. Potential triggers for readers may be present, including a discussion about PTSD.

Also by Kara Liane

***

Playing Heart to Get—A Tryst of Fate Series Novel—Book 1

Every Heart Inch—A Tryst of Fate Series—Novella 1

Heart to Follow—A Tryst of Fate Series—Novella 2

***

Dedication

This book is solely dedicated to all the heroes of the United States military, past, present, and future. I thought this would be a fun, romantic way to bring a side of your story to life—with a little bit of spice. However, I need to touch on the dark, the deep, and the pain. You're out there in the trenches each and every day, and the men and women serving this country have my unwavering support. God bless you for what you do! I am only here today with the ability to be a writer because you gave it to me. Each service member plays a part. To the families that are left at home, I acknowledge you as the unsung heroes; when the military serves, you serve too. Much love, thanks, and appreciation from my military family to yours.

Table of Contents

Prologue

Brenneth

June 2003
Baghdad, Iraq

Motherfucker, this is not what I signed up for! The more I look around the tent that I currently call home, the more pissed off I get. It's dusty as shit from the sand and hot as hell from the sun—which already went down, but you wouldn't know it from the scorching temperature. I'm not a whiny pussy, so don't start on me. I just thought things would be different with serving in the military.

And don't get me wrong, I know I'm the one who chose to join and take the sacred oath. But shit, who could have predicted we'd go to damn war? It is my duty, and I am proud to serve, but a part of me wonders how long this will go on. Right now, it doesn't feel like there is an end in sight.

I just turned twenty a couple of months ago, and every single goddamn day I am reminded that I am not invincible. I am reminded that I could be "next." I am reminded that war is hell. And I am reminded that it doesn't matter if I'm on the front lines or not—when my number is up, it's up.

I am a cargo loader, well, technically an aerial porter, working right on the flight line. We're called the port dawgs of the air force. You could say that getting shot at constantly adds to the stress. When you're out uploading or downloading an aircraft, what the hell do you think the enemy is aiming for? If you answered "the fucking aircraft," then you're correct. So those of us on the ground working the missions are just casualties—the result of being in the right place at the wrong time.

Part of my job is HR, which means "human remains." Loading dead bodies takes its fucking toll on the mind. Every single day, I'm tempted to snatch the satellite phone and call back to Texas to hear my parents' voices. I am also desperate to talk to Little Bit. I miss my baby sister; she's only nine. I dread not being there while she's growing up, especially without my protection. But I can never find the courage to call back home. I am weak and pathetic. I can't let my family know I'm over here bleeding fear. So I opt to write letters instead; letters are a safe choice. No internet means no email, so snail mail is all we've got.

Where the hell is home now for me, anyway? I was stationed in Oklahoma, and after only being there a little over a year, I got tasked for deployment to this shithole. Neither BMT (Basic Military Training) nor tech school could have prepared me for this. I joined in 2001 but before September 11, before America was forever changed. Yup, I was just fresh out of high school and thought I knew what signing on the dotted line meant. Shit, I had it all wrong. Would I do anything differently, though? Hell no! I get the feeling I'm meant to be here.

The siren is going off again. Another mortar attack coming in. I won't even bother to get under my bed this time for shelter. What's the point? I'm just an A1C (Airman First Class), and no one cares about a young rookie airman. I might as well bend over and kiss my ass goodbye. Hell, I am just another number, just another pawn in this game that I will never understand.

Everyone is shouting outside my tent.

Then, dead silence.

Chapter 1: Falling Up the Stairs

Brenneth

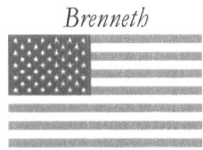

December 17, 2016

I was sitting next to my brother-in-law, Alexi, at my little sister's college graduation from Temple University. We were packed in the auditorium like sardines, and my air force blues uniform was suffocating me more each minute. The air tasted stale, and I was constantly fidgeting—to no fucking end. Let me be clear, though, in saying that I did want to be there. I was so proud of my little sis, Caylan, who happens to be Alexi's wife. She graduated with honors with a bachelor's in environmental science.

I am in awe of the woman she has become. I've always been incredibly overprotective of her, so after a recent attack and kidnapping by a pseudo ex-boyfriend from our home state of Texas—and when I found out I had been left out of the ordeal of her first attack the year prior—I went ballistic. God, that's a long story in itself. But as a family, we've worked through everything and agreed there would be no more secrets. I know why they kept me in the dark, though. They knew I would have gone after that worthless, doesn't-deserve-to-live, piece-of-shit Greg after the first assault.

When he pursued her a second time, Alexi and I came to her rescue. We found her in an abandoned warehouse down by Penn's Landing in Philadelphia, Pennsylvania. I had my finger on the trigger and the gun aimed right at Greg's head. I almost fucking blew away the scumbag, but Caylan stopped me. With her being pregnant and scared, and in such a vulnerable state at that moment, it was a sobering experience. It snapped me out of my crippling rage. I had realized I couldn't let her witness me become a killer, even if the bastard deserved it.

But it's okay; he got it in the end. Moments after we fought off Greg and saved my sister, he fell into a hole in the floor at the warehouse that was on the river. All three of us watched the lowlife drown in the murky water at our feet. I still hadn't lost one night of sleep over his death. What I had lost sleep over, though, was thinking about what she must have endured. The details of her attacks turned my stomach.

Christ, she's my baby sister. How was I supposed to forgive myself for failing her? I've been trying to get better about realizing she's not mine to watch over anymore. Well, of course I always would watch over her, but Alexi was the main man for the job now; the fucker makes that quite clear at every opportunity.

Caylan was right: I would have been discharged from the military and consequently thrown in prison if I had acted on my impulses about what to do to the little shit. I should be grateful in some ways that she never told me previously about the horrors. All that is holding me together these days is knowing I have a career and a job to do. This was a calling for me. I bleed fucking red, white, and blue. But my PTSD was bad, hence the problem I was having being stuffed into that place like cattle.

I kept wishing Greg had been there for me to take out all of my anger and frustration on. *Pfft,* he got off easy. I would have derived so much satisfaction from using him as a human punching bag, pummeling him into oblivion. That would have been well worth whatever consequences I would have faced. I wouldn't have divulged that little fantasy to anyone, though. They'd have locked me up in some loony bin and thrown away the key. I'd surely have gotten med-boarded after intense psych evals, and my long fifteen years of military service would have been for nothing. No, no one could know my innermost thoughts.

I intentionally nudged Alexi in the side but played it off like it was accidental. I liked giving him a couple shots here and there. Don't get me wrong, I like the dude, and he is good for my sister. But let's face it—no guy will ever be good enough for Caylan. And damn Alexi for trying to do things his way all the time! Like I said, I'm still learning to step back and let him handle things when it comes to her, but it's hard. I'm eleven years older than she is, so you have to understand that she's always been my responsibility. I've never felt burdened by it, though. I love her so much.

I couldn't believe I was going to be an uncle. Caylan was seven months pregnant at the time, with my niece. She wore pregnancy well. She glowed, and it was a sight to behold. There was no baby name then, so I'd taken to calling her "Lil' Bits" since I used to call Caylan "Little Bit." I hoped I wasn't going to get deployed again anytime soon, that I'd actually be there for the birth. My "tempo band," or deployment window rather, fell right around the time she was due. I had not been tasked yet, but I figured inevitably someone in my squadron would not have been able to fulfill the slot. That they'd probably send me back to one of the various wastelands. I was all healed up from my surgery the previous May. The doctors repaired my leg after an injury I sustained while I was in Afghanistan. I went through intense physical therapy for months, but I was fully cleared and ready to go.

Alexi had turned to me like he had something to ask, but then we heard the name we'd been waiting for announced from the stage.

"Caylan Bree Graham," the announcer called out.

Caylan walked across the stage, and we all cheered, hooted, and hollered. Shit, I was so damn proud! She was going after her dreams. I need to take lessons from my little sis; I've wasted too many years not going after some of mine.

Once my sister's name was announced, I couldn't sit a moment longer. The walls were closing in on me. I was sweating profusely, and I knew I was about to rip my uniform to shreds any damn second, clawing it the hell off me. What a disgrace I'd be to my branch then.

I had to get the hell out of there. I abruptly stood up and damn near crushed the gift bag at Alexi's feet. What a friggin' pussy that one is. He spoils my sister, but I guess I should be grateful she has someone to dote on her. Damn, I only got her a card!

My parents and cousin Meg all had concerned looks on their faces as I darted out of the stadium seating. They probably thought I was losing it, but I didn't give a fuck because I was. My heart was pounding so hard, I thought it would thump right out of my chest. I was clambering for the nearest exit. I frantically looked in all directions. It appeared up was the way to go. I continually stumbled and fell up the stairs trying to get my footing. What a freaking embarrassment. My shiny black shoes were surely scuffed up. This was not how I wanted to present myself to the world when I was in uniform. Being an airman is a way of life, not just a job.

I made it out through the exit and down the corridor. I was looking in both directions to find the goddamn restroom. The area was completely empty, which made me breathe a sigh of relief. I decided to turn right and head that way.

Out of nowhere, I ran into a woman.

It was a hard hit. After all, I am a big fucking guy. I just saw a mass of blonde curls and arms and legs flailing about.

"Shit!" I exclaimed as I tried to stand up.

Add a dirty uniform from the dusty floor to the list of things going wrong. I brushed off some of the dirt and then realized she was still on her ass with her head cast down. I didn't know who ran into whom, but where the hell were my manners? I guessed they up and left with my goddamn brain when I ran from my seat. I've always tried to portray a gentleman when I wear my blues, but that day I was failing miserably on all counts. I reached down for the woman's hand, and she looked up with disdain and annoyance etched on her face. I sucked in a sharp breath. If I wasn't already sweating, I'd have been a friggin' tidal wave of perspiration by then anyway.

Fuck, she was hot! She looked to be about my age, so I felt tongue-tied at first. Her face was heart-shaped and framed by bouncy golden spirals going off in every direction. She had emerald-green eyes and freckles splashed across her dusky-apple cheeks and narrow nose. Her lips were a delicate pink, and she had a dainty silver nose ring in her right nostril—it was sexy as hell. The matching silver hoops in her ears stuck out noticeably, but I didn't make it past her face because she interrupted my gawking.

"Well, shit. What a nice greeting, soldier," she grumbled.

I righted her onto her feet and took in the rest of her body. Unfortunately, it was well hidden behind layers of clothes. But I could tell she was lean. I'm six one, and she looked to be about five nine. She was wearing some kind of denim ballet slippers or flats—whatever chicks call them. Her flowy, ankle-length, patterned skirt gave her a bohemian-chic look. Her top was white and tucked into the skirt to give it that billowy effect. She'd paired those with a cropped denim jacket.

Shit, it's a good thing I know a few terms about fashion from my baby sister, I laughed to myself.

Whatever this chick was wearing didn't really matter, though. She could have been in tatters, and she would have looked just as alluring. How she'd stayed warm in it through the December cold was beyond me. With her golden skin, she belonged on a beach, not in Philadelphia. She began tapping her foot, clearly waiting for something.

She ran into me, I realize when I replay the scene in my mind.

What, like an apology? Tough shit, cupcake.

"Airman," I stated back.

"What?" she questioned me with snarkiness to her tone.

"I'm an airman, not a soldier. Airmen are in the air force. Soldiers are army. Big difference, sweetheart," I clarified.

She scoffed and returned with, "Does it really fucking matter at this point? And don't call me 'sweetheart.' I'm a woman. Big difference, buttercup."

Wow, she had a damn mouth on her. I didn't know if I liked it or not yet. With my hackles up, I decided to set the young woman straight.

"Fair enough, *ma'am*," I said sarcastically.

She narrowed her eyes into tiny, piercing slits. If I know anything, I know women do *not* like to be called "ma'am" unless they're much older. No woman likes to seem aged before her time. I stifled my laugh. Shit, she was easy to rile up.

This could actually be fun.

Normally the women I screwed around with just wanted a good time in the sack or some company to go to dinner and a movie with. I'd go out to bars or find lonely women who were fellow NCOs around the base to keep me company.

I'd never had a serious relationship. It was just too hard with all the deployments. Who in her right mind would voluntarily sign up for this kind of life? Being married to a service member is like being married to a ticking time bomb. You never know when the hell we might go off; I mean this in many different respects. We're a unique breed because we have to be.

I looked at the lanyard hanging from her neck. It appeared to be some kind of a press badge. I reached for it. She must have thought I was going to grab her tits, because she blocked me with lightning-fast reflexes. She swatted my hands away furiously.

"Whoa there, Karate Kid!"

"Hands off, buddy," she admonished. Then she followed it up with a sugary-sweet, sarcastic tone, "I mean . . . airman."

My dick was pissed off and turned on in equal measure. How the fuck was that possible? This woman pissed me off *and* made me want to cover her in cum. I smiled at her. I realized I had to take back control of the situation. This was a game I was willing to play all day—and night—if I had to.

"Technical sergeant, actually," I corrected her.

She tilted her head to the side and narrowed her eyes again while pursing her lips. I could see the wheels turning.

Before she could respond, I went on to say, "I am an airman, but it's more of a generic term, much like *soldier* is. I should be addressed by my rank, which is technical sergeant."

She laughed in a haughty manner and retorted, "Oh, I'm sorry. Is this introduction time? Well then, you can address me as 'Your Highness.'"

Wow, this woman was thorny and hot as hell.

Thorny and horny rhyme, hmm.

I just grinned widely back at her. She tapped her foot again. It was cute the way she got so mad.

"By the way, Your Highness, I wasn't reaching for your tits. I was looking at your badge," I claimed.

She looked confused at first, then glanced down at her chest and back up to meet my gaze. "I knew that!" she announced, but clearly she *hadn't* known.

I bit my tongue to keep from quipping back with something just as sharp as her bite. I had a sneaking suspicion this would not be the last time I'd cross paths with the woman, so I tried to rein in my need to rib her. Call it intuition or whatever you want, but I felt surely we'd meet again.

For some odd reason, she held the badge out to me, away from her chest, in acceptance. It still dangled on the lanyard around her neck.

I took a step closer. Her neck was so delicate; I could see her collarbones stick out from the sides. I found that feature so sexy. I wanted to lick her right there. Once I was closer to her, I could smell a light scent of cucumber and melon. I held the badge in my palm and flipped it over. It read, "Everly Reynolds, Reporter, *Philly Timez.*"

Hmm never heard of her—or the publication, for that matter.

I let the ID fall from my hand. It swung back to rest again on her chest. I watched the movement. Shit, I wished I knew what her body looked like under those flowy clothes. She took a deep, shuddering breath. Gone was her bristly-cactus attitude. Before me suddenly was a more serene, peaceful woman with a hungry look in her eyes.

I was left thinking, *What the fuck?*

Then she shook her head as if to clear it, and the prickly side of her came back again.

"Okay. Well, I have to go, creampuff. I'm covering a story about college graduations and the success rates of students obtaining immediate employment," she explained.

She cleared her throat as if realizing she didn't, or shouldn't, have to explain anything to me. I just kept staring at her, wanting to know who she really was and what she was about. After glimpsing a taste of how she might be under that barbed exterior, I wanted to know more. She didn't give me a chance to learn more, though. She just turned and started walking off in the opposite direction I came from. I stood there for a second before I finally reacted.

Wait. What? She's leaving?

I yelled down the hall to her, "See you around, Your Highness." Then I bowed for added effect.

She smiled and actually laughed a hearty, girly laugh, if that's possible. I loved it. I wanted to throw her down and fuck her senseless.

Shit, she's beautiful.

In return, she saluted me and said, "Technical sergeant."

She then disappeared.

I returned to my seat in the auditorium with a bounce in my step. I managed the stairs just fine this time. When I sat down next to my brother-in-law, I was sporting the biggest, goofiest grin. Alexi looked at me like I had been smoking crack.

"What gives?" he asked.

I smiled and responded, "I just met a royal pain in the ass."

Chapter 2: Never Really Came Back

Brenneth

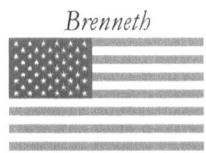

February 14, 2017

My niece arrived after thirty-nine weeks and three days. I am happy to report that my sister delivered the most beautiful baby girl the world has ever seen. I'm told Lil' Bits came out screaming, so I think she takes after her father. I was petrified to look at her, so even holding her seemed out of the question. But Caylan insisted I take a turn, so Emeline Valentine Graham was placed gently in my arms. Once I held her, though, I knew I wouldn't drop her for anything. The last time I held a baby was when Caylan was born. I was scared shitless then, and I was scared shitless now. I'm a messed-up person, so being entrusted with something so small, pure, and fragile was terrifying.

There's something about holding a baby, though. Gazing down upon my niece and feeling her in my arms was like holding an angel. She weighed as much as a damn feather at six pounds, five ounces, and she was twenty inches long. I marveled at her tiny features: petite nose like her mother, and long fingers like her father. I couldn't yet see her eyes since she had them tightly closed, but my sister said they were the brightest blue, only rivaled by hers and Alexi's. I kissed the top of her head and inhaled that new-baby scent; sorry that sounds fucked up, like I'm comparing it to a new car, but babies just have that smell. Come on, people, back me up here!

Caylan lay there in her hospital bed with the most tranquil look on her face. It was one of utter contentment, and she looked so genuinely happy. She occasionally glanced up and beamed at Alexi, who donned the biggest grin. I found myself both jealous and sickened by their display of affection. Would I ever have that with someone? Chances were probably slim considering I wasn't ready to settle down yet, if I ever would be, but a part of me longed to fill the void that years of loneliness had caused. The gap kept getting bigger and wider over time. The longer I stayed a bachelor, the more likely I'd remain one for eternity. It was a life sentence of disappointment, signing up to be my spouse. I didn't wish it on anyone. Conflicted much? Yeah, that's an understated question.

Out of nowhere, an image of Everly Reynolds popped into my head. I hadn't seen or heard from her since the graduation two months ago, so what had just made me think of her at this moment? Odd. I shook my head at the bizarre visions that flashed through my mind. I was picturing Everly holding my niece. These types of images were so foreign to me. It was like watching someone else's life, or a movie playing in my mind of different scenes in which Everly starred. Of all the things or people that could have popped into my head, I couldn't believe this woman was one of them. I remember she hadn't been wearing a wedding band the day I met her, so I hoped that meant she was single.

Wait, what?

Just then, as if Emeline was startled by my inner rant, she opened her eyes. I looked into the deepest, truest blues I'd ever seen. My breath lodged in my throat, and I was frozen in place. That baby was looking into my soul. She blinked a few times, did a little stretch, and drifted off to sleep again. In that moment, though, I knew. I knew I did not belong there. I was poison, and she was too pure and precious. I'd end up tainting my niece somehow. Fantasies of Everly—or any woman, for that matter—sharing moments like this with me would never come true. It was not in the cards for me; I should have realized my deck had been stacked a long time ago.

What was I even thinking by coming here? I had no right. I stood up and carefully laid her in my sister's arms. Sweat was pouring down my face. I was about to lose my shit . . . again. Caylan looked up at me with worry and distress hanging in the shadows of her eyes. She whimpered slightly, knowing I couldn't stay; she knew me too well. I bolted from the room before the walls closed in and anyone could question me. It wasn't fair to my family to ditch them all, but my need to survive was propelling me forward. I couldn't concern myself with anyone else's feelings. Fight or flight, right?

Fuck, I can't make it work anywhere. There's nowhere I can go, nowhere I can hide. I might as well be in the shitty desert at this point!

I never truly came back home all those years ago. I realize that now.

***

A week later, I found myself outside the door of my Unit Deployment Manager's (UDM's) office. I had just met with my commander, first shirt/sergeant, and UDM. I slumped against the door and accepted the fact I had just fucking volunteered to go back into hell. One voice inside my head told me *"You're a stupid motherfucker!"* The rational side said *"You're doing the right thing"* I kept thinking how I didn't belong there.

How would I tell my family I was going again? They were so upset when I PCS'd (made a Permanent Change of Station) from Oklahoma to New Jersey with a new assignment. At least when I was in Oklahoma, they were close, being in Austin, Texas. We had spent years apart as it was. However, when they moved to Philly a year and a half ago, it was luck that I was now stationed in New Jersey. I felt like my parents, Milly and Fred, were secretly relieved I got injured during my deployment in 2014. That probably sounds shitty because my parents are like Ward and June Cleaver, but my mom wanted me safe and at home.

Maybe if Caylan didn't have Alexi, I never would've walked into my UDM's office, but she was taken care of, and so were my parents. So, there was nothing else keeping me home. I didn't want to be a burden, the head-case brother hanging around. I know people probably think I'm so fucked up, and if that's the situation, then why would I even go over there again? But the truth of the matter is that war centers me. It rages on, and in the middle of the turmoil and stress, I've learned to find my own sense of calm, right in the eye of the storm. I've come a long way since I first went over in 2003, and at first glance, probably appeared to be pussying out. Jesus, I was just a boy then. Well, that's what has changed. I became a man, and the desert is my "home."

Christ, I didn't want to lie to my family about this deployment. I decided to omit the truth—that I volunteered this time. Before, I'd always gone because it was just my rotation. This time around, however, all the slots had been filled. But since I volunteered and another guy was trying to get out of his tasking because his wife would be having a baby soon—well, it just all worked out. We were the same rank, so it was an even swap. This would be my ninth tour to the Middle East. Fuck, that sounded like one too many. My family would deem me a hero, but I knew I was no hero. I was a coward. I was hiding, and there was no other place to do it. Over there I would be nothing to no one, and I could just concentrate on the mission.

I was scheduled to leave in a week, on the first of March, so time was ticking. I had a lot of shit to get done—the type of stuff that no one ever thinks about until they're faced with it. I'd have to put my vehicle into storage again, purchase more life insurance because I was a firm believer that my Servicemembers' Group Life Insurance (SGLI) was not enough, get all my bills and mail in order, pack, and out-process from the squadron.

The list was a mile long. On top of all that happy horseshit fun, I would also have to move out of my place. My roommates would want to fill my room. Even though I would gladly keep paying my portion of the rent, we had all made an agreement a while back about deployments. The agreement was that it's better to have a body in the house because no one likes to be responsible for the deployed member's possessions, so it just made more sense to leave. Then, somewhere in there, I'd have to find a way to break the news to my family and spend a little time with Caylan and Em. I liked calling Emeline "Em" for short; I guess you could say I was really partial to nicknames.

I decided to clear my head. I was still on my lunch hour and didn't feel like eating anyway, so I thought going over to the base exchange (BX) would be a good way to kill time. It's the department store on military installations, so I figured I'd walk around there. I ventured into the movie section and decided to do some perusing. Movies were my thing when I wasn't at the gym, at the local bars, or chilling with friends from my squadron. I wasn't into video games like most of my coworkers. My favorite movie classics, which were on offer at the BX, included the greats like *Top Gun*, *Jaws*, and *The Exorcist*. I of course already owned all those, so I'd have to settle for buying a new release or another classic I didn't have.

As I scanned the shelves, my hand hovered over a title that made me laugh out loud. I threw my head back, and it felt good to let loose for a second. Once again, thoughts of Everly were on my mind as I picked up the DVD for season one of *Royal Pains*. I knew what I would be binge-watching that weekend. Damn you, Everly!

I hated to admit it, but I had thought of Everly off and on over the last few months in another context. Hell, I jacked off thinking about her. Yup, she was at the top of my list when I conjured up my spank bank material. No woman should be that friggin' gorgeous. She was a danger to herself and me. It was probably best I never saw her again—even if I had the feeling I would.

***

Everly

February 27, 2017

I stirred from the vestiges of my peaceful slumber. I stretched my arms high to the sky and made that squealy girl noise that sounds ridiculous on me. A very ungraceful yawn followed as I worked out all the kinks in my muscles. I was glad to be alone because I'm a very vocal person, both in and out of the bedroom. God, it bordered on embarrassing sometimes, the noises that came out of my mouth. Some people probably think I'm oblivious to how I act, but I assure everyone—I'm well aware.

Mmm . . . I had just had another yummy dream in which Technical Sergeant Peters was the man-meat star. I still didn't know what else to call him because he had never told me his first name, the douche. Actually, he never told me his last name either—luckily I read it on his nametag. At least with my amazing powers of observation, I had noticed he didn't sport a wedding band. So I didn't feel guilty fantasizing about him—I don't go after married men, just for the record.

I was half tempted to dig up some information on him using my investigating skills as a reporter. But I remained steadfast in my decision to refrain from doing such things because I didn't want him to get any more under my skin than he already had. The man made my blood boil in more ways than one. He had challenged me the second I met him, and yet I couldn't believe how instantly I felt attracted to him. It was like a laser beam pulling its target in for a kamikaze shot. Just being in his presence, I could tell he was beyond manly, lethal, smart, prideful, and in pain.

He wore pain like I wear pain. It's not the kind of emotion that people tend to wear on their sleeve. No, this type of pain is deep, burning, and only seen in the eyes. Eyes that tell a story. Eyes that are haunted. Eyes that have a past. I usually run from those types of eyes because they are the kind that I know I also have; they reflect the kind of pain I have never, and will never, share with anyone. Peters would be bad news for me.

I had to giggle at my own cheesy news pun.

He and I were surely better off just being acquaintances. But I had this crazy feeling somehow we'd meet up again. Maybe I just felt that way was because I was going to the air force base the next day.

Hmm, maybe that's why I dreamed of him again.

I thought it would be ironic if I ran into him. I happened to have an interview scheduled for a story I had been working on regarding the military, and I couldn't help but wonder if he was stationed on that exact base. The odds were good, considering he had been at the Temple University graduation two months ago and the air force base in New Jersey wasn't too far away. It was the closest one I could think of.

I was already putting way too much effort into thinking this out logically. I needed some coffee. I ran on copious amounts of coffee, energy drinks, and Cheetos. Don't ask me how the hell I stayed 120 pounds, because I couldn't tell you. I didn't work out, and I was one of the least healthy people I knew when it came to nutrition. Okay, okay, I'd occasionally sneak some salads and fruits in there, but I rarely had the time. I'd pitch a story idea to my managing editor or I'd get a tip, and I was off and running.

Oh shit, I guess I do get exercise!

Anyway, I had to push thoughts of Technical Sergeant Peters out of my mind and stop wondering what was under that uniform; my libido couldn't handle it. It had been months since I'd fooled around with anyone. I was too damn busy writing for a living and trying to pay the bills. My shitty little apartment in South Philly didn't offer much, but it was home— and still quite expensive. My cat, Pussy, is my sidekick and companion. Side note: I know it's unoriginal and ridiculous to call her that, but she's a prissy cat so the name just seemed fitting. Also, I hate my nosy neighbor, so imagine my sheer satisfaction getting to yell "Pussy" through my dump of a place, knowing damn well that the *B* next door will hear.

Pussy jumped up on my bed as if summoned from wherever she was licking herself and immediately started kneading my chest. Shit, I hated that, but she was an attention whore, as I guess most cats are. She was a big ball of fluffy, snow-white fur. Her yellow eyes always assessed me, and she loved to stick her ass in my face. I'll admit I had a little bit of a soft spot for the finicky feline anyway. I figured I'd be more of a dog person, but cats were easier to care for when you lead a life like I do. I'm gone for hours on end and keep a weird schedule. Reluctantly, I started petting her, and she purred like a motherfucker.

I so did not want to get out of my comfy, sumptuous bed. That is the one luxury I absolutely will splurge on, besides good coffee. I have to have a nice down comforter and at least six-hundred-thread-count sheets, or forget it!

Okay, enough stalling.

I did one final stretch in bed, ran my fingers through my unruly curls, and stumbled as I got on my feet.

"Pussy, it's time to get your ass moving," I said aloud. However, I didn't know if I was talking to my cat, or myself.

Chapter 3: Schmooze for the News

Well, that interview didn't go as planned. I couldn't even blame it on the fact that it was the end of the workday for the officer I was seated opposite. I know no one likes probing questions, accusations, or finger-pointing, but I thought I approached it with professionalism. I wonder how much more sarcasm I could drip into that line. Who was I kidding? I am a hard-ass when I'm grilling someone, and I make no bones about it. My mouth gets me into trouble a lot, but I won't apologize for trying to get to the truth and the heart of the subject. When I take on a story, it becomes a living, breathing entity. It is a rush unlike any other. It's almost up there on the same level with sex; that is, if I could remember what *that* even felt like these days. The big *O* was a bitch to me, so I snubbed her right back.

Oh boy, that Peters was obviously wreaking havoc on my senses, considering going without dick for a while normally never bothered me this much, or to this extent. I never did serious relationships. It was always a casual thing, because serious equated to having to share something of yourself, and that just wasn't me.

I know it's ironic that I dig for the truth and stop at nothing to attain *my* goal, when I myself clam up faster than an oyster with a precious pearl. But it is what it is. I know I can come off a bit on the abrasive side, and I understand I may be too headstrong for some guys. That's why I need a man like Peters to take charge and push back. I don't need to open up fully where feelings are concerned, but I'd open fully in other ways. Was there even such a man up for the task?

See, the men in my "office"—well, the rinky-dink publication was one giant, open office save for a few desks reserved for upper management, but I digress—those guys didn't like a confident, strong woman such as myself strutting around the place. Let's just face it: they are penvious. Yup, not only do they suffer from a sort of penis envy because my nonexistent balls are still definitely bigger than theirs when it comes to chasing stories, but they're also envious of my writing skills. I can match wit for wit and tit for tat any day of the week and twice on Sunday, thank you very much! My editor knows I'm the best. When a promotion comes up again, I'd better damn well get it, or I'd have to try and move on or go freelance.

Either prospect is scary, but I've always managed to land on my feet. I've been on my own a long time. I'm thirty-two years old and I've never gotten anything handed to me—and would never want to start now.

I stood up from the desk across from the medical officer I had just abruptly finished interviewing. I nonchalantly thanked him for his time, even though he shot daggers at me, and walked out with an air of Everly confidence. The airman, who was my escort for the time I was on the base, walked with me as we moved down one of the corridors at the medical clinic. We rounded a corner and *bam!* I smacked right into the chest of another freaking airman.

But not just any airman, mind you.

When I saw the nametag, my nipples instantly hardened, and heat with a gush of liquid pooled between my legs. I slowly let my gaze wander up to the face of Technical Sergeant Peters. I sucked in my breath and held it. His probing stare analyzed my face, and the look of recognition was a boost to my ego; clearly he remembered me too. Lust swirled momentarily in his hazel eyes before he schooled his features into that military-rigid pose he seemed to don so well.

His features were just like I remembered. His chin was strong, as was his jawline; it was cut to perfection. His thick brows were shaped nicely and framed his face over his sculpted nose. Those amazing eyes meant double trouble. The flecks in his irises were alluring—I had forgotten how much I wanted to get lost in them.

My fantasies had not even done the man justice. He clearly was a fine specimen of what the opposite sex should be. The way his eye color morphed from brown to green and then back again indicated that he was a person who was constantly shifting—and who would constantly keep me guessing. Even under the fluorescent lights in the hallway, his powerful appeal and aura could not be masked. My thoughts were interrupted by the cacophony of thundering beats my heart was letting out. I could feel the blood pounding and pulsing in my ears. I had never been this undeniably and inscrutably attracted to another being.

If he didn't talk, it would be a miracle—because inevitably he'd fuck up the moment with his smart-ass charm. But at the same time, I wanted to hear that gravelly, sandpaper voice caress my ears with his wicked tongue. And that smell! Oh, how it made my mouth water. There was a hint of salty sweat mixed with a mountain spring, but not of course girly or floral by any means; it was earthy and masculine and unique to him.

I let my stare venture down his body.

Holy hell, this uniform is much better than the blue one.

He was wearing the camo fatigues that all the girls swoon over. They hugged his body just right, allowing me to make out the mountains of his muscular arms, the broad shoulders, and the thick thighs. I wished it was even tighter so I could have made out what was right *between* those thighs . . . but hey, I could still fantasize. I was not ashamed of eye-fucking him to my heart's content. His short, caramel-brown hair, cropped close to his scalp, completed the look.

He was all military man, and I was about to be in trouble again. What exacerbated the situation was the blatancy of impatience and annoyance that met my stare; his irritation was back with a vengeance. It was unnerving and arresting to hate him for being an asshole, yet to be so attracted to him that I wanted him to throw me against the wall and screw me until I couldn't walk. To hell with anyone who watched. If he did just that in this moment, I would, for the first time in my life, be comfortable with voyeurism.

"Damn it, woman. What is with you fucking running into me?" Peters bit out.

I noticed he called me "woman," not by my first name. Interesting. Either he was stupid and had forgotten it, or he was purposely acting like an asshat.

"Hey, soldier. I didn't see you there. And for the record, *you* ran into *me* . . . again," I grumbled out.

I noted I could easily work him up too.

"You know damn well to address me as 'technical sergeant,'" he retorted.

"And you know damn well to address me as 'Your Highness,'" I said in the most sinister tone I could manage.

Stop being a dickhole! That's what I wanted to shout at him, but it would have clearly been inappropriate given the time and place.

We held each other in a staring contest for a moment, then both our lips began to twitch as we tried to hold back a smile or laugh. I heard a throat clear behind me and realized it was my escort. I didn't break the connection with Peters, though. He needed to make the first move. His lips curled into a panty-splitting smirk, and I found myself grinning back.

"Everly Reynolds . . ." He just said my name, and let it hang there in a wistful way.

I didn't even know how he could do that.

But like a loon, I secretly loved that he had remembered my name. I glanced down at my chest to see that my press badge was flipped over to the blank side, confirming that he hadn't just read it again, he had actually remembered it. He followed my action by looking down at my chest too, and we both burst out laughing, remembering our last encounter and the same scenario. Talk about déjà vu. The tension was broken. It felt good to see this side of him.

I noted the perfectly white, straight teeth that I couldn't believe belonged to a man.

The military must have a good dental plan, I murmured to myself.

I figured it was time to return the favor by addressing him with the proper title. "So, Technical Sergeant Peters . . . do I have to keep calling you that, or have you got a first name?"

He looked at me like a puppy who is perplexed by his new owner, and then it clicked with him that he had never told me. He held out his big, callused hand, and I placed my slender one in his. These were the hands of a working man. These were the hands of a strong man. And these were hands that needed to touch me . . . everywhere. His fingers swallowed mine, and he grabbed them with a firm grip. He was letting me know right then and there exactly what kind of a man he was. He was the take-charge, no-questions-asked, take-it-or-leave-it kind of male. I felt flutters in my belly, and the evidence of more heat was coating my panties. Thankfully, I didn't wear thongs, so I had a little protection in my bikini briefs.

Just that small contact of hand in hand was a zap to my system. I knew he felt it too. It was like a force of nature right there in the hallway. Correction. *He* was the force of nature right there in the hallway—one I couldn't wait to tumble in the sheets. He licked his lips and, in turn, I licked mine. We were practically fucking in the hall just with our body language.

"You don't have to be so formal with the title either. You can say 'tech' instead of 'technical.' And I'm Brenneth. But I'd prefer if you called me Brent, Everly." He rasped out the end of the sentence as if it was difficult for him.

He gave my hand one final squeeze, and we both let our arms fall back to our sides. My hand continued to tingle where we had touched. My breasts were aching and felt full from being so aware of him. I needed to snap out of the trance.

What is with me?

This was so not me. I was never this affected by someone.

"So it's Brent, huh? I never pictured you as a Brent," I said cheekily.

"I didn't know you pictured me at all," he fired back with mischief in his eyes.

Damn, he got me there.

"Touché!" I admitted with a little snip of reluctance.

I had forgotten about the airman standing behind me again. He very noticeably, this time, cleared his throat and shifted his position.

I turned my head and asked, "What's up?"

He looked chagrined and stuttered to say, "Umm, ma'am? I need to escort you back to your vehicle."

Before I could even respond, Brent beat me to it. "No!" Brent stated without even looking at the young'un behind me.

Both the airman and I looked at him with puzzled expressions.

"I will escort Ms. Reynolds wherever she needs to go. I know the rules. As long as she remains with me, I will sponsor her," he said matter-of-factly, leaving no room for argument.

My momentary fit of woe at the thought of being booted off the base was instantly mollified by the hunky, beefy man in uniform. I turned to the pipsqueak. He looked like he wanted to argue at first, but then thought better of himself. I may not have understood the whole rank thing—whether he was an officer or enlisted—but I could see well enough that Brent had more stripes on his arm than that guy. So that had to mean something.

I waved my fingers in that gesture snooty girls do to dismiss someone and said, "Too-da-loo!"

He huffed and scampered off, and I turned back to Brent.

He had a satisfied look on his face. He spoke conspiratorially, "I have an idea."

God, he was hot.

"Fuck . . ." I whispered, not actually realizing I had voiced it.

I knew my pupils grew large, and that I probably had a panicked look on my face like those little stuffed animals with the grossly enlarged googly eyes.

The wicked gleam in his hazels was evident as he replied, "Exactly."

***

Brenneth

"Wait, so how does this 'fuck' game work again?" Everly snickered.

Her eyes were alight with merriment, and she was already slightly buzzed from the few drinks we'd been nursing. Hell, I was so horny and hard for her, it was difficult to sit next to her. The bar top was not doing a good job of hiding my very painful, very obvious erection. Occasionally her hand would land on my thigh, torturing the shit out of me. She knew exactly what she was doing.

Damn minx of a woman!

After we left the clinic, I had told her I needed to swing by my place to change into civilian clothes. She didn't object to hanging out with me, so I figured I could totally stand the company of a beautiful woman for my last night in the States. She stayed in my truck waiting for me while I changed, which was wise because having her anywhere near a bed would have been very bad for both of us. We then headed over to one of the local watering holes, and I decided to introduce her to my own version of the drinking game, What the Fuck?

"We can play it any way we want. It's practically like any other drinking game, with the ultimate goal being for me to get you drunk," I joked.

Truth be told, I don't like my women sloppy drunk. I'd never take advantage of a woman like that. I don't prey on vulnerability or any degree of inebriation. With Everly, though, I liked that I could rib her. She was like a dude when it came to giving me shots back. The banter was fun. But let me make it perfectly clear: I did *not* see her as a dude. Shit, she was just a cool chick, and one I could see myself being friends with even if we never ended up rolling around in the sheets. But if I had it my way, there would be fucking soon enough. I liked that I could joke around with her and not have to be so damn gentlemanly. It was a relief to—almost—just be myself.

"Okay, how about we table the drinking game for now? Tell me, how long have you been in the military?" she hedged.

Jesus, she cuts right to the chase.

That spark of reporter bled out as I stared at her beautiful face. Her curls caught the light here and there, making her glow. I knew she must have been damn good at her job—I could just tell. It's not like any of this shit was top secret about my life, but I just didn't like talking about myself. I know this is how you do things when you're on a date, though.

Did I just say "date?"

I hoped I could keep my tone casual as I replied, "I've been on active duty for fifteen years now. It will be sixteen this coming summer, actually."

I even surprised myself when I came to that realization. *Sixteen* years? Wow, the years had been flying by.

She nodded, but tilted her head as if reading something else in my features.

Damn perceptive woman.

Maybe she could see my hesitancy, picked up on the fact that I not only hated the idea of talking about myself but also had reservations about discussing my career.

Civilians who aren't accustomed to this life don't understand that some people in uniform just don't want to talk about this shit. I lived it each and every day. Another tour through the desert meant I'd have yet more baggage to carry with me for the rest of my life.

Maybe I needed to turn the tables on her. I decided to broach a safe subject. Talking about family was safe for me, so I knew I could reciprocate when she asked me about mine.

"So tell me about your family," I demanded more than asked.

It was subtle, but I saw her grip the stem of her martini glass a little more forcefully than she should have. Shit, for a second I thought it might even shatter. She became incredibly tense. I just knew that, although family was a safe subject for me, it was not for her.

Yup, there's definitely a story there.

Chapter 4: Prickly and Dickly Rhyme

Brenneth

After I witnessed her panic, I decided to let her off the hook. So before she could even respond, I jumped in again. I felt the need to protect her somehow. I could tell it was a painful subject. It was almost like we could both sense each other's pain. Weird.

"So my sister just had a baby. My niece was born on Valentine's Day. She's a cutie," I offered.

Her tense face relaxed immediately, and I knew we were treading in safer waters. She smiled back at me. I couldn't help but smile when I talked about Em. I think she also seemed surprised. I know I don't look like the baby-loving type, and I wouldn't want one myself, but I love my family to death—plain and simple.

"What's her name?" she asked.

"Who? The baby, or my sister?" I wondered.

"Well, both actually," she said with interest.

It felt good to know she seemed to genuinely care. Maybe it wasn't the idea of "family" that turned her off—maybe it was just *her* family?

"My sister's name is Caylan. She's twenty-two. I'm eleven years older. She just married a cardiologist and graduated college. And on top of that, she had my niece, Emeline," I said, all with the most sincere fondness in my voice.

"Oh, so *she's* the reason you were at the Temple graduation. And that makes you thirty-three." Everly seemed to have a knack for detail.

I nodded my head, confirming she was right on both accounts. I didn't tell her I would actually be turning thirty-four soon, or that Caylan's birthday was at the end of January. So technically my little sis was twenty-three already, but that was neither here nor there; as a dude, I'm lousy with keeping track of this kind of thing.

"I'm thirty-two, so suck it." She laughed and then took a mouthful of liquor. She seemed to get a kick out of one-upping me, which is what she had done the entire drive over to the bar. For her next question, she posed, "So, should we talk about the elephant in the room?"

Where the hell did that come from, and what elephant?

I must have had a look of perplexity stamped on my forehead because she just threw her head back and chuckled. I raised my brows at her, and she continued to seem amused. I'm not one for being obtuse, but I couldn't for the life of me figure out where she was going with this. I didn't like being laughed at or being the butt of a joke—in this case, though, I didn't think she was being bitchy. And I couldn't help myself for loving how her face lit up and changed so much with her smile.

She's a gorgeous woman, but when she smiles, she's softer somehow. All the pain, the secrets, the burdens she carries melt away. The edges get softened, and it's a sight to see. What you're left with when all that happens is a stunning creature before you. I held her gaze, and we found ourselves once again locked in a significant moment.

Could it always be like this? Always devouring each other just with our stares and with our demeanor? Always so connected?

Evidently, I was charmed by more than just her beauty; her mind was also a beautiful thing. It was a lethal combination.

That smart mouth of hers I could really put to use—along with her blunt tongue. My eyes must have been smoldering, because I could see and feel the burn reflected in her. She had to have been having similar thoughts. I think both she and I were on the same page, and clearly our minds were both in the gutter.

I looked down at her amazing breasts. They were just pecking out from the white, button-down shirt she was wearing, and they seemed to swell before my very eyes. I suspected she had dressed more professionally today because of her trip to the base. Although I realized I still didn't know what she was there for earlier; I assumed it was for some kind of a story she was writing. I was curious to discover what her true style of dress was. I suppose it wouldn't matter anyway—she could probably master any look, as I had said when I first met her.

The gold necklace she wore hung right in the *V* where her breasts met, and it was a mouthwatering view. It was also such a goddamn tease. At the end of the necklace sat the initials *NGU*; I was momentarily thrown off by the unusual letters because they weren't her monogram. How odd. I was going to ask her about it, but my brain—I mean cock—had other plans. I just kept staring at the way the pendant was nestled just so into her tan skin. She didn't have huge tits by any means, but they were at least a handful, and I was more than fine with that. In this outfit, I could ogle her a lot better than when she had worn that flowy shit. But I'd kill to see her in some sexy lingerie.

She had her shirt tucked into a black pencil skirt with black nylon stockings and those trendy boot-shoe things girls wear; they were black too. I loved the kinky curls of her hair, how they bounced in her face and sprang around her shoulders when she moved. It amazed me how she could have hair like that, which screamed youth, but have a mouth and body of a very worldly woman. The irony was not lost on me. I couldn't help but stare at her nose piercing again—this time she wore a tiny gold stud.

Why the fuck is that so sexy? Maybe because I want to know if she's pierced elsewhere? Shit, she drives me wild without having to do anything.

Just then, someone yelled across the bar, startling us both and ruining the moment. Damn drunk bar patrons! She shook herself loose and laughed again. She licked her lips. I forgot where we left off. But leave it to her to pick the string of conversation right back up.

"How the hell did we end up meeting again today? Don't you find it a little strange? Hence the elephant?" she asked, as if it should have been clear that I knew what she was referring to in the first place.

She was right, though; it was strange. Strange, but wonderful. This was exactly what I needed, and I hadn't even known I did. Rather than question it, I wanted to go with it. So I held up my Jack and Coke glass to her martini.

"Well, here's to trysts—and quite possibly to fate," I toasted.

She clinked glasses with me, but couldn't hold back her skepticism. "Feeling whimsical there, Sparky? *Fate* and *trysts*? Not two terms I'd guess would come from your lips," she managed to say around a mouthful of her drink.

"And once again, I didn't know you thought about my lips, Everly," I had to quip back.

She almost choked when she realized she had walked into that one too. She shot me the red-ring-of-death stare, you know, the kind of ring exhibited when your fancy video game system shits the bed? Yeah, that look. Hey, I said I didn't play the game systems, but that doesn't mean I don't know what they are.

"Ya know, you can be quite prickly sometimes," I surmised.

"And you can be quite dickly," she came back with.

Fuck! Why does her filthy mouth turn me on?

I grinned at her and ran a hand over my head. Even though there was no hair to grab, it felt like one of those kinds of moments that would help relieve the crushing weight of the situation. She followed my every movement, of course, with her sharp and cunning eye.

How the hell can one woman have me pissing blood and semen at the same time? She wraps my nuts in a vice, and yet I want to challenge her to do it even harder.

Everly Reynolds is definitely a one-of-a-kind woman, so I told her just as much. In return, she just blew it off as if she'd heard it before. Well, maybe she *had* heard it, but I bet no one really appreciated that aspect of her. I wondered if she'd ever been serious with anyone. Why did I even care?

Instead of discussing relationships, thank God, we talked for a little longer about other things. We discussed her goals as a reporter, and I shared how it was growing up in Texas. She was surprised to find out that I grew up in Austin, considering I have no accent, but it's more city there than "country." She asked me more about my sister and niece, and I was happy to oblige with details.

I stayed away from the subject of work, and she stayed away from the subject of her family and her upbringing. The only thing I volunteered regarding my job was what I actually do in the military. I quickly explained to her what an aerial porter is, and she listened with rapt attention. Not many people realize that military personnel actually load the aircraft by hand; I think there's this misconception that some big machine or robot does it for you. I mean, of course we have equipment to aid us, but ultimately we're the ones doing heavy lifting and wiping our brows from the sweat we produce. It's grunt work, and there's a lot of elements that go into it.

At one point in our conversation, she asked if I ever went to college. I was embarrassed to admit that I hadn't. I wish I was more like my sister. In high school, I was popular and excelled in academics; I wish I had made some different choices, but I have to always remind myself not to dwell on the past. I informed Everly that I felt like I had let my parents down since I was the star athlete in high school and had attained amazing grades.

But the military just seemed right for me. She assured me there was no shame because, in her experience, she thought those already in the workforce had a jumpstart compared to the students just entering the workforce. Nowadays it seemed like skills and experience were more accepted than in the past, when you had to follow the traditional route of schooling and then try to land a job. I hoped that was true. I was planning to retire in four years, and I had no clue what I was going to do next. Maybe something in logistics? To tell you the truth, I don't know *what* I might like to do outside of the armed forces. There's a program where the government helps troops become teachers, so that could be something to pursue. I do like kids, even though they scare the shit out of me. There would just be the obstacle of getting the actual degree.

She talked about attending school at Penn State and how she graduated with honors in journalism. She said it was tough finding a job at first, but that she got lucky when she stumbled upon her current position. I enjoyed listening to her fill me in on the freelance work she had done for a while, and how she had to make ends meet. I knew she was tenacious, with an independent spirit, and could certainly hold her own. All those qualities were sexy on her.

Everly even revealed that she had been at the clinic to interview a medical officer regarding the lack of care today's veterans receive. She wanted to get the perspective of clinicians not working at VA hospitals. As she suspected, no one would touch that subject with a ten-foot pole; well, not if they wanted to remain in their current position, of course.

I had yet to divulge that I was heading out for Afghanistan the next day. A part of me cringed to think about going back to the very place that had crippled me for a while. I didn't know if it would make a difference either way to tell her about my leaving, but somehow I didn't feel like bringing it up. I thought it might spoil whatever we had going. Whether this was friendship, companionship, or whatevership, I wanted to see where it went . . . at least for right now.

As I said before, I'd never wish this kind of a life on anyone. It wouldn't be fair to her to start up something. I wanted her, though—that much I knew. It was evident things were comfortable between us, like we were old friends. We could share things, but just not any of the nitty-gritty details. I could live with that.

She had no filter when it came to her verbal delivery, but I found it refreshing. She riled me up, but also served as a calming presence. However, underneath that comfortable exterior was a sizzling, crackling heat just waiting to bubble to the surface. I needed to harness that kind of spark and utilize it to my advantage; well, it would be a mutual use of resources in this case.

After a few hours of discussion, I'd more than had enough. It was time to cease talking and put the story to bed!

***

We ended up going back to my place because her apartment was entirely too far away, across the city. I actually have two roommates, Todd and Ben, who both happen to work in security forces—they're base cops. But luckily, they work the graveyard shift. Since it was well after ten o'clock by the time we got there, they had already left for work. I had filled her in on my living situation earlier in the evening anyway, so she knew what to expect with my arrangements. It was nice to have the whole place to myself at night since I worked days, but that meant on my days off I usually tried to be out and about so they could sleep without me disturbing them. The house we shared was decent enough. We each had our own bedroom, and there were two full baths and a nice finished basement where we could all hang out with our respective work friends.

We also had a communal dog. He was a four-year-old black Labrador named Maverick; I told you I was into *Top Gun*, and I don't give a fuck who thinks I'm a dork. Well, I guess the dog was more mine than anyone's, but the guys would take good care of him for me while I was gone. I knew my parents would have taken my dog too, or even my sister, but they all had enough to worry about. They didn't need to add my pup to the mix—especially when he still thought this place was his house.

When I came home next, though, I'd have to see if there was still a room available, or I'd have to get my own place. Truth be told, I was tired of sharing a home anyway. I had been doing it for years to save money. With all the deployments, I also didn't want to worry about having to find someone to housesit for me in my absence. So it started off as a money-saving measure and convenience thing, but shit, it was getting beyond old having to move constantly, find new roommates, and try to start over again. I could easily afford a down payment on a house now.

The queen-size bed that was currently in my room—and all the other furniture—had come with the house, so renting this place had been ideal. I was hoping Everly wouldn't ask me why my room looked so bare. Maybe she would just automatically assume I was a neat freak; by the way, I *am* somewhat of a neat freak. I would be able to save up plenty of money during the coming deployment with hazard pay and whatnot, so purchasing furniture when I came back would be a breeze too.

I had already moved all my other belongings into storage over the weekend. The next morning, my parents were coming to see me off, and my dad would take my truck and put it in storage. I hoped Everly wouldn't also notice the two camo duffel bags in the corner, which were the telltale sign of my departure—just ten hours away. If I could distract her somehow . . . I still wasn't prepared to have a conversation with her about leaving. I preferred to just lose myself in her first, then see what happened next. As I said, I felt a sense of calm around her, so she made me want to forget about all the other shit that surrounded us. Yes, I'm a selfish bastard, though, for not telling her. I realize that.

We let Maverick out to piss and shit and gave him fresh food and water. When I told her his name, she seemed surprised. I was going to ask her why, but she changed the subject and commented on the state of the laundry room; the blame for the messiness definitely fell on Todd and Ben. I couldn't stop watching her interact with my dog. She was a natural with animals and struck me as a "dog person." Maverick wouldn't stop licking her face and sniffing her crotch; yup, that's my boy.

I couldn't help bursting into full-on fits of laughter when she informed me about her "Pussy" cat. This woman was just too much! She didn't think it was so funny, but her ire only spurred me on more. And the more pissed off she got, the hornier and hotter for her I became. We hadn't even touched yet in a sensual manner—or otherwise—and yet I felt like we were already intimate somehow.

I was fire and she was ice; I liked the duality of our personalities. I knew she had to be a stone bitch, but I don't mean that harshly—that's the way she had to be in her world. I had to be a hotheaded, red-blooded, quintessential military man through and through. It was encoded in my DNA. Some things just *are*. Everly and I were the red and blue that blended seamlessly together to create a whole different color. Well, shit, if she could hear my inner monologue, she'd think I must be a fucking poet. At least my sister would be proud, since she *was* an actual poet.

I grabbed Everly's hand, and we left the mudroom. We walked together until we reached my bedroom door. Thankfully, the softly lit bedside lamp perfectly set the mood. I could feel her palm get sweaty in mine. The ice was definitely melting.

I wondered when her last time with a man had been, but that was her business. Hell, I had just been with a woman a few weeks back. It was nothing—never was. Just a casual hookup with a fellow NCO from another squadron. Everly was a stunning woman, so I suspected she had plenty of men beating down her door. I would show her, though, what all the others lacked.

As much as she obviously liked to be in charge of most situations, I had already gleaned from our two encounters that she would like to be dominated when it came to sexual interactions. So I was lucky there would be no power struggle between us, or rather between the sheets. It was clear from her body language, responses, and her eyes that she wanted someone else to take charge in the sack. Regardless of what she thought, she couldn't hide from me in every respect. I *saw* her. Did she see me too?

I couldn't focus on that right now, though. I let go of her hand, and she turned to face me. That fucking outfit of hers had to go. My patience had long ago evaporated—I was surprised I'd made it this long.

I said in a husky tone, "Strip."

She sucked in a ragged breath. I could see her pulse beating in a vein on the side of her delicate neck. Her pupils dilated, and I knew she was wet. I couldn't wait to fucking smell her, taste her, and make her mine. Yup, tonight she would be mine. I'd show her who was "dickly" now.

Chapter 5: Parting of the Seas

Everly

He said the word, and I froze. I knew subconsciously that he meant "strip" my clothes, but I couldn't help feeling like he also wanted me to bare my soul. I was not willing to do that; I was not willing to strip away the layers. I was so surprised I was feeling so much so quickly for him, and a part of me wanted him to break through my shell.

I had never experienced anything like this connection before. It was an overwhelming feeling swelling inside me. I had never wanted to really know someone before. With Brent, though, that feeling was there. Would he want the same in return? I reminded myself he was trouble— what he made me question just confirmed it all the more.

The years it had taken for me to shove away memories and perfectly cultivate this shield I had could all come crashing down any instant. That's why I knew I had to run. I was about to bolt. I didn't care that I was stuck at his place without a vehicle. I'd walk back to the base or call a cab if I had to. I didn't give a shit that it was freezing cold outside either. I could handle the weather, because the ice in my veins was already thickening again. The longer I stood here and contemplated my escape, the more I would cool.

I was about to run, but Brent's hand touched my cheek. It shocked my entire body, almost like rebooting a computer.

His electric touch paralyzed me. I was forced to stay rooted in place as his other hand cupped the other side of my cheek. I closed my eyes; it was all I could do. I couldn't speak. I couldn't think. I couldn't move. I took a deep breath to try and fill my lungs with precious air. I recognized this for what it was.

It was a panic attack.

Motherfucker!

It had been years and years since I had been so shaken up like this. I had never got help for the attacks, because there was no one to go to. I would not be talked to by some shrink like I was crazy or an idiot, and I had no one but myself to depend on in this life. I had learned to control the attacks over time, not let them control me.

I suppose Brent knew what this was.

Shit, why do I have to have one right now in front of this man? It's because of him!

Only . . . he also somehow stopped it and chased it away.

How did he do that? How can he turn me inside out like this?

I think he's a menace to my very existence one minute, and the next, he's the guardian protecting me from myself?

"Don't run from me," he begged in such a cajoling tone.

How did he do that? How did he know I was going to run?

I wasn't even miffed by his tone because I knew it was sincere. He was showing me a side of him that was vulnerable. Did I owe him that in return? I also knew he wasn't trying to get me to stay just because he wanted to fuck me—it was because he wanted to heal me. Well, he couldn't heal me. No one could. And I wouldn't let him even try. No, I would just let him make me forget . . . for one night only.

I opened my eyes, and he sighed in relief. He sensed I was back.

I licked my lips, and he brushed the pad of his thumb across the lower curve of my mouth. I kissed his thumb, and he growled. I was becoming bolder. My tongue shyly slid out between my lips again, and this time I sucked his finger into my mouth. He stared at the movements. He was completely and totally transfixed by the action. I knew what it probably looked like. I knew it had to be erotic as hell and sexy as fuck. He shoved his thumb in a little farther. I bit down, exerting just enough pressure to give him a taste of my abilities.

He growled again, and this time a full-body shiver moved through me. I saw his eyes change to a darker green. They practically glowed in the low light, and I figured any patience he had had finally disappeared.

I was ready. I was ready to be taken. I didn't want to be in charge for once. I knew he would dominate me, and I welcomed that. No man I'd ever been with had been able to before. They were too intimidated by me. They all thought I wanted to be in charge, when in fact the exact opposite was true. Brent got it, though. I needed him to be an unstoppable force and move through me like the relentless storm I recognized him to be.

He attacked my mouth. There was no finesse or workup to it. He just took, and I gave willingly. It was incredible. I didn't need him to be gentle or easy, even though I suspected he was capable of both. I realized he would be a generous lover. I could sense it in his kisses and taste it on his tongue. He had a talented mouth, and I wanted to be consumed. I wanted to exploit all his assets. By this point, I was already making very loud, obnoxious noises in my throat. I just hoped he wasn't turned off by them.

**

Brenneth

Fuck, she was perfect! The noises she was making were causing me to burn hotter with each passing second. I had never taken a woman like this. I knew I could be demanding, bossy, dominant, cocky, and stubborn, but she brought out the beast in me. It was instinctual and natural, being with her.

She made me want to fuck her so hard, to rut into her like an animal on steroids. I was raging like a machine pumped full of testosterone. Lust more than clung to every pore of my skin. I understood she didn't deserve this type of approach, but I had this gut feeling it's what she craved. My dick was so hard, it pretty much hurt. I couldn't wait to fuck her—if only I could stop myself from kissing her over and over again.

We were both starved for oxygen, and yet we couldn't break apart. We were pressed so close together and our noses were smashed into one another's faces that it was hard to breathe. It was friggin' amazing. No woman had ever wanted me with this much fervor. I loved her moans and groans. She was so vocal. It was the biggest damn turn-on knowing I was doing this to her.

I wasn't about to mention her panic attack. I certainly cared, but we both needed to ignore it for now—for her sake. Bringing it up would only embarrass her, and I know what it's like to need to move on and forget, to take advantage of distractions.

I ventured with my hands down from her cheeks and to the front of her shirt. I grabbed each side of that crisp, white business shirt and pulled it apart. She gasped as the buttons flew off every which way and pinged around the room.

Good, that got her attention. She sighed and melted into me further. I pulled the shirt from her shoulders, but kept it around her elbows so her arms couldn't move too far. I wanted her to feel a sense of helplessness. Sometimes giving up control means you're actually taking back control. I wanted to provide that for her. I didn't want her to do anything at the moment but just feel . . . feel *me*.

Reluctantly, I removed my mouth from her succulent lips. I had to taste the rest of her. Her mouth was luscious, so I surmised that her lips had to be equally juicy elsewhere. She had her eyes closed, lost in the moment. She was just breathing and moving her head from side to side. I loved watching her reactions. Her whole body was so expressive and responsive; it was an addiction, being with her.

I wanted to always feel that good, from there on out. She was exactly what I needed. I was discovering quickly that she could be a healing balm to my overwrought, shattered nerves and spirit. Once I had tasted this side of paradise, how could I possibly not want to indulge again? I had told myself at the start of the evening that this would never happen, or at the very least, it would only be a one-time thing. But now I wasn't so sure.

She was dangerous for me. She could be my kryptonite.

How can she cripple me and draw me to her all at once?

She was a siren calling to me, beckoning me to taste her forbidden fruit; I would take one bite of the apple for sure. But this wasn't a damn fairy tale, and I was no Prince Charming. I was the dark knight who did *not* rescue the fair maiden. I was no hero, despite what others tried to tell me. Heroes are meant to be idolized and have their shit together, and I was a fucking mess. I was not worthy of such a title or distinction. I wasn't even worthy of a task like rescuing anyone else, since I couldn't even straighten out myself. Christ, I was not worthy of her. I shoved my thoughts of self-loathing and despair deep down into the pit of my stomach and let the lust overcome all else. Lust I could work with.

I kissed my way down her neck, licking and biting her here and there. Her body twitched and quaked with each motion. I licked her collarbone and then sucked on her earlobe, and she went wild. I moved on to the swells of her tits because those beauties needed attention. She wore a plain, white cotton bra that suited her. She was sexy like this. It made her seem vulnerable somehow. I would have expected spikes, black leather, and chains, but once again, I realized the exterior didn't match what was truly underneath. She really was a remarkable woman. I loved her softness when she was like this with me; it made it all the more real.

I kissed the top of each breast and then bit her nipples through the fabric of her bra; they were straining against the material and easy to see, so it was not difficult to hit my target. She squirmed, and I caught a whiff of her feminine arousal. It was musky like it's supposed to be, but also sweet, like ripened cherries. It was the finest of smells. I could only imagine the delicacy that awaited me.

I looked at her face. She still had her eyes locked tightly closed. Maybe she thought it was less intimate this way, not having to look at me, but I felt closer to her because she was concentrating on every little thing I was doing to her. I would expose her soon enough, and she would be forced to take what I had to give. I placed wet, sloppy kisses down her rib cage and all the way down to her navel. I swirled my tongue around her sexy belly button and dipped it in the hole, ravishing her beautiful skin as I went.

Sure enough, she had yet another piercing—in her belly button. It was a silver hoop with a dangling diamond. It looked so yummy, hanging there. I had never thought piercings were particularly hot, until she came long. I lightly tugged on it with my teeth. Even though her arms were still trapped, she managed to find my head and grip my scalp. I suddenly wished I had more hair for her to grab. However, it still felt good—and her touch told me all I needed to know. I was more than getting to her now.

"Please," she whimpered.

I chuckled. I knew what she needed and wanted. She thought I was teasing her, but oh no, none of this was a tease. I was sure going to deliver. Call me UPS, because I'd get the package to the door. It was no hardship for me to be on my knees in front of *this* woman. I normally didn't like going down on a chick, but she was different. I knew I was good at eating pussy, and I liked the taste and act of it, but to be honest I usually only did it because I was not going to be one of those asshole guys who didn't reciprocate. With her, though? Fuck, I'd suck her juices and flesh all night long and not ask for a goddamn thing in return.

I found the side zipper to her skirt and peeled it down her tan thighs. Now I was staring at the center of her beauty. Fuck, I was so far gone at this point. I was ready to attack her cunt. She wore a pair of white, cotton bikini briefs to match her innocent bra, and my mouth watered. Her black, thigh-high stockings could stay on for all I cared—and so could the boots. She looked hot that way, but the panties had to go. The bra could stay; all those other things could come off when we moved to the bed.

Before I removed the material covering her secrets, I stuck my face right in between her thighs and inhaled. God, she had the prettiest cunt the world had ever seen. If I had it my way, no one else would ever see it. It was all mine for the night. I knew she'd be perfect and taste good, and it would make it that much harder to leave the next day. I kissed her pubic bone. She screamed in ecstasy, her head fully thrown back in the throes of passion. If she kept it up, I'd come like a clumsy teenage boy. Her noises were driving me out of my crazy fucking mind.

I slowly pulled her panties down her legs with my teeth. Once they were past her knees, I let them drop the rest of the way to the floor. Her pubic hair was very short, and a shade darker than the curls on her head. I licked my lips in anticipation of the treat I was going to feast upon. I took my thumbs and splayed open the lips of her sex. What awaited me was, in fact, paradise. Her satiny, pink lips were juicy and beautiful. She was the epitome of the female form, and could rival any goddess etched in history.

I felt her tremble in my hands. I was savoring her smell and the sight of her center. Her clit was already engorged, and I wanted so badly to lick and suck it. Before I could do that, though, I needed to taste her and enjoy the flavor. I started at the middle with my tongue, then swiped upward, all the way to the hood of her clit. She moaned so loudly. I was right about the taste—fucking cherries jubilee, she was. Yup, it was everything I thought it would be. I knew I would never taste, touch, or see paradise like that again. After our night together, she would just be a mirage.

***

Everly

I was not going to survive. He was going to town, licking my pussy. The sounds of his sucking and lapping were driving me wild. I wished he had hair that I could grab onto, but I just kept rubbing and gripping his scalp. It had never been like this before with any other man. I was never this unhinged, nor was I ever this thoroughly pleasured. Honestly, I didn't even like a guy going down on me—but Brent was the exception, clearly.

After a few more minutes of the oral treatment, he ended up throwing my left leg over his shoulder. Not only did that open me more fully to his viewing, it also let him insert a long, thick finger into my channel. The insides of my vaginal walls clenched his finger tightly.

"Fuck! You're so goddamn tight. If it's this tight around one finger . . . holy fuck, you're going to grip my dick so hard you'll break it off," he groaned.

"Shut up! You're ruining this for me," I admonished.

He chuckled and went back to his ministrations. Of course I was enjoying every moment—nothing he said could have ruined it at all, but I would never tell him that. Although I think he knew, the bastard.

Fuck! Why does he have to be so good at this?

I had no shame at this point. I was more than happy to give myself over to him. Never before had I wanted to watch a partner eat me out, but this was different. For the first time ever, ladies and gentlemen, Everly decided to look at a man chowing down on her.

I slowly opened my eyes and watched him move between my thighs. This was a liberating occasion for me. It was so hot, I can't believe I didn't come right then. I was purposely dragging this out, though, and trying so hard to hold off because I didn't want it to end. I didn't want to see him again socially or otherwise, so I had to make it count. I was rocking into his face at that point. He inserted a second finger, which made me want to climb the walls. I probably looked insane and sounded insane between what was coming out of my mouth and the way I was moving my body. I was a woman possessed. If this was what true ecstasy felt like, then he had surely ruined me for anyone else. The jerk!

I was so wet. Between his saliva and my secretions, his fingers were so slippery going in and out of my hole. I knew I was about to fly to the moon any moment. I could feel my pussy clenching and contracting even harder, and then there was that feeling like I was about to shatter; God, it was hovering right on the horizon. I never knew watching that act could be so captivating. I had never had the urge to look before—I guess I was always uncomfortable. With Brent, though, he put me at ease and made me want to do *everything* with him.

How does he do that?

"Give it to me, Everly," he rasped.

He then gently bit my clit, and that was it! I screamed so loud, I thought for sure I was going to pass out. Wave after wave of juices were flowing from my core. He kept drinking from me like he was dying of thirst in an endless desert. I was so sensitive, but in my mind, I just went to another place and rolled with it. I was beginning to sag, so he had to help hold me up. I don't know how many minutes passed before I finally returned to myself, but I suspected it was a while.

I finally let go of the death grip I had on his head, and he lightly removed my leg from his shoulder and placed it on the ground—but not before giving me a kiss on the inside of my leg. Wow, that gesture was sweet and unexpected. I started to feel myself get weird again, like I didn't want him to show me affection, but I tried to stay in my happy place. We both deserved that. I breathed a heavy sigh. That sigh said everything I couldn't. It expressed my relief, my utter joy, my thanks, my admiration, and it conveyed the fact that I had shared a part of myself with him that no one else had ever experienced. He stayed kneeling at my feet, and I felt cherished.

I gazed down into his eyes and smiled. He looked so surprised at first, but then his initial shock wore off and his expression quickly turned to one of genuine happiness. He smiled back at me.

Jeez, am I really that big of a bitch that he doesn't think I'm capable of being nice?

I had just worked up the courage to tell him how I felt. Before we had sex—note that I'm calling it *sex* as I couldn't possibly reduce it now to just *fucking.* Anyway, I wanted to tell him that I wanted to see him again even before we slept together. This was so not me, so I hoped he'd have mercy on my awkwardness. He beat me to speaking first, though.

What he said was the last thing I ever expected to hear. It changed everything.

He started with blurting out, "Everly, there's something I have to tell you."

From there, it all went to shit.

Chapter 6: Never Ever*ly*

Brenneth

March 18, 2017

Yup, I'd really gone and done it. I thought back once again to that last night in the States and the way I left things with Ev; I liked calling her that—too bad she'd never know my pet name for her. I was sitting there, alone, in my tent at Bagram Airfield in Afghanistan. Tent city was set up for temporary housing until we could be moved to more dormlike living quarters. That only happened as rooms became available. Even though I was an NCO, I certainly wasn't a senior NCO, so the conditions were expected for someone like me.

      I'd been there two weeks but still hadn't adjusted to the time, environment, or food. The three-day trip required to even get there takes its toll before your tour even really begins. The countdown is on, though. The six months couldn't go by fast enough. You're exhausted, you smell, you're hungry, and depression sets in before your boots hit the ground. Military aircraft transports turn into long bus trips, which then turn into sitting around at briefings and receiving a laundry list of things to do—before you are even issued a bed to collapse on. The famous military motto of "hurry up and wait" certainly applies here.

      Inevitably, you get sick as soon as you arrive at a foreign base. Trying to get used to the air, water, and food wreaks havoc on your system. I willed my body to try to adjust as quickly as possible; you get twenty-four hours to basically play catch-up on your sleep before you're thrust into doing your job again. If I sound like a whiny bitch, then I'm sorry. But loading cargo is demanding work and very labor intensive. I had to stay focused and keep my head in the game for the safety of myself and those around me. I was finding that to be quite difficult.

It was so hard to concentrate on anything but Ev. I kept regretting the night before I left and playing it in my head over and over again, just torturing myself. I was driving myself absolutely fucking crazy.

Goddamn it, who am I kidding? I am crazy!

I thought I'd be settled once I got overseas and would feel at "home." But I guess I had some unfinished business back in the good ol' US-of-A. That's why I couldn't concentrate properly. I think it was a dick move, the way I abandoned my family. I couldn't even bring myself to look at pictures of Emeline that I knew were waiting in the dozen emails that sat unopened on my computer. Seeing Em would just be a cruel reminder of what I was missing, and a reminder of the fact that I *volunteered* to do a shitty tour again. What a dumbass!

I also knew things were unfinished with Everly. God, that fucking woman had crawled right under my skin. Her barbed exterior burrowed its way right under the nail beds, and no amount of jacking off or hardcore exercising to get her out of my system was working. I was doing everything I could to tire myself out during the day so I'd literally pass out at night. I was actively trying not to have to lie in bed alone and think about the monumental fuckups I'd caused.

I had yet to talk to any of my family by phone. The only person I had responded to so far was my mom, via email, and she said she'd let everyone know I was okay. I knew if I opened up Caylan's emails, she'd have some choice words for me about how I'd ducked her. I couldn't handle disappointing yet more people in my life; I think that's why I've mostly been a loner. There was no point in getting too close to people if you move around so much; if you're not the one doing the moving, then they end up leaving. Either way, someone's always moving on. That seemed to be the story of my life.

I hung out with Alexi and his best friends a few times before I left. We had officially met at the hospital during Caylan's recovery. I'd also seen them at the wedding and at Caylan's graduation party in December. They were pretty cool dudes. Caleb Daniels is a lawyer and is rumored to hit on every cougar. Gil Morris is some bigwig in finance or some shit. Alexi had mentioned once that he had shared the same women at times with his best friend, Anthony Parker, but I didn't know or care because that was their thing and their business.

Anthony is a doctor too—a doctor of what I couldn't quite remember—but I think it's pediatrics. He was engaged to a redhead, which shocked the hell out of his friends when it happened since another one in their group fell prey to a woman. Her name is Shanna Sullivan. She's a sweet, Southern girl from Oklahoma. I never visited her hometown while I was stationed there, but then again I didn't know she existed, let alone her little hometown of Payton. It's a small world sometimes—some people's paths don't ever cross, but eventually they lead to the same point.

But anyways, Shanna's gorgeous—and taken. Anthony didn't take too kindly to me talking with her at the graduation, so I hadn't seen her since. I doubt I had been a great conversationalist at the grad party, because I was still reeling from having met Everly earlier in the day. I was damned amused about Anthony's attitude toward me, though. I'd never move in on someone's love interest, but I get it that those guys are protective of their women. I say good for them.

When I went out with that group of guys, we just did the drinking thing and talked shit. The only remaining bachelors in the circle were Caleb and Gil; well, I guess you could throw me in there too. Again, I liked those guys, but what it boiled down to is that they were far too smart for me to hang with. I certainly tried to hold my own when I was with them, though. However, no dude likes to feel inferior. There was always that fucking unspoken pissing contest and whose-dick-is-bigger competition with them, no matter what. Regardless, they were good men, and good friends to Alexi. They treated my sister well and were there for her and Alexi during her abduction, so they were okay in my book.

I circled back to thinking about how Ev seemed like a loner too. Not only did she not talk about her family, but she hadn't mentioned any friends either. It's funny how you pick up on things after the fact. But I've had a lot of time on my hands to think; well, that's all I seemed to do at the base. Maybe that's why Ev and I would have been a match made in heaven? Or in my case, hell? I felt like I have been in perpetual hell, lost and completely stuck in the abyss of my thoughts. It's a cruel thing when you can't surface and keep sinking to the bottom. You're teased a little bit and given a gulp of air only to be pulled right back down moments later. But enough of that crap—look at me, being all philosophical.

My supervisor was giving me a raft of shit for some rookie mistakes I had been making with the loads. Fuck, I was better than that. I felt like a moron because you'd think I was fresh out of tech school and hadn't been doing the same job for over fifteen years. I had just finished another shift; the next day would be my first day off since arriving. Eventually I'd be on a schedule of six days on and one day off, so I was looking forward to that. There was just too much work to do at the moment to take a break. I don't think the general public realizes how hard we work at home and down range. No matter where we are, the workload is tremendous because we are a smaller military with more jobs to do these days. But fuck, I really couldn't complain, considering it did help keep my mind from wandering into a dark place—or even into a light place that housed a blonde-haired, curlicue beauty.

I had made it back to my tent and I was sitting on my cot. I put my head in my hands and sighed heavily. I desperately needed another shower, but it wouldn't help get clean; you were always "dirty" over here. You'd step out of the shower and immediately be covered in dust, dirt, and sweat. I bet if they fucking tested my blood, the vial would be brown, not red, from all the shit swirling around in the air. The burn pits are the worst; the smell wafted right toward my tent. The shit pit, where we dumped all the sewage, made things extra fun.

What was the point of trying to sleep? You had to wait for sleep to come to you, and sometimes she could be a fickle bitch. Forgive me, but I curse her a lot to the depths of hell. I breathed deeply for a moment, trying not to choke on dust, and thought about Ev. About what went down after I spent time in heaven between her thighs. What happened when I fucked it all up, that is. I flashed back to the night before I left, replaying everything.

***

I knew I needed to tell her I was leaving before things went any further. I wanted to kiss the inside of her leg again, but she stared down into my face so tenderly, it was crushing me. My insides were caving in. The avalanche was going to occur any second. Fuck, it was the guilt that was eating me alive. She deserved to know. I got the sense that it was a one-time thing for her, but then I kept second-guessing myself because of the way she was acting with me—but maybe I wasn't as observant or perceptive as I thought. I prided myself on being observant, so this threw me off; well, actually, she threw me off in general. Shit, I don't know. How could she have unraveled me so quickly?

Without even thinking, I blurted out, "Everly, there's something I have to tell you."

I could see the surprise in her eyes. I could tell she was retreating. This woman had perfected control of her facial expressions, and on command could school them into her "normal" appearance. She was bracing for something bad, because her face pinched up. All that work I had done to bring out the relaxed, pliable woman underneath vanished in an instant. Fuck. Even so, I had hoped I'd get the chance to one day find out what had hurt her so much and to cause her to be so guarded.

I stood up from where I had been kneeling by her creamy skin and reached for her, but she stepped back. Okay, telling her was not going to be easy—she had already gone on the defensive.

"Everly . . . I am leaving in the morning," I said with reluctance.

She looked confused for a second, then her eyes darted around the room until they landed smack-dab on my bags settled by the wall. Her lovely green eyes narrowed into slits, and I could see the wheels spinning. Her hair practically came alive as she turned her head, as if Medusa-like snakes were weaving in and out. If I didn't have a thing for her already, I'd have been afraid she'd turn me to stone with just one look. I knew she had figured it out, though, from the bags. Shit, the woman should have been a detective. She figured things out in a nanosecond, but I'd already gathered that the she wasn't so good at discerning genuine feelings; maybe they were just too foreign of a concept for her.

"Just like I thought. You were going to fuck me and discard me. You fucking soldiers are all alike," she spat at me. It practically gave me whiplash.

It was not lost on me that once again she used the term "soldier" as an insult and reduced me to something I was not. The "fuck" and "discard" comments were added hurtful digs. I had no idea why she would be making such a comparison between me and another military person. I had no clue what her frame of reference was. I knew I wouldn't get the chance to ask; I just knew she was shutting down. This was it. I needed to think fast, but she started pulling her top up—the one that had been scrunched around her elbows. After most of the buttons had gone flying off around the room, I imagined there wouldn't be much to hold the material together. But, being the resourceful woman she was, she tied the ends up, which made her shirt into the most alluring crop top. Goddamn her for always having the upper hand. Her belly button jewel winked at me as if to say, "Not on your life, buddy."

She pulled on her skirt, straightening and smoothing it into place. I was distracted by each movement of her sexy hands running over her body. What a fucking vixen! How could one woman be so lethal?

I was going to try to explain everything to her. In my head, saying all the right things, but instead of it coming out the way I needed it to and wanted it to, of course I failed in the most epic sense. I guess my defense mechanism is sarcasm too.

"Yup, that's it! I was going to fuck you and leave you. You got me all figured out, don't you? Well, at least you can return the favor and suck my cock before you storm off!" I fired back with an absolute lack of feeling.

She recoiled at that—it was a slight reaction. If I hadn't been paying such close attention, I might have missed it. After the words were said, I felt my stomach bottom out. I do not by any means like to hurt women. My sister would have twisted my nuts off if she had heard what I said. Hell, my mom would have used one of those melon ballers on me—we'd have had a de-nutting party going on. What a bastard I was!

If my vile words hurt her, she didn't let on. She wouldn't have let me see if they did anyway. She was too tough for that. That's why she was stronger than I am. I don't know how she did it. She just huffed as if she was bored by our conversation. I can't believe she didn't cry at that moment. That was such a cruel, shitty, and disgusting thing to say, but she took it like a man. She put her hands on her delicious hips, which only accentuated her dangerous body all the more. My dick was crying in a lonely corner of my pants because I had fucked up the situation. And let's face it—sex is something you absolutely need in order to relieve stress, especially before getting deployed. But not just any woman would do. I wanted her.

She took two steps toward me. I couldn't tell if she was going to throw a punch *or take me up on the distasteful offer I had laid at her feet. She did neither of those things, though. Instead, she stared me down with the rays of a thousand suns and said the thing that cut the deepest.*

"I can't say it was nice meeting you, Tech Sergeant Peters, but I wish you good luck and hope you return home safely to your family." She spoke firmly.

Then she turned on her heel and walked out of my room, slamming the door behind her. In the distance, I heard the front door slam too. I also heard Maverick bark. I knew I was utterly alone. A part of me wanted to run after her to make sure she would get home safely, or at least give her a ride back to her car. But I was absolutely frozen in place. I could not for the life of me move because of the finality of the situation. I would have welcomed a bitchy attitude, but when she wished me luck and a safe return, I couldn't process or handle her words. I think it made me realize she had just cut me out of her life in that one second. She had made a choice for both of us, and it sliced me to the core.

I sank down to the bed and gripped the sides of the mattress so hard with my fists, I was white-knuckling like I never had before. Sweat poured down my face in stinging streams, and my eyes watered and burned from the salty mixture.

Fuck, I hoped she would make it home okay, especially in that sexy outfit she donned. I prayed she'd call a friend or a taxi, because it was a cold night. Hell, I didn't even know where she lived so I wouldn't be able to check on her. I realized I didn't have her phone number either. She was a mystery lady to me in so many ways, and yet I'd never felt so totally connected to a woman in all my life. But I guess you could say we were both "gone."

***

Fuck, it sucked thinking about that night again. I took a deep breath and laid down in my bed with my boots still firmly laced on my feet. I let sleep take me. She was merciful tonight, and for that I was truly grateful.

I spoke these words in my mind as I drifted off: *Everly . . . wherever you are out there in the world, I wish you good night and the sweetest of dreams. And whether you want me to or not, I'll come home to you and I'll make this right somehow.*

***

April 11, 2017

I was still nowhere near ready to reach out to my sister. I didn't need to pile anything on her. I figured I'd worry her more if I talked to her. Of course I saw the inbox in my email folder was filled to the brim with all manner of begging, shouting, and threatening emails from my family—especially because of the significance of the date.

Just focus on work. Yeah, that's good.

That was something I needed to do. In Afghanistan, there was just the sand and time and silence. I don't particularly like the silence because being alone with my thoughts was not good. But what choice did I have? I didn't even tell anyone on the base it was my birthday. I blew out an imaginary candle on the imaginary cupcake I was holding in my hand. I did this while I stood in the crummy makeshift shower with the water raining down on my large form, all while trying to wash away my torment. I made a wish . . .

It wouldn't come true anyway. Wishing was for the weak.

Chapter 7: No-Go Zone

Everly

July 4, 2017

I sat in my apartment, staring at my computer screen. Pussy just jumped up on the kitchen table and stuck her ass in my face. I swatted her away. She gave me a snotty look and scampered off to sulk; she had been a needy, clingy bitch lately. What was up with her? I was not in the mood for her shenanigans.

It was after ten o'clock, and the sky was covered in thick clouds; no stars in sight. It smelled like rain was looming in the air because of the humidity. Some of the fireworks had died down after the big celebration during the day's festivities around the city. Since I was surrounded by apartments, there wasn't much activity in my area. Down by the water, however, that was a different story—there were shows celebrating the mighty Independence Day, and I'm sure all the happy little families were enjoying themselves. Where my place was nestled, though, it was hard to celebrate. Besides, you needed a permit to light fireworks anyway since Pennsylvania is one of those persnickety states when it comes to these things. They only allowed them at places like theme parks or event venues.

Once in a while, I'd hear someone shoot off some kind of whizzing thing from their rooftop, or I'd see a kid across the way with a colorful sparkler. But that was as much activity as I'd probably get. Nope—no fireworks in my bedroom either. Pussy was seeing more action than I had, since she began making eyes with the tabby cat down the hall. I had caught her trying to sneak out a few times when I opened my door. I had never got around to getting her fixed, but I was in no way ready to be a grandma. I had to be better about keeping tabs on her.

As I continued to sit there, cursing at a blank Word document, I realized the only action I had had in the last four months was the night I was with Brent. His lips, tongue, and teeth had felt so good on me. I was mad at myself for constantly using his sexy face as the hero in my fantasies when I was pleasuring myself. My vibrator, which I had bitchily named "Soldier," did the trick time and time again. Damn that man for being the one who made me come whenever his rugged good looks entered the picture. Good thing he'd never know.

I put the back of my hand to my face and felt my skin, which was kind of feverish. Brent did that to me, though. Just thinking about him made me want to rip my clothes off and lose myself in him. The night before he left, he had made my skin so sensitive from the onslaught of oral treatment. My flesh had been so hot and aching for him, it was unlike anything I could have ever dreamed. I had wanted so badly to glue his mouth right between my thighs and keep him there forever. But, like usual, things got fucked up, and I cut and ran.

The idiot didn't even chase after me—but it wasn't a game. I certainly hadn't expected him to run after me, if I'm being honest with myself. I was the one who ran, and I own up to it. Luckily, I called a taxi after I strutted out of his place. When I made it to the base, the gate guard took mercy on me and let me get my car so I could return home. I'm sure the outfit I wore helped my case. I never reached out to Brent after that night. It didn't matter, because I had no way of contacting him anyway. Sure, I could have dug a little to obtain his info, but by that point I didn't want to.

I didn't appreciate what he had said to me, but I guess since I didn't reciprocate in the oral department, I'm sure he was pissed and just being a total douche about it. I didn't want to send him off to war with blue balls—but that was his problem, not mine. He should have been honest and up front about being deployed. I had been a moron for letting him get to me in the first place. Not only that, but I stupidly missed out on having what was sure to have been the best sex of my life, and for what? Why did I really care that he was leaving? Nope, not going to examine that one because I wasn't sure which side of the fence I wanted to be on in this dilemma.

Better to leave than be left, am I right? Everyone leaves at some point, I just happened to make the first move. It's like a game of chess. I strategically place my pieces on the board, and some moves may be foolish or genius. Either way, I'm the one who gets to call "checkmate." I'm the one who gets to end the battle on a high note.

I knew it was pathetic that I didn't have any girlfriends to call up and hang out with or vent to. I had a neighbor down the hall named Dawn, not to be confused with the *B* next door that I taunted. Anyway, Dawn and

I would converse once in a while, but we weren't that friendly. Granted, I didn't like doing much of anything, but since things were slow at work and my dickhole editor was still not giving me the good leads on stories, I was getting bored—a lot. This boredom led to me masturbating—a lot.

I had tried my hand at doing some crafty shit I had found on Pinterest. That crap lasted for two seconds. I ended up burning my finger with a hot glue gun, wasted over a hundred bucks on supplies that I'd never use again, and drank a whole bottle of wine while I attempted to make my wreath resemble the origami thing it was supposed to. Yup, I needed to get some ass.

But hold on. I'm not that desperate to jump just anyone, and I'll prove it. They hired a new intern at the *Timez*. This kid—I'm totally going to call him a kid—wouldn't stop texting me. His name is Stuart, and he's twenty-four years old, so to me he's just a baby. He has a lot of growing up to do and whatnot. I'm not going to front and act like I'm not attracted to him. I have eyes and perfectly working hormones, thank you very much. But I was not going there! He had that surfer-stoner vibe thing going on anyway, and I was so not attracted to that persona. I also make the conscious effort not to shit in my own backyard.

As I said before, it's hard enough for a woman like me to make a name for herself, mostly because *they*, the men in my field, want literal head to help me get ahead. Therefore, beach-bum boy was not going to help me in any way, regardless of whether his daddy did happen to own the building where our newspaper was housed. I could continue to give myself orgasms, and no one would get hurt. I did realize quickly that Stuart had a crush on me, and I don't have time for that shit. I didn't even do the whole dancing-around-the-subject thing.

I told him flat out: "Don't go sniffing around this bush, because it will bite your pecker right off."

He turned green at the gills at my words, so I thought that had done the trick. Yup, I thought he had gotten the hint, but in his boyish brain he probably thought it was hot that I told him off. Ugh, this isn't a kindergarten fantasy where the mean boy—girl in this case—teases you or taunts you because he likes you! I would kick him in the nuts if he tried anything, so I hoped his daddy was ready to pay for reconstructive surgery.

I had set a specific chime on my phone just for him, so I knew not to bother checking his messages.

Of course it went off just then with a text: *Happy Forth! :)*

What a dumbass! He couldn't even spell "fourth." Naturally, I didn't reply. I just snickered at the offensive phone sitting next to my computer.

I had switched from wine to coffee. I had added way too much sweetener, but I couldn't bring myself to throw away my precious coffee. I took in a whiff of my hot-chocolate-scented wax melts. It was a calming thing for me to smell the aroma. I heard the chime again, and the fucker broke my Zen. The tone was that annoying alien-sounding buzz. I wanted to throw the damn thing across the room.

I stood up, squealing the chair legs against the floor in the wake of my abrupt movement. God, I hated that noise too! I took my phone and put it on the nearby couch, then proceeded to put a throw pillow on top of it to suffocate the defenseless thing. Looking satisfied with my handiwork, I turned and went back to my kitchen table. I needed to get my act together and start planning my next story. I was thinking of doing a column piece, or maybe an advice piece. But since I'm shit at advice, I dumped that idea just as fast as I thought it up.

I wanted something trendy and on-point, but it was hard to come up with things when I didn't feel inspired. I hate when a story doesn't come to fruition, and lately I hadn't been as clever and witty as I normally was, which led to my editor being even more disapproving than he normally was. I needed something to reenergize our readers. We were lucky that our publication didn't have to stick strictly to news, weather, politics, and so forth. We had some leniency with our stories. At times we went borderline into tabloid territory, but not quite that far—if that even makes sense.

I also wanted to lure in a younger, more hipster crowd. I figured with a younger target audience as readers, we could appeal to a whole generation that we weren't currently tapping into. I mean, let's face it, that black-and-white print thing is out. I get it that millennials like their news on a tablet screen and not in print. But there is something about the printed version that makes my veins sing. I love holding a paper in my hands and sniffing the ink. I love when the black smudges across the page and I get my hands all dirty. It's like confirmation that something is going on in the world, that there is something beyond what each of us is currently doing in that moment.

I had also recently discovered that some groups in the younger crowd were getting back to brick and mortar by going to libraries and ditching the tablets. I thought the same trend could transfer to these groups picking up a paper, so I figured I'd have as good a shot as any if I tried to reel them in too. I knew my managing editor, Steve, wouldn't like the direction I was heading, but what the hell at this point, right? How cliché of me to remark this, but I was going to do it anyway.

I said aloud, "You do only live once." So I was going for it!

Even if it was a challenge—and anyone in my profession has to like challenges—I still nixed writing about things I wasn't well versed in, like politics or economics. And I definitely avoided stories about the Middle East because I wasn't prepared to come across anything to do with Brent, accidental or otherwise. I didn't even know where he was on the planet. It was better that way.

So I decided to write a piece about things girlfriends talk about that guys don't realize is being said. I know it's ironic that I chose this topic considering I had no girlfriends to talk to, but therein came the challenge. I was going to focus on how guys think women should be prim and proper, but yet the majority of us are just as raunchy and dirty as they are. I think it's therapeutic to discuss certain topics. For me, this piece would help my own psyche by being able to reach women. Since I obviously couldn't do that on a personal level, well, I'd settle for a professional one. I didn't want to alienate men; the idea was more to educate them—and this story would help.

My fingers began flying across the keyboard as I started to get to work. I was so jazzed and excited to have a new focus. I made a mental note to remind myself to stop and pee at some point. Sometimes when I'd get so into a story, my bladder would cry until I finally realized I'd have to pee myself, go right there in the sink, or start wearing diapers. TMI, anyone? Sorry, that's gross, but that's just how it is. Clearly, I'm passionate about my work. I was typing snippets of information and some general thoughts I had. I couldn't wait to go out and interview women to confirm that I was hot on the trail of what was typically exchanged among besties.

I thought back to conversations I had had with peers in college, had overheard while eavesdropping on the train, or had witnessed while sitting in the park. Girls did talk about all kinds of things. Nothing was sacred, secret, or off-limits. It was a good, refreshing feeling knowing women could be "real" too. After all, we're not *just* women. We have brains and libidos that are just as active as men's. Sometimes I think our dicks are bigger than theirs. I've had conversations about the best method or practice for shaving your asshole—once, my college roommate's boyfriend walked in on us demonstrating by air shaving. You know, like when bands play an air guitar? Well, we were air shaving. It was hilarious and ridiculous, and I loved every minute of just being "one of the girls." That story was definitely going in there!

I also wanted to find out whether flavored cum was a myth. I heard that if a guy ate a bunch of pineapple, consequently his cum would be sweet. I had to research that one, and, of course, everything would be tactfully or scientifically written, so as not to offend anybody—God forbid the news be blunt!

I also owed it to ladies to discuss certain unfamiliar slang terms. Half the time I'd have to look up things on the internet because I didn't know what a "pearl necklace" was, for example. I was proud, although maybe I shouldn't admit this, that I knew what a "golden shower" was and what "tossed salad" meant. I remember a guy telling me about "the shocker." Let's just say I was less than impressed when he informed me it was "two in the pink and one in the stink." It made me roll my eyes so badly when he told me that it gave me a headache.

I couldn't wait to empower women with this knowledge, and, of course, learn a few things along the way. I even wanted to interview women to find out if they had certain buzz words that weirded them out or made them squeamish. For the record, mine is "taint." That word is just all kinds of wrong, and I shudder whenever I hear it, see it, or say it. It gives me the willies—yuck!

I typed for maybe another three hours. By that time, my back was sore. My bladder was past the point of crying; she had gone numb and was in shock. I once again stood up, and the chair squeaked as I ran for the bathroom. Once I peed and wiped, I stretched my back and moved my neck from side to side. Oh my God, I knew I'd feel this in the morning. I felt satisfied, though, that I had a good start to my story.

Once I made amends with my bladder, I decided I was a little keyed up because of my chosen subject matter. So, I padded over in my purple, fluffy spa socks to my intimates drawer and grabbed Soldier from his box. I smiled to myself and knew that either Brent or Soldier would be going to town on my clit. I just hoped the batteries lasted.

Chapter 8: Scared or Scarred?

Brenneth

July 8, 2017

It was eating away at me. The guilt. The guilt was overwhelming. It suffocated me at times. I had finally broken down and responded to Caylan's email, but I still couldn't bring myself to talk to her on the phone. I knew if I heard my niece in the background, I'd completely and once and for all lose my mind. Alexi threatened by text to come over and personally kick my ass, then proceeded to apprise me how the stress I was causing his wife by avoiding her was cruel and inhumane. Well, that finally did the trick and broke my silence. I sure as shit wasn't afraid of Alexi—he could bring it on anytime—but I was afraid of what I was doing to my baby sister.

I still harbored so much anguish and pain over what had happened to Caylan. For me to abandon her like this, right after she had given birth to my niece, was something unforgiveable. What I was doing wasn't fair to my family. I knew it. I was an absolute, total asshole of the highest degree. But that girl didn't have a mean bone in her body, so I knew she'd love me despite my scars and flaws. My mom and dad were the most loving and giving parents. They never gave me guilt trips; they let me find my own way, in my own time. I did deserve a swift kick in the rear, though, and Alexi had sure provided that. He brought me back to the reality I needed. But having done so, disrupting the little fortress I had built in my mind, also meant the floodgates opened to make me once again think about Everly.

I wondered if Ev had celebrated Independence Day. I wondered if she had gazed up at the fireworks and held hands with some dickwad and kissed and fucked him under the stars. See, this is where I get myself into trouble—on one hand, I can spout a bunch of shit claiming I don't care, and then on the other hand, I realize I do friggin' care, and it kills me. I guess par for the course of having PTSD. I know I have a problem, as I've admitted before, but it's not something I need to talk about with any damn head doctor while sitting on a couch, no less. I choose to deal with it in my own way, and so far I've managed just fucking fine.

I sat down on the Fourth and decided to write Everly a letter. I'm never going to mail it, but it was good to write it out. Caylan is always giving me crap, telling me I need to write about my feelings. I'm not into that girly, hokey-pokey, pansy shit, but no one would need to find out. So what's the harm? Caylan is a damn good writer, and I thought she'd be proud of me if she knew what I was up to. I know it's not Shakespeare, but it will do. I even went as far as addressing the letter to Ev's work. I knew she worked at the *Philly Timez*, and I looked up the contact info one day while I was at one of the community computers they had set up for communications.

However, I have a laptop set up now in my room. I'm lucky I'm in a real room finally. I have a piss-mate, well, really a roommate is what he is, but that's what we call them here. It's not too bad, though, because we work opposite shifts, so we make it work. Harold Jefferson is his name, and he's a cool dude who works in comm. He's normally stationed in North Carolina. He gets his jacking-off time, and I get mine. He doesn't snore and neither do I, so we seem to get along just fine. He's not married either but is desperately trying to hook up with an old flame, so sometimes I listen to his tales of woe. When we both need private time, I'm sure we both do the exact same thing and make desert jellyfish in the tub; yes, what I'm referring to is jizzing in the shower.

Anyway, I made a habit of pulling the envelope out of my cargo pocket as I sat on my bed. There's no time to think or do anything but focus on work when I'm on duty, so my room is the only place, besides the bathroom, that affords me the solitude I need. I read over what I wrote. It made my heart and balls ache all the more when I looked again at the words I had penned.

I wish I would have gotten laid before I left. Five months without sex really fucks a guy up, ya know? I scanned the letter. The creases were becoming more prominent, as was the dirt from the number of times I had pulled it out, folded, and unfolded the note over the last four days. It was my only connection to her, so I grabbed it like it was a lifeline. I had also tracked down her email address, but I wasn't strong enough to try that route. No, this letter was safe; I could say what I wanted without fear of being judged or having to feel her pity. I didn't have to worry about her ever reading it, and I definitely didn't have to worry about seeing her face when she did. I read it silently.

July 4, 2017
Everly,
I'm sorry about the way we left things. I don't know where to begin or how to explain. You kept throwing me off. From the moment I met you, I felt so completely out of my element. You're so damn beautiful, you scare the shit out of me. You're the smartest woman I know, and you're so strong and brave. I can tell you have pain in your eyes, though. Your pain matches mine. I know you feel it. I feel it too. I wish you would have let me explain things that night. I wish you would have given me a chance.

I'm a dumbass for not coming after you. What I should have done was run out the door, scooped you up, and brought you back to my room. I would have made love to you all night long. It wouldn't have been just a fuck, Everly—at least not for me. I would have worshipped your body like the goddess you are. Every inch of your skin would have been covered by my mouth, and I wouldn't have let you leave the next morning without the promise from your gorgeous mouth that you'd be there waiting for me when I return.

You make me feel things I've never felt before with a woman. You make me feel like a man worthy of your beauty, charm, and wit. I know I can be screwed up at times, but I'd never let you down. I would be your protector, even though you would say you wouldn't want me to be anyway. I'd keep the evil at bay since I know it still haunts you. I don't know who or what hurt you in the past, but I wouldn't hurt you, ever.

I wish you'd give me a chance. I wish you'd let me be your man. I wish for many things. I have many regrets and too much time to think about where I went wrong while I'm sitting here in this sandbox. I know you'll never get this letter because I'm too much of a chicken shit to send it. But it brings me comfort knowing it's out there in the world.

I wish things had turned out differently for us. I just want you to be happy. I don't even know you, but yet I feel like I already do. Is it the same for you? There has to be a reason why we kept running into each other. I mentioned it to you at the bar, but maybe it really is fate. Anyway, I hope you're well. I think of you . . . always.
Regards,
T.Sgt. Brenneth Peters, USAF

It was a shame she'd never get the letter.

***

Everly

July 22, 2017

It was a Saturday, and I was bored to tears. I had already finished my article and placed it on Steve's desk the day before. It was a waiting game now, because we weren't a daily newspaper—we were a weekly publication. So my story wouldn't run until the following Friday, if it ran at all. I wasn't too worried. I had to believe in myself and be confident that my article would make it. After I pitched him the idea, he knew I had something. I could see the gleam in his eye and that spark only journalists can understand.

I had so much fun going out and interviewing women and taking formal and informal polls on the subject matter and material for the story. Since I had six days until it would hit the stands, there would be plenty of time for edits. I hoped there wouldn't be too many edits, though, because I'm very meticulous and an anal-retentive person when it comes to perfecting my work. But Steve is just as big of a perfectionist as me, which was equally good and bad. I cringed every time he slapped down an article of mine on my desk with red lines everywhere. It made me feel pathetic and weak momentarily, and then I'd remember that he was just doing his job. I'd come this close—picture me making the universal sign for "small"—to stabbing him with one of my heels the last time an article of mine looked bludgeoned to death.

I know I have a temper on me, but it helps in this industry. I think my gut instincts also act as a good barometer for measuring the quality of my work, and it serves me well often. I was playing with my hair incessantly at the moment, running my fingers through the wild curls. It was a thing I did to calm myself, twisting my curls around my finger and then pulling my finger out to see if I'd get a knot. I know I'm weird, but these are the quirks that make me . . . well, *me*. Without my idiosyncrasies, the world would certainly be a dull place indeed.

I moved on from playing with my hair to playing with a spoon and trying to balance it on the tip of my nose; I know, I lead such an exciting life. I finally remembered to heat the curve with my breath so it would help hold. Don't judge me, I saw it in the movie *Overboard* as a kid, and it's fun to try; well, that is when you're alone and not trying to impress anyone. That movie was one of my faves growing up—mainly because it was one of the only movies I ever got to watch. My all-time favorite movie, though, is *Top Gun*. It's funny how to me it's a classic, but if you talk to anyone under the age of thirty today, they have never heard of it. You are not my friend, or even worthy of being my foe, if you have not watched that movie.

That's why when Brent informed me of his dog's name, I was in complete shock. I couldn't believe we had anything in common, or that it was that easy to click with someone. I was going to ask him if it was because of the movie and make some smartass remark like "Where's Goose?" but I refrained from doing either. Instead, I changed the subject because I was a coward. This is why I felt so torn. I read about people finding one another when they weren't even looking, but it couldn't be that easy. Could it?

I randomly hiccupped, and it hurt like a son of a bitch. I hated when that happened. I rubbed the necklace I always wore around my neck; I had a habit of reaching for it when I needed to soothe my nerves. The pendant was my reminder of what life was all about. I touched it without even realizing it half the time, thus drawing other people's attention to the initials. They would always ask what it meant. I never told anyone, though, because it was too private and personal; it was just for me. Sometimes the worst scars are the ones you can't see, and that's all I'm going to say about it. And my reply when people asked what it meant was literally "nothing."

Pussy broke the trance I was in. I let go of the necklace and let it settle back against my throat. She started purring uncontrollably and rubbing her head on my leg. I knew she was buttering me up so she could try to sneak out to visit her boyfriend. Eh, what the hell. I was in a generous mood, so Pussy could play away. She could accompany me down to get the mail at least. I'd go through the motions of checking the box, but it wasn't like I expected to receive anything of significance.

Chapter 9: Pussyfooting Around

Everly

I stood up and opened the door. I looked down at myself and decided my outfit of sweatpants, tank top, and toe socks was totally and completely, 100 percent appropriate for grabbing the mail. I walked out my door with my mailbox key in hand. Pussy strutted behind me to some imaginary beat, trying to wave her pussy around. That cat cracks me the hell up, but it's guaranteed she gets more dick than I do. I made it down the three floors to the lobby. Pussy was meowing like crazy, either letting the tabby know she was around or bitching because he was nowhere in sight. I grabbed my stack of mail and walked back up to my floor with her trailing behind.

After her lazy butt made it through the door, I locked up and turned to her to say, "Sorry, Pussy, but I think we're doomed to be partners for life."

At that comment, she stuck her tail up in the air and ran off. I swear she knows exactly what I'm saying. With that little move, she was telling me to go fuck myself. Apparently it would just be a lonely party of one, with me being the only guest. Not even my cat abided by girl code.

I started sifting through the stack and weeding out the junk mail. I got to the bottom of the pile. The last envelope was from my office.

I could tell it was Steve's writing, so I opened it immediately thinking, *Shit, is this a pink slip?*

Inside was another gross-looking, dirty envelope with a note wrapped around. Steve had scrawled something on his favorite canary-yellow, lined notebook paper. I read aloud.

> *Evy,*
> *This letter came Friday right after you left for the day, so I figured I'd mail it out to you in case it's important. You might not get this until*

Monday anyway, but I guess there's always a chance you'll get it sooner. I'll get cracking on your edits; don't get all bent out of shape yet. I like where you're going with the story. I know I don't tell you this often enough, but you do a damn good job. You really have something, kid! See you Monday.

Steve

For the record, I hate that he calls me Evy, but he does it on purpose. I try to take it as a compliment—he could call me something far worse. It also amuses me that he refers to me as "kid." Again, I try to take it as a compliment since he does it to anyone under the age of forty. Plus I did it to Stuart, so I guess it's only fair. Steve's only fifty-six, but he clearly thinks of himself as very old and wise. I was also bowled over by the praise. *Jeez, that's the nicest thing he's ever said to me.* I was surprised I wasn't hyperventilating into a brown paper bag at this point. That letter was definitely getting pinned to my fridge like a preschooler's first finger painting.

After the shock of Steve's praise wore off, I paused to further examine the dirty envelope. I was trying to assess its features. It was tattered, but it had clearly been crisp white—once. Now it was caked with dirt and grime. Sadly, it was just a mess of an envelope now. *A hot mess much like me, ha!* It was so creased that I was surprised the thing didn't fall apart in my hands like when a vampire turns to dust in the sun. There was no return address, and I didn't recognize the handwriting. Surely no one who was pissed at me would send me anthrax through the mail, right? I decided to go ahead and open it, casting cautionary measures aside. I pulled out a well-worn letter. Attached to it was a large sticky note. *Jesus, another note inside a note! What the frick is going on?* I read that one silently. It was quite brief.

July 13, 2017

Ma'am,

I know you don't know me, but I room with Brent. He'd never send this, and he'll be angry when he finds out I did. I snatched it from his pocket last night because it deserves to be sent. I'm a hopeless romantic and I lost my girl once. I don't want Brent to lose his. Forgive the intrusion, but maybe you'll both thank me one day?

Forever hopeful,

T.Sgt. Harold Jefferson, USAF

Bagram Airfield, Afghanistan

I couldn't move or breathe.

Afghanistan! Holy Mother!

I'm not such a total twit I didn't think he wouldn't be in harm's way, but I had been hoping for some other, safer, location. I had hoped for him not to be smack-dab in the middle of the shit!

God, he must hate me right now.

My hands shook as the reality finally set in of what a complete and total bitch I truly had been to him. I didn't grow up around military. I had one experience with an ex-soldier that I don't care to go into, and it had soiled my view on military guys. Let's just say he left a bad taste in my mouth—for many reasons—and leave it at that.

Shit, sometimes I'm such a hypocrite. I dig into people's lives for a living, and yet I couldn't put the clues together to come to the realization that Brent was a hero. Even if he never saw combat, I could still appreciate his sacrifice and sense of honor and duty. Even if he wasn't on the front lines—I would never know—he was still a hero.

I never cried. It was something I just didn't do. Tear production wasn't in my DNA. I always thought blubbering was for pussies. How wrong I was. At that moment, a tear slid down my cheek and dripped to the floor at my feet. I could have sworn I heard the splash when it hit the tile. I felt destroyed, because it finally hit me that I had let this man slip through my fingers.

"Tech Sergeant Jefferson, I have no idea if I should thank you or curse you right now," I tried to get out through the horrible knot in my throat.

I slid to the floor and just sat there with the letter next to me. I couldn't bring myself to read it. I was not worthy of *his* words.

There was no way to describe what I was feeling. I think the problem was that I had too many emotions. When a journalist can't even formulate a coherent sentence and string the necessary words together to articulate what her brain and heart are feeling . . . I knew I was in trouble. I finally made it from the floor to my couch—baby steps, people! At least I had my signature coffee in hand, which helped calm my fried nerves. All synapses were firing, but I still felt the signals weren't making it to all parts of my body. It was an effort to get every component to work together.

After a good chunk of time passed by, I finally felt ready to digest the letter and examine it with a critical eye, from a professional standpoint, naturally. This I could do. I was not ready for the personal aspect yet. After assessing the letter from all sides, I would pursue the hardest part: reading it as *me*, as a woman, and as the intended recipient.

I should have realized this before, but Brent was a man who had probably seen too many horrors in his life. I felt that pull to him that he described. I'd admitted it enough times to myself, but failed to let the sensations ensnare me in their grip. I had done enough research on veterans for my articles to realize Brent probably suffered from post-traumatic stress disorder. He had referred to "pain." I pictured him in front of me with the look in his eyes that can only be described as "someone who's seen too much shit in their life." It's the mark of a combat veteran. How did I miss that before? Maybe I didn't want to see it because then I'd have to admit something was also wrong with me on a deep level. But it was clear as a new pane of glass that his suffering called to me. I had finally met my match in the pain department.

That's why, subconsciously, I pushed him away. I was the chicken shit, not him. No, not this brave man. He was so strong, not just in the physical sense, but also in his mind and spirit. I was in awe of him. Maybe I *could* trust him. I realized he put me at ease. Maybe, just maybe, I could open up to him. I know the petals on my bud are locked up tighter than any flower on the edge of a winter-to-spring day, but if you only knew why, then you'd understand.

I had thought I was too messed up to be with him. But maybe I'm not. Maybe we could heal each other. It sounded like a lot of work, something that would take a lot of time and effort. We'd have to expend a great deal of energy. So the real question was this: is he worth it? I guessed there was only one way to find out. If he was willing to take the leap of faith and ask me to give him a chance, then I should do the same. I realize he didn't intend to send the letter, but he still put it out there, laid it all on the table.

I read the letter so many times I probably had it memorized. I nursed my coffee long after it had gone cold. I heard that annoying alien chime from my phone, but I ignored it; Stuart was at it again. I realized I should look into blocking his number.

I went back again to thinking about—or rather overthinking and overanalyzing—each line and point Brent made. I responded, rather loudly I might add, to his pleas and questions in my mind.

He had me just as thrown off. I can't believe he hadn't noticed that. But I think I have a pretty good poker face. With that bitch vibe I give off, I know I mask certain things. I was pissed at myself, though, for being so transparent with him that he could tell I was scarred by pain too. A small part of me was relieved that someone could realize I have feelings too—it meant maybe I was human after all. But I spent years cultivating that facade, so it also felt uncomfortable to be discovered.

And for the love of all the saints, why the frick didn't he just scoop me up and throw me in his bed? Damn him! I would have willingly done anything and everything that night. If he only knew what I needed and wanted from him. He might have been a man with needs, but I'm a woman with just as much pent-up frustration, sex deprivation, and lust. I think men often overlook the fact that we're also creatures with sexual cravings. I get all the jokes about claiming to have "headaches" and being tired and all that shit, but we have just as much of a voracious appetite as they do.

I also would have waited for him. Hell, I *have* been waiting for him! He just doesn't know it. Quite frankly, I didn't realize that was I was doing either . . . until now. If you recall, I was about to tell him I wanted to see him again, but then he opened his mouth and ruined the moment. I couldn't stay mad at him, though. He's a man of honor, and he was taking the right course of action by telling me he was leaving. I get it now. These missed chances and missed opportunities were just sad. He talked about fate, and then fate goes and rebuffs us.

He was damn right about one thing—I *don't* need protection. Who the hell would I need protection from? I would have to let that thought marinate a little longer. I scanned the ending again. I agreed with him. I felt like I knew him too. I sighed heavily and reached for my necklace, once again seeking comfort in the here and now. I licked my very dry lips, and realized my lids were starting to droop. I was out of coffee and finding myself very exhausted by the feelings the letter unearthed.

I folded the letter into a neat-but-dirty square. I grabbed my phone, dragged myself from the couch, and kept the letter lovingly tucked into my palm. I went to my bedroom and put the small square next to my phone on the nightstand so I'd remember to put it in my pocket in the morning. I would take it with me wherever I went until he came home.

As I finally climbed into bed with Pussy kneading herself a nice little spot next to me, I had one more thought. I kept coming back to one key point. What stuck out the most was when he said he wouldn't hurt me.

So me being the optimist that I am—ha ha—I would definitely hold him to that. If he did step out of line, then he'd be sorry when he found out what I'd do to him. PTSD would look like a picnic compared to the EBRD I'd give him. In case you're wondering, that's for Everly Ball Removal Disorder.

Aww nuts, was that too harsh?

Chapter 10: Hopefully a Home*coming* to Remember

Brenneth

July 13, 2017

Maybe dreams can come true . . . that cucumber-melon scent I fucking drooled over hung in the air. I could smell her, all of her. All senses were engaged as I locked on to my target. Everly Reynolds certainly knows the way to a man's heart—and it's not through his stomach. Nope, it's farther south, ladies. She was standing at the foot of the bed in the hotel room I was staying in, since I still hadn't found a place to live. She shimmied out of her denim skirt and threw off her black top.

Before me stood a goddess more beautiful than any who had come before. No other woman could compare, and those that would come after her wouldn't either. Well, actually, there wouldn't *be* any after her. I was lying on the bed with my arms folded under me, propping up my head, just admiring the show. I was clad in only my black cotton boxer-briefs, and the flagpole was raised. I couldn't help but grin and think about how lucky I was to get to watch this woman strip for me.

Ev ran her palms over her gorgeous breasts. I groaned, enraptured by the sight of her stiff nipples doing a taunting, hypnotic dance through the sheer material of her bra. The ripened, juicy tips would be in my mouth soon enough. I'd suck and lick them like they were my favorite piece of candy. I'd devour her on the first go-around and then do her all over again, slowly. That way, I could savor her properly. She brought out a different side of me, one that channeled my base instincts.

The nude-colored satin of her panty-and-bra combo made my

mouth water. My balls tightened up in a fit of lustful need. She was exquisite. She was perfection. And she was mine for the taking. Oh, I'd fucking *take*, but I'd also give right back. There was no other woman on earth I could, or would, give more to. She made me think long-term as time ticked by with each moment I was in her presence. With a body built for sin and a mind built for great things, she was a force to be reckoned with. She held all the cards and she knew it. She could play her hand better than any woman—or hell, even man, for that matter.

I couldn't wait to bite her in that spot where the shoulder and neck meet. It's my favorite erogenous zone to go for. When you're in the throes of passion, it's sure to get a girl to scream. Her creamy nectar would spill forth for me instantly—I just knew it. I was licking my lips and salivating just thinking about getting a taste of her.

And I couldn't fucking wait for her to finally taste *me*. I had been fantasizing about it long enough. I wanted to command her to suck my cock, but I didn't want to be forceful or a hasty bastard. I was hoping she would *want* to do it, without being prompted. There is nothing sexier than a woman taking charge of the situation when it comes to sucking dick. I would certainly give her a hefty amount of throat coat once she sucked me good and thoroughly. I was getting lost in the possibilities that were piling up in my dirty mind.

"Am I boring you?" she questioned.

Her eyes pierced me with their emerald glimmer, and I found myself speechless. I loved it when she brought out this sassy side. There were times I wanted to rise to the occasion and take the bait, and then there were other times I wanted to let her steamroll me. Either scenario would be fine as long as *she* was involved.

"Fuck no!" That's what I wanted to yell at her, but I refrained and went in a different direction.

"Everly, you're fucking torturing me is what you're doing! There's so much to look at and play with that I don't know where to begin. I'm fucking dying over here just thinking about what I can, and will, do to you. Or what *you'll* do to *me*." I said the last part with very little restraint.

Then I waggled my eyebrows, trying to be cute and playful. She giggled and arched her back while an erotic moan escaped from her lips. My patience was about to evaporate completely. She had no idea how alluring she was. I doubt she could comprehend the depths of my feelings or desires. I wanted to finally be with her, to lose myself in her luscious body. My dick was clawing its way out of the opening in my boxers, trying to get to her. The desire to finally make love to her was boiling under my skin. I was so desperate for her.

I closed my eyes for a brief moment, to focus and center myself. I needed to dig deep to tell the swimmers to stand down for now and to man their battle stations. I wouldn't survive this if she climbed on my lap.

As I thought that very thing, she moved to the side of the bed closest to me. I felt her there, and my eyes flew open. I growled. I fucking growled like the goddamn caged animal I was. I grabbed her hips and planted her on top of me. She squealed at the swift movement and gulped when she felt my clothed erection line up with her panty-covered pussy. It felt like perfection, even with the material separating us. I could see the change in color on her panties where the wet spot of her arousal had soaked the front. Fuck me, I even had a spot to match with my pre-cum. What a pair.

She arched her back again and closed her eyes. I took advantage of the moment to inhale her scent. I had to touch her in some way. I licked right between her breasts. Goose pimples raced down her arms, and her pink-tipped nubs puckered up under the cups of her bra. I could see the pulse at her neck beating frantically. Her skin was hot to the touch, incredibly smooth, and tasted like paradise. Then I bit her in that spot I said I would between her neck and shoulder, and she did scream in pleasure.

I grabbed her ass cheeks and flipped her over so she was sprawled on her back. She yelped and stared up at me with wide eyes. I was sure my predatory glare was either dangerous or sexy. Either way, I was coming for her. She had to know there was no escape.

I marked the outside of her lips with the tip of my tongue and then plundered her mouth. I ate up her cries and moans, which matched my own groans of passion and ecstasy. I was saving her pussy for last. I couldn't go right for the gold, and it was gold—well, golden, that is. I bit each nipple through the fabric and then moved back up to suck on an earlobe. She cried out, and it was music to my ears.

I decided to change direction by heading for the farthest point of her body. I gently picked up her right foot. She was about to question me; she started to sit up on the bed, but I put the kibosh on that by silencing her with a firm look. She immediately settled back down and just gazed at me, breathing heavily. It was glorious, watching her tits rise and fall with her respirations. As I said, I just liked to watch the show. There'd be more time later for that. Right now, I was on a new mission. And being the good airman that I was, I would fulfill my duty to the best of my abilities.

I kissed and lightly sucked the arch of her foot. She squirmed and tried to kick me away. I knew it didn't tickle—I just suspected it was sensitive and a new feeling for her, one that elicited all kinds of sensations. I examined her big toe and fell in love with her dainty feet. She had long toes, and they were sexy. Her second toe was the longest on her foot. You know what they say about people with a big second toe, right? You'll have to find out for yourself if it's true.

She had painted her nails in a red so dark that they looked like black cherries. It was sexy on her—everything she did was the exact opposite of the frilly, girly, predictable women I was used to. That even extended to the fellow NCOs I had occasionally screwed around with. Everly always managed to surprise me and keep me on my toes. Speaking of toes . . .

I took her big toe in my mouth and sucked. She bucked so hard and moaned that I thought something was wrong at first. But it wasn't wrong. It was oh-so-fucking-right. I bit down slightly, just to draw more vocals from her. She closed her eyes tightly and thrashed from side to side. Oh yeah, I was in the right spot. I thought to myself, *Oh Everly, I'm just getting started.*

I continued to suck on her toe for another few seconds, and then gently laid her foot back down on the bed. She slowly opened her eyes, and I smiled brightly at her with a cat-got-your-tongue look. She smiled back at me. She was the most stunning woman I had ever encountered. I was so thunderstruck by her beauty, inside and out. If only she'd let me tunnel into her mind the way I wanted to tunnel into her body. She had more tight passages in her—and on her—than I could count.

I was about to tell her as much, but suddenly her face fell. I looked at her in utter confusion. I was about to ask her what was wrong, but then she disappeared right before my very eyes. I yelled out her name and reached for her, but I couldn't grab anything but air. I looked down at my empty hands. They were covered in blood. Nothing but dark, cherry-red blood. I felt sick. I was going to hurl.

When I looked up again at the room around me, I realized I was not in a hotel. I was in the middle of the desert, just on the outskirts of the flight line in Afghanistan. I couldn't move my leg. I couldn't really process what was going on because of the fog my mind was in.

Oh, right. I have a concussion. I looked around. The dust was still heavy in the air from the IED explosion.

Pain. Immense pain is what I felt. It lanced my body. But the pain from my injuries paled in comparison to the pain I had felt when Everly disappeared. I closed my eyes and realized this wasn't a dream I was having—it was a nightmare.

Fuck! Wake up, Brent! I screamed at myself.

But I couldn't save myself from my nightmare any more than I could have helped myself on the day of the original injury. I was lost in an alternate universe, and I just hoped I'd get out of it soon.

***

I woke up from my nightmare and abruptly sat up in bed. I was gasping for breath. I was trying to take in mouthfuls of air. I choked and coughed as sweat soaked my shirt. I'm sure my sheets were like a wading pool. *Fuck!* Thank God my roommate was out. I didn't like anyone to see me like that. It was embarrassing, and I felt like a failure when people realized I was certifiable. I ran my hand over my hair. It was a little longer than normal because more time kept passing in between cuts; I didn't have as much opportunity to get groomed as I did back home.

Home. Fuck, I want to go home.

I knew where that was now—and it wasn't Afghanistan.

I reached for my uniform pants, haphazardly slung over the back of the chair at my computer desk. I had taken them off last night and climbed into bed, forgetting to remove her letter and put it under my pillow. I needed the letter now, though; I needed that small reassurance she was out there, even if she wasn't mine. I needed the letter pressed against my flesh as if it was her body; I needed it now more than ever to help keep the nightmares at bay. Running my fingers over the letter helped me in the same way stress balls or fidget spinners help other people. I stuck my hand in my pocket and came back with—nothing. I dumped the pants upside down, but nothing fluttered out. I tried every pocket again, even though I knew I always kept it in the same spot.

I was losing my mind—and getting really fucking angry—as each second passed. I started tearing the room apart like a wild man. When I got done and the cyclone had stopped spinning, I couldn't believe I had trashed the place the way I did. I'd managed to upturn anything and everything not nailed down. But no friggin' letter appeared.

It had vanished, just like Everly.

Where the hell could it be? That letter brought me fucking comfort. Hell, I liked to think I could have even worked up the courage at some point to actually send it. I suddenly wanted to return to my nightmare. The mess I made of the room seemed symbolic of the mess my life was at the moment. I needed to clean up both. Shit, where to start?

Chapter 11: Is This Girl for Real?

Everly

August 20, 2017

Brent's words plagued me. They haunted me. They wrapped their greedy fists around my soul and squeezed as if trying to extract truth from me, like the way you would get the last of the toothpaste out of the tube. They were wringing me out, little by little, each day. I felt out of control of my emotions. How had he slipped through my defenses? I let this happen. Did I *want* this to happen? Maybe on some subconscious level I did. He had finally worn me down. I was helpless against him, defenseless. I surrendered to the idea of . . of . . . us.

If my calculations were correct, Brent would be coming back in the next few weeks or so, which gave me time to do some investigative work. I would put my journalistic skills to use, and this time in a personal capacity. I was going to locate his sister and find a way to reconnect with my man. *Oh fuck!* I just referred to him as "my man," didn't I? You know what? I decided to own it. It's out there; I've said it. I vowed to start thinking in serious terms until he gave me a reason to do otherwise.

Hell, I'd been faithful the whole time he'd been away anyway, like a dutiful girlfriend—so I might as well become one! I don't need the label, though; whatever we decided to be would be just fine. I'd just realized that I wanted to try to give "us" a chance and see where it goes.

I would set my plan in motion the next day, as soon as I got to work. For all Steve knew, I would be working on an article—and not on personal queries. I had a few tricks up my sleeve. I wanted to give Brent a homecoming he would never forget. I could be downright, positively devious when I wanted to be. Oh, Tech Sergeant Peters . . . you'd better be ready for me. I'm coming—and I mean that figuratively *and* literally!

***

It wasn't hard to track down Caylan Bree Graham. First, I started with social media. I found a Facebook account for Brent, but he had the highest privacy settings turned on; I assumed because of the military. No luck there. I got sneaky and called an old friend who worked in the journalism industry and who happened to have access to records that, let's just say, the everyday person didn't. He pulled Caylan's school file, which was listed by her maiden name; that led me to finding her married name. From there, he obtained her address and phone number from alumni records. I knew everything was sure to be current since she had only graduated eight months prior. I thanked my contact profusely, which wasn't in my nature, and hung up.

I drummed my fingers on my desk. It's not that I was a pussy, too afraid to make the call. I cold-called people all the time in my line of work. It was just that, once I went down that path, there would be no turning back. Well, I had already put my feet on the track, so I might as well sprint to the end! I went for it. I picked up my cell phone and dialed Caylan's number. It rang three times before she picked up. I hardly ever get nervous, but this time I swallowed audibly.

"Hello?" a sweet voice answered.

"Um, hi. Is this Caylan Peters, I-I mean Caylan Graham?" I stuttered. I hated that I sounded so ill-prepared.

"Yes, it is. Who's calling please?" she questioned.

"You don't know me. Forgive me for calling like this out of the blue, but I know your brother," I rushed to say.

I heard a gasp on her end. "Oh God! Is he okay? Please tell me he's not . . . I mean he isn't . . . I mean . . . Please just tell me what's wrong," Caylan begged.

Wow, I wasn't expecting that. I didn't think she'd panic and assume something was wrong just because someone mentioned him. I had to fix this—fast.

"Caylan, I'm so sorry. I didn't mean to alarm you. Nothing's wrong. At least I don't think anything is. I haven't talked to your brother since the night before he left." I was sorry to hear myself admit that.

I heard her crying on the other end. *Aww, crap!* I didn't know what to do about that. Sometimes I'm not good at the whole girl thing—or tears.

I should have a set of nuts instead of a slit between my legs, because I didn't do the emotional thing the way women expected me to. I mean, Christ, I have feelings. It's just that I can't cry over things I imagine most women do. I waited her out and let her tears fall. Finally, she seemed to rein herself in. I heard the sobs subside.

"I'm so sorry about that. I haven't talked to Brent since before he left either. He won't talk to me. I finally got an email from him at the beginning of last month, but that is all. He mostly emails my mom when we finally threaten bodily harm. I've been so lost, not talking to him. I worry about him constantly. I love him so much, and it hurts that he's shut me out," she sniffled. "Goodness gracious. I'm babbling, aren't I?"

She loved her brother, that much was obvious. I felt bad for her and recognized her distress. This seemed to be very hard for her to handle. I was beginning to realize that deployments affect everyone linked to the military member who is sent overseas. I had to figure out if I wanted to be a part of that equation, because it seemed like a big burden to sign up for. If Brent was worth it, though, I'd certainly do it. Considering all signs pointed to the fact he was worth it, well, I guess my mind was already made up. I realized I had yet to respond to her, so I snapped myself out of my own thoughts.

"You're not babbling. To be honest, I listen to all sorts of stories for a living, rambling or otherwise, and then I write about them. I'm not writing about this, although I am a journalist. I met your brother the day of your graduation," I explained.

"Oh wow, that's amazing! I don't know any journalists. That's really cool. I'm a writer myself, well, mainly of poetry. But come to think of it, did you use your skills to get my information? And what prompted your phone call today anyway?" she switched tactics and asked quickly.

I knew there was a protective side to her—here it was, coming out full force. I could hear the skepticism in her voice, so I knew I needed to un-muddy the situation quickly.

"I'll be honest. Yes, I did have to go to some lengths to track you down, but please give me a chance to explain. As I said, I met your brother at your graduation. Then we ran into each other again right before he left. I really liked, I mean, I really *like* him. He sent me a letter. Well, he didn't really send it; his roommate did. I want to see him again when he gets home," I admitted.

Jesus, now I was the one who was babbling. *Why did I explain all that?* I had this feeling Caylan was very easy to talk to. She seemed so sweet. I don't know why, but I felt at ease with her even though we had only been talking for a few minutes. I also realized that as much as I don't do the girly thing, I could so see Caylan's appeal. I instantly liked her. She was adorable, and not in an annoying way.

"OMG! Gah! He has a girlfriend? Okay, well, maybe not yet, but you want to be, right? Oh my God, this is amazing. I've always wanted my brother to settle down and find someone. I *knew* there was someone out there for him. He is the best—the absolute best. I know he has his issues, but who doesn't? Anyhoo, he is just the best. Yay! I can't wait to see the two of you together. And he sent you a letter? How romantic is that? This is just the sweetest thing ever," she squealed.

Holy shit! Even though I had no clue what she looked like, I could practically see her jumping up and down and clapping her hands together on the other side of the phone. I needed her to put on the brakes, though, because this wasn't a done deal. I guess in her eyes, it was. *Fuck me!*

"Whoa, Caylan. I love your enthusiasm about the situation, but pump the brakes, girl! He doesn't even *know* I got the letter, and therefore, he doesn't know I'm still interested in him." I sighed and then continued, "It's a long story. I'll be happy to tell you the whole thing some other time. The reason for me calling, though, is that I need your help. I need to know when Brent is coming home so I can meet up with him."

"Okay. That I actually *do* know. He is set to come home the morning of September fourteenth, at the Baltimore airport—unless something changes, of course. If you aren't familiar with the military, well, let me just tell you that stuff changes all the time. My parents are going down to pick him up. Then the next day, we're having a cookout here, at my house. Of course Brent doesn't know we're going to ambush him with a small homecoming party, but he's pee-wee'd me off long enough. He's going to have to show up and darn well enjoy it! I'm dying for him to see Em—that's my daughter, you see. She's six months old, and he's missed so much of her life already. I don't even know if he's gotten the pictures I've sent, and it makes me so sad," she said, whispering the last part.

Crap, I wanted to hug her. For the record, I am not a hugger. But again, this girl made me want to form some kind of a sisterhood—pants traveling, whatever-the-shit that thing is—or bond with her. I wanted so badly to make her feel better.

"He told me he loves and adores the both of you. I can see why. So, are you in? Can you help me surprise him?" I was asking for help, which was also something I never did.

"Guuurl, I can do you one better. I will help you prepare and execute. This will be so much fun! I can't wait to see the look on his face, and I can't wait to meet you. We'll have to get together for lunch before he comes home so we can plan. Yay, this is going to be amazing! I am so excited, I might pee. Well, that would suck since that means I'd be leaking from both ends. Oh my God, I'm sorry. That is probably TMI! But I already went there, didn't I? Well, anyway, I'm still breastfeeding, and I forget not everyone probably wants to hear about all that baby stuff. I'm sorry. My husband is a doctor, so he lets me talk away about all the bodily stuff too," she giggled.

It was TMI, but for her, I suppose it was normal. I was okay with it, though, because, well, she was his sister, I guess. It's odd how this woman had already charmed me into being her friend.

"No problem, Caylan. You're fine. You can share whatever. Hell, I may share stuff that's TMI too. It's nice to talk to another female, and it's refreshing to talk about something that's not job-related. I could get used to this. And yes, we should plan lunch. Just let me know when and where. You have my number now, so feel free to call or text me, and we'll get together. I'll work around your schedule—you're the one with the baby," I stated.

We chatted for a few more minutes and then ended the call, but not before she promised that she would contact me soon to meet and conspire. I pulled my cell away from my ear and placed it on my desk. I smiled at the phone. It felt so good to talk to a girlfriend. I sure hoped things worked out with Brent. But in the event it didn't, I called dibs on his sister in the breakup.

***

I got home later that night and still felt buzzed from the amazing call with Caylan. It had put me in a good mood for the whole day, in fact. I needed more positive people in my life, I realized. I groaned when I heard Stuart's telltale chime. *Ugh!* That boy was becoming a stalker. I had repeatedly told him I wasn't interested, but clearly he still wasn't getting it.

I rolled my eyes at the phone and walked to my bedroom. I put my phone under my pillow to muffle the sound and decided to treat myself to a bath—and maybe much later, after said bath, an orgasm.

I had looked up some of Caylan's poetry at work and printed out a collection of things she'd written. I decided to read some of it while I soaked. I opted for wine tonight, red to be exact, and I burned a pear-scented candle in the corner of the shower stall. The bubbles were stacked high, just the way I liked it, and I still gave myself a beard with them for kicks, like I had in my youth. Although, I remembered with a twinge, in my younger years it was a rare occasion when I actually *got* a bath. I also made my hair into a Mohawk. Some things you just never grow out of, I guess.

After I was done playing and being childish—blame nostalgia and Caylan—I started to read. I couldn't believe the first poem I picked from the small stack. I was awestruck, because it hit too close to home.

I've Been Waiting for You
The hours have ticked on and the clock signals the loss,
My bleeding heart has not found the path that you cross.
I've been waiting for you to return to me, you must know,
But the colors have no clarity, and frolic to and fro.
I'm waiting for the light to make the picture clear,
I'm waiting for the time when you will reappear.
I'm lost in the darkness, stumbling around,
I cannot find the beginning, the end, or the ground.
I've been waiting for you to return, can't you see,
Why did you go in the first place, why did you leave me?
So I'll sit idly by and keep watch from the tower,
Ticktock, the clock signals hour by hour.
I'll stand guard and observe you riding right to my door,
I'll be ready and waiting, always and forevermore.

I had cried last month for the first time in forever at Brent's letter. And
tonight . . . well, tonight I cried again, but this time because of his dear
sister.

Chapter 12: Ambushed

Brenneth

September 14, 2017

Finally! I fucking touched down on American soil, in Baltimore. I turned on my cell phone as we were still taxiing in, and a million messages flooded my screen. The message senders included my parents, sister, brother-in-law and his buddies, my former roommates, and various other people. All were welcoming me home. It was the best feeling to be back in the land of the free. I relaxed in my coach seat and just sifted through the texts as we pulled in. I liked to be the last one off the plane, so I had some time to kill as all the hasty passengers tried to make a swift exit.

One of the first things I was looking forward to doing was taking off my smelly boots. I wanted to burn them. I had worn them too damn long. The trip home had been exhausting, as always. Traveling is the worst part of any deployment, because of the anticipation.

I wanted to make fists with my feet like Bruce Willis did in *Die Hard*; that movie is another classic, by the way. But anyway, I desperately needed a shower. I couldn't wait to rid myself of my uniform and general travel filth. I also couldn't wait to wear civilian clothes again. On Monday, I'd have to go to the base to in-process, which involved a lot of paperwork because of transferring back to my normal squadron from my deployed one. But I had the upcoming weekend to just be me—whoever that guy was now. Once my in-process checklist was complete, I'd also be on R & R for two weeks, and I was going to take another two weeks on top of that because I had use-them-or-lose-them days built up. It would be amazing to take a break and get some headspace. I had a list a mile long of things to do, starting with finding a place to stay, then getting my dog back from the guys.

I had a lot on my mind, as usual. I had never found out what happened to my letter, and it bugged me more than you can imagine. Nevertheless, I had survived another deployment. July marked my sixteen-year anniversary in the military, and these next fucking four years couldn't go by fast enough to reach the big twenty-year mark signaling retirement. I was ready to start a new chapter in my life, whatever that entailed.

I looked at my phone again. My mom's text explained that they were in baggage claim, anxiously waiting for me. I definitely wanted to see my sister and niece, but I was hoping it was just my parents there for now. I wasn't ready to face the firing squad quite yet. Yup, I'm a big, fat pussy. As I darkened the screen on my phone, thoughts of Everly swirled in. I longed to hear from her. How I wished one of the texts had been from her; I secretly hoped she had managed to get my number somehow. It was wishful thinking that she'd be around to welcome me back, though.

***

Thankfully, there had not been a big parade or damn scene at baggage claim. That would have had Caylan's name written all over it. It had been solely my parents there to greet me, and I couldn't have been more grateful because I didn't want a big to-do. I stayed with Mom and Dad, at the condo that Alexi and Caylan lived in when they were dating. My parents had made the place into a nice home. It was such a departure from its previous look. I had been in the condo when it still screamed "bachelor," back before my sister Caylan-ified it, when Alexi was simply dating her. Eventually, Alexi and Caylan bought a house, then he went into private practice, and consequently they gave my parents the condo.

My parents were hardworking people, though, and assured Alexi they'd pay him back over time. Alexi had more money than he could shake a stick at, so it wasn't a big deal to him. His parents were rich too. I was happy my baby sister was taken care of and that their daughter would be cared for her whole life. There was no jealousy on my end, because I was comfortable with my lifestyle in spite of its flaws.

The condo now had that homey feel that can only come from a mother's touch. My mom was the best. She was sweet, loving, and giving, and everyone just adored her. Although I grumbled—okay, damn well barked at her—when I found out a surprise welcome-home cookout was planned for me at my sister's house later that afternoon. But I was partly grateful. It would be good to finally see the rest of my family, even if in the back of my mind I was still pussying out.

Before we left my parents' residence, I noticed their orange sedan had finally transitioned from Texas license plates to Pennsylvania ones. The 'rents were supposed to surrender the plates a long time ago, but I think they had been holding on to a piece of what they thought was "home." Now I think we all considered the East Coast home and finally felt settled. We were all at peace with where we were, and that was a comforting prospect. We had been through a lot as a family, so I smiled to myself as I climbed in the car and realized the simple plate switch meant my parents had embraced their present and future here. I had decided to let Mom and Dad chauffeur me around for the day, but I planned to get my truck out of storage the next day.

We pulled up to a huge house on an amazing plot of land. My sister and Alexi sure had good taste. Their home would be the perfect place to raise a family, and I knew my niece would be adorable toddling around in the yard in a year. I had missed so much already, being "over there." I felt awful. I remember when Caylan was born, and how she seemed to grow every single goddamn day. Emeline surely was a completely different baby by that point.

My chest ached, and I started sweating. I rubbed the spot in the middle of my chest where I felt intense pressure. *Oh no, not now.* I tried to stay in the moment and breathe deeply. *Here goes nothing!*

We walked into the house and were immediately greeted by staff I assumed had been hired for the day to help out with the "cookout." I knew that term was a euphemism for "party" and the explosion that was probably waiting for me in the backyard. Caylan sure didn't do anything in a small way. My sister had a huge deck, patio, pool, gardens, hot tub, and tennis court, so their house and grounds could easily accommodate a large crowd. To my surprise, I didn't see a lot of people as I looked around outside. I scanned the gathering of people and surveyed the area for any threat—a force of habit from being trained to observe and take in my surroundings. I was never going to break myself of that cycle since I did it everywhere I went. I always had an exit strategy for those just-in-case scenarios when things might go south.

The backyard was decorated with elegance and taste, and Caylan's minimalistic approach actually made it perfect. She had really made this a wonderful, understated homecoming, and it was awesome. Even the banner wasn't obnoxious or loud. I was proud of her for making it a great event. My cousin Meg was flitting around the crowd, snapping pictures. Man, that girl never stopped with the camera. She was a budding photographer, and from what I hear, a damn good one. She's also my sister's best friend. I had missed Meg's college graduation in the spring; it was just one more family milestone I had missed.

I walked by three familiar faces and nodded my head at Caleb, Anthony, and Gil. They each appeared to have brought a plus-one to the shindig; I couldn't help but wonder if two of the companions were only temporary—arm candy. These guys were the ultimate bachelors, but as I said, one by one, they were pairing off. Anthony was with Shanna, of course—the green engagement ring still shone brightly on her finger. As far as Caleb and Gil were concerned . . . well, I couldn't picture either of their respective statuses changing anytime soon. But maybe I shouldn't judge. After all, that's where Alexi had been a year ago. Look at him now! It's amazing what the right woman can do for a man.

I saw one of Alexi's nurses from his practice, Liz, over to the side. She was talking to his parents. Liz seemed like a cool chick. I barely knew her, but from what I did gather, she was an army brat. She was also a beautiful woman—and not just beautiful "for her age." I think Alexi said she was in her forties. Apparently, she had three teenagers and an alcoholic husband.

Alexi's parents, Juliet and Randolph, were pleasant enough. They came from money, so they acted as I expected. There were a few people I didn't know mingling about, but I assumed they were friends of Alexi's and Caylan's. It suited me fine, not socializing with everyone, because it didn't appear I needed to entertain anyone.

My ex-roommates, Todd and Ben, were chatting up two women by the bar in the corner. I didn't know the women, so either they also brought plus-ones, or they were also mutual friends somehow connected to my sister. I kept scanning the yard, looking for something. No, not something—*someone*. I knew I was being foolish. Just then, I heard a squeal. I turned rapidly to gauge where the noise had come from.

My sister, as tiny as she was, came barreling toward me. She practically took me down with the force of her attack. She kissed my cheek repeatedly, and I had to bend down to her level to accept the assault. Tears were streaming down her beautiful face, and I couldn't understand a friggin' word she was saying due to her excitement and sobbing. She held on to me for dear life, and I felt like I was about to cry too. My baby sister could do no wrong, and I loved her to death. It felt so good to see her.

Then, she reared back. For a second, I thought she was going to slap me. I got off lucky: she scolded me with her pointed finger instead.

"You're in big trouble, you meanie. I have been through hell for six months because you didn't call or email me. Don't ever do that to me again, or I'll cut off your manhood," she said deadpan. Her red-rimmed eyes burned into me.

I didn't know if I should laugh or cower in a corner. She never threatened me like that. I knew she couldn't bring herself to say the word "balls." It was almost as if she was taking lessons from Everly. My chest ached again at the thought of that blonde-haired beauty.

I didn't know what to say to my sister except, "I'm sorry, Little Bit. It won't happen again."

I scooped her up once more and held her to my chest. She looked gorgeous, as always. Motherhood suited her. She had on a beautiful pink, flowy dress and a jean jacket. My baby sister was a grown woman—married, with a daughter. I still couldn't get over it.

"You're damn skippy it won't!" she said with a resigned sigh.

Then she smiled and looked like her normal, sweet, happy self. "Em is napping right now. Alexi just went to check on her . . . I suspect to give us a moment to talk. He wants to pound your butt for what you put me through, and I'm debating about whether or not I should let him. The funny thing is, you know I can't stay mad at you very long. Especially now that I'm a mama and realize how precious life is. Oh my God, I can't wait for you to hold her. She's so stinkin' cute. She giggles all the time and is the happiest little baby. She's trying so hard to crawl. I bet it will be any day now, and then look out! I can see Alexi following her around with a pillow until long after she's mastered the skill. Good Lord, that man is driving me crazy with how protective he is. But I'm the luckiest girl in the world. Wait until you see the pink headband with the enormous pink bow on top of her head." She laughed with abandon.

I knew she mentioned the bow and had the baby wearing it to purposefully drive my brother-in-law nuts, and I was all for it. Any chance I could get to gang up on him with Caylan was well worth it. I was about to tell my sister that we could gang up on him more often now that I was home when I heard a bark in the distance.

Funny, I didn't know my sister got a dog.

The barking got louder as the animal got closer, then I saw Maverick weaving his way through patio furniture and people to get to me.

He jumped up into my arms and started licking my face. He let out a part-cry, part-howl kind of noise. Then he ran around in a circle and repeated the process of licking me. I missed him and told him as much. He's a good dog. I didn't expect to get to see him so soon, but it made sense since Ben and Todd were there. I was scratching behind his ears and petting him on the head, telling him what a good boy he was, when he jumped up again. I could have sworn I smelled cucumber-melon lotion on his fur.

Impossible!

"Maverick, sit! Good boy. When we get home, wherever the hell that is, I'll give you a special treat," I assured him while laughing at his display of excitement.

"And when do I get *my* special treat?" asked an all-too-familiar but

73

unexpected voice from behind me.

I sucked in a huge breath and froze. I knew that voice. I'd know that voice anywhere in a crowd, even though I'd only had the privilege of hearing it twice. It would be locked in the very deepest recesses of my mind for all of eternity.

I turned in her direction. It was one of those moments like in a movie, you know, when the records skips, the music goes dead silent in a jam-packed room, and then all the attention turns to the main character. Temptress Everly had invaded my senses every single goddamn day since the last time I had laid eyes on her. I raked my gaze up and down her delectable body and worried I'd bust a nut just from being in her presence.

She was wearing skinny jeans, white strappy heel things, and a red fitted top.

Fuck me, she's my own patriotic princess.

But was she mine? Her tits looked perky and amazing. Her tan skin begged to be sucked. Her pert ass filled the jeans out like she had been poured into them. I was probably slobbering like Maverick, but I'd gladly take a doggy bag to go if it meant I'd get to take that exquisite being home.

God bless America, ladies and gentlemen! The flag was raised high and proud in my pants, waving in the wind and at attention.

You could probably have put a hook in my mouth from the way I was gaping at her like a caught fish. I imagined everyone thought I'd just seen a ghost. Maybe I was hallucinating.

This can't be real, can it? Fuck, did I get blown up again? Am I lost in some kind of a dream or coma?

If that was the case, I never wanted to wake up. I needed someone to pinch me.

What the hell did she just ask me again?

I watched her assess my choice of dress too. She eyed up my build and devoured me with her gorgeous greens. I was wearing dark-washed jeans, black boots, and a tight, white T-shirt with a checkered, short-sleeve button-down over it. Watching her eat me up with her stare made my groin tighten painfully. I couldn't even adjust myself to relieve the throbbing because we were in public.

If she was standing there in front of me, it meant she was there to see *me*. A jolt of emotion and heat overtook my body. My spirit felt light and airy from the relief of seeing her. I hadn't felt so good in as long as I could remember. That moment was everything. I was reunited with my family, and I was reunited with my woman. Yeah, I could talk in terms like that. She wasn't going to get away—not this time. I had already decided I would go after her when I got back anyway, but as always, she beat me to the punch.

She had better be prepared to pull an all-nighter, because I have six months to make up for.

 I never answered her question. She laughed, knowing full well she caught me off guard . . . again. This woman could do that to me anytime she wanted, though. I was about to tell her as much, but of course she spoke first.

 "Well, Tech Sergeant Peters, should we talk about the elephant in the room?" she asked with a captivating smile.

 I smiled back. I couldn't wait to play her game again.

Chapter 13: The Heat Is On

Brenneth

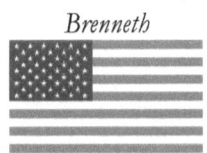

I still hadn't said anything to her. I couldn't. I couldn't think about anything but the need to feel her body and ravish her fully. I'd have to be careful not to be too forceful and attack her, but I'd friggin' ambush her like she had ambushed me.

I moved toward her like a heat-seeking missile. I reached for her arm and yanked her toward me. She let out a squeak, but I think it was out of surprise and not discomfort. I looked into her eyes. Her breathing was erratic. Her pupils also gave away how affected she was by the situation. Nope, definitely not afraid. She was turned on and in tune with my body, just as I was with hers. I felt her soft curves mold to my hard build perfectly. I groaned and stared her down.

She knew what was coming. I cupped her face and moved in. I tongued her in the deepest, wettest, most scorching way a kiss could ever be delivered. I devoured her like my life depended on it. I had never been so starved for a woman. I wanted to fuck her right there on the pristine patio table next to me. I wouldn't care who watched either. To hell with the food and dishes that would be destroyed in the process.

In a small part of my brain, I heard throats clearing. I registered my sister clapping and jumping up and down. But I could care less. The gawkers and voyeurs could watch me swallow her up. The best part was, she didn't seem to mind or protest. She was lost in the moment with me. I was a man on a mission, and a man who had been deprived for six months was not one to be trifled with.

I didn't just want to fuck her, though; I wanted to make real love. It would be everything, because she was everything. There were so many unspoken things between us still, but all that shit could be worked out later.

I wanted to scoop her up and carry her off into the sunset like the scene in *An Officer and a Gentleman,* but I knew I couldn't abandon my family so soon. My dick was crazy angry, my heart burned deeply, and my mind raced uncontrollably. I could hold out a little longer to get her alone. She was worth the wait.

***

Everly sat next to me at the patio table—yup, the very table I had just fantasized about making love to her on. Inwardly, I smiled to myself at that idea again. Then I had to tell myself "down, boy" so I wouldn't rethink my choice. We comfortably conversed with my sister, Alexi, and Mom and Dad. The party was pretty much over by that time and all the guests had left, but the people who mattered most remained. It had gotten a little cool once the sun went down, but the staff had turned on the deck heaters. Soon enough, a cozy and tranquil ambience was created. Lights were strewn about the back deck; my sister had quite the little utopia back there. Very fucking romantic, I might add. Ev's skin looked even more tan and glowing in the light that they cast.

I was making funny faces at my niece, and she was squirming and squealing away in my sister's arms. God, she was the cutest kid. I blew kisses at her adorable chubby cheeks and affectionately admired the bow on her head. I couldn't stop laughing at how much Alexi grumbled about that headband. Secretly I knew the bastard loved it; he was the happiest, luckiest son of a bitch. Maybe I would be as lucky one day.

I kept looking over at my girl. Whenever we locked gazes, we made a charged connection. My need for her matched the strength of a powerful electrical storm. Neither of us said much to the other, but we didn't need words. My parents took to her immediately, and she seemed more than content with my sister and brother-in-law. Clearly I had missed a lot while away, because the two women giggled and chatted away like they were old friends. It was an amazing sight to see, though. There was no awkwardness at all; she fit right in with the most important individuals in my life. I needed to pinch myself again.

Everyone steered clear of asking me any questions related to my deployment. My family knew better, and I was grateful they didn't pry for details or information. I was not the sharing type with that shit, probably never would be. No one could understand what it was like unless they'd served. I'm sure the journalist in Everly was burning with questions, but she refrained from asking any either. It was comfortable. Everyone just let me be; it was the best homecoming ever.

I was finally *home*, and I knew I would never have to contemplate where that was again.

My parents did do one thing I didn't expect: they announced to everyone that I had made the next rank. I never made a big deal about those things, so I was relieved that my parents had waited until only our small group remained before spilling the beans. I had tested out of cycle because of the deployment. Luckily, my board scores and test scores were enough to get me the promotion. I'd be sewing on master sergeant (M.Sgt.) stripes soon—probably the next month. Some people moved through the ranks fairly quickly, and then there were others, like me, who didn't. There was always the worry about being high-year tenure, which could ultimately lead to your being discharged from the military. Basically, if you don't make rank within a certain amount of time, then you're discharged. My goal was to retire as a M.Sgt., so at least in four years that dream would be realized. After the round of congratulations rang out from everyone, we finally moved on to other subjects. I knew everyone was proud, but I could do without any fuss.

At one point, I heard Ev's phone chime with an irritating sound. She didn't even look at the screen, just made a passing face that showed her annoyance. I made a mental note to remember to ask her about it later. As I said, there was a lot we had to work out. I was anxious to get her alone so we could do just that—physically and verbally.

I'm sure no one wanted the night to end; well, besides my libido and maybe hers. But it was getting late. Mom and Dad were early-to-bed-early-to-rise types, so they were ready to head out. Em needed to be put down for the night too.

I was more than ready to put the story of Everly and me to bed once and for all. This drama had gone on long enough; it was time to take action. I was willing to get a hotel room, but she swooped in before I could again, informing me she had already planned the sleeping accommodations. She leaned into me just as my parents were getting up from the table.

"By the way . . . you're staying with me tonight, at my place." She delivered the news with absolute conviction and control.

Fuck! She was so sexy, it was scary. Where had she been all my life? I closed my eyes. I needed a moment to get myself under control—and to absorb the fact I would get to have her. Finally.

I responded in the most simplistic terms, "Fuck yeah, I am."

She gave me a saucy grin. She knew exactly what she was doing. I would let her. I would have walked on hot coals to be with her. I worshipped her. She was everything I wanted in a woman, and everything I didn't even know I needed.

We bid good night to my parents. I told them I was going home with Ev. They didn't even bat an eyelash. My mom just kissed me on the cheek and whispered a sweet warning for me to "behave." My dad clapped me on the back and then pulled me in for one of his famous Dad hugs. They were the best in every way. I was so damn lucky. They also took Maverick with them. I said I'd collect him later.

I smothered Emeline in kisses and shook hands with Alexi as he carried his daughter off to bed. The staff was tending to cleaning up the rest of the mess, so Ev and I were left with only my sister. Caylan was having a hard time letting me leave, but I got it. She needed reassurance I would come back again soon. I held my baby sister tightly, extracting all her love and support in that embrace. She infused me with relief, acceptance, and trust.

"Caylan . . . you know I'm coming back," I reminded her gently in her ear.

She sniffled, and I hugged her even tighter. I let her collect herself before I released her. When I pulled back, she gave me a lovely, watery smile.

"I know. I just love you. I missed you. I'm just so glad you have Everly," she replied.

I could see Everly blush out of the corner of my eye. I was surprised. It was a new thing to see her almost embarrassed by sentimental words. But just as I loved everything about the curly-haired siren, I sure loved the way she reacted to that phrase. That moment was such a stunning thing to be part of.

"I love you too. I won't be a stranger, I promise. We'll get together very soon. I need to spend time with you guys, and I need for Emeline to get used to having an adoring fan of an uncle around," I said.

Caylan smiled and dried her eyes with her fingertips, and nodded in agreement. She walked over to Everly to give her a hug too. Everly enfolded her in her longer arms. Seeing the two women together like that melted my fucking heart. I knew Caylan was loved by everyone, but for Caylan to love Ev right back . . . wow, that was sheer heaven. Ev said goodbye. Caylan turned to head into the house, then stopped to say one last thing. And in true Caylan fashion, she botched it.

"It is so fan*testical* that you're both here together. I mean . . . fantastical. I mean fantastic. Gah! Good night, I'm sure you two can show yourselves out, all the while behaving." She giggled, realizing her Freudian slip, then ran off into the house. But somehow she still managed to end the situation on a carefree and light-hearted note.

Everly and I laughed at her retreating form. My night was just getting started. It was sure to be "fan*testical*" indeed.

***

Everly

I would explain everything to Brent at some point about how the whole night came to be. We were heading to my place. He was behind the wheel, and I was in the passenger seat, a prisoner to my thoughts. I was reflecting on the night and all the planning—or, rather, I should say conspiring—I did with his sister to make it happen. I even made sure his parents drove so both his truck and my car wouldn't be left at his sister's. I had coordinated with Caylan to ensure the cookout was planned in every detail. She wanted to make a big production of it, but in the end, we both agreed a small-scale welcome-home party was best given Brent's nature and state of mind.

I had come to love Caylan just in the few weeks I'd known her. She was like my sister from another mister. We'd gotten together a few times to plan and to just be women. It was the best thing, having a friend like that. It was something I'd been missing for thirty-something years. I finally had an actual girlfriend that I could just pal around with, and it was amazing. I took to her like a duck to water. I couldn't get over the fact that his parents were so loving, giving, and supportive. I sure didn't have that growing up, but enough on that sorry subject.

Caylan did say one thing that stuck with me when we were sitting at lunch a few weeks ago. Her words had been hovering in my mind. As she casually did her mommy thing and breastfed Emeline, she told me something that resonated with me.

"Mamas give you roots and wings: the roots to your family and the wings to fly to wherever that may be one day," she imparted.

Caylan had no idea how profound and meaningful that statement was. It hurt my heart that I had never had—and never would have—that. She also said the saying might mean something different to each person, but I didn't even know what it really meant to me. I just know the phrase had been toying with me.

My first impression of Caylan reaffirmed the fact that I believed she was a very astute individual. Again, it was no wonder her husband adored her and her brother idolized her. It wasn't lost on me that she had subtly slid into our first real conversation the story of how she met Alexi. She also kept driving home the point that you didn't have to know someone forever to fall in love with them.

"When you know, you know," Caylan kept repeating with goo-goo eyes and merriment written all over her face.

Jeez, she really wants this thing between Brent and me to stick.

She must have thought we were a done deal. I was trying not to think prematurely about our relationship, though. Things would fall into place the way they were meant to happen. I kept thinking about his letter and about Caylan's poem. I sighed to myself. I needed to forget everything about yesterday, today, and tomorrow. I just needed to think about Brent and the way he made me feel in the moment. I tried to let his words from the letter float through my bloodstream, to give me the courage and strength I needed to bring my heart in sync with my brain and body.

I looked over at Brent. He was handling my older Jeep like a pro, and even managed to do the "Jeep wave" at passersby in the "Jeep club." Good thing I had him plug the address to my apartment into the GPS in his phone; I was lost in my own head and would have been useless to help him navigate even to my own place. I realized I was also fairly useless at keeping him company at the moment. However, it was a comfortable silence between us; I think we both had a lot on our minds.

Or maybe we just had one thing on our minds.

I was trying not to overthink things. I was nervous, excited, anxious, horny—you name it. I had tried to plan everything for tonight, but maybe I was trying to plan too much. Better to just let things unfold. I had even methodically planned my outfit so it would reflect a patriotic theme; maybe that was over the top as well, even though I was going for charming with a hint of come-hitherness. He hadn't said anything about it, so maybe he wasn't impressed.

I didn't know why I was second-guessing myself all of a sudden. I was second-guessing *everything* the closer we got to my apartment, probably because of nerves again.

Ugh, this is hard . . . I mean difficult.

Now I sounded like Caylan, with all the innuendos. Man oh man, I needed a stiff dick.

I mean drink. Shit!

We finally pulled into my apartment complex. I knew it wasn't the nicest area, but it was what I could afford on my salary, and the location was convenient. Brent didn't seem like the judgmental type. I was grateful for that, especially after seeing Caylan's house. I was not jealous; she and her husband earned what they had. Actually, I was the exact opposite of jealous. I didn't covet what others had when it came to material possessions. I wanted to earn everything on my own, and I'd be damned if I ever had anything handed to me. I didn't like the feeling of owing anyone anything. That's probably even why I had assumed Brent reduced our encounter to just a fuck—because *I* didn't want to owe *him*, emotionally speaking. I misjudged him. But his parting words about "reciprocating" really stung. That's why I found it hard to let him in again. The letter changed all that, though.

I led him up the three flights of stairs, and he entered my place. It was a good feeling, having him there. He looked around. I could tell he was trying to get a sense of my style. I loved the way I kept everyone guessing. I thought I could pull off just about any trend when it came to fashion and clothes, but what I went for in terms of home décor, though, was comfortable and just simply "Everly."

Pussy came out for a second, and Brent moved to greet her. She snubbed him by sticking her pretentious tail in the air and walking away from him. She strutted down the hallway, shaking her ass. She's a twat and can be very cunty. I can't say I blame her; after all, she is a product of my influence, and I don't easily let people in either. I'm sure some would say I'm the toughest nut to crack. Not only is there an outer shell, there's also an interior one. Brent thought she was adorable, and I loved him all the more for it.

Wait . . . what the frick did I just say to myself? Nope, never mind. I'll just hit the backspace button on my mental keyboard and delete that shit faster than I even thought it. It never happened.

After he laughed at Pussy running off, Brent became as still as a statue. I realized that he was breathing heavily. I turned toward him. Sure enough, he was standing there, fucking me with only his gaze. I never, ever blushed, but I did then; come to think of it, I think I had earlier too.

Goddamn side effect of hanging out with Caylan! She was an angel, though, in so many ways. Namely for taking on a friend such as myself. I made a conscious effort to push thoughts of her to the side just then, though—because of what I was about to do to and with her big brother.

I had been taking the lead all night, so I wasn't sure if he was waiting for me, or if he wanted me to wait for him. I was about to come out with one of my famous smart-ass comments, but there was no time.

In two seconds flat . . . well, I was.

I was flat on my back on the couch with his big, solid, muscular, oh-so-fucking yummy body hovering over mine. He was supporting himself just enough to keep the bulk of his weight off me, but he was still pressing against me so I could feel the presence and heaviness of his entire manly form, from head to toe. It felt so good to have him against me. We both groaned, and he hadn't even done anything to me yet. We were still fully clothed, but it was erotic, delicious, and intense all the same.

Damn. The man could make me feel so much for him, it was scary. My knees fell to the sides as I opened my legs wider so he could fall farther into place. Everything of his aligned perfectly with my most intimate, moist parts. He smelled my hair, and I moved in to suck his earlobe; I couldn't help it. I didn't even know I had a thing for earlobes, but with Brent, apparently I did. He had used that same move on me the night before he left, and I had always thought it was the ultimate erotic act. So I sucked and bit down gently, hinting at the tonguing action I so wanted to give his ball sac. He growled and reared back. He got up off the couch and stood there. He was clearly trying to calm himself down—I could tell by his overactive respiration.

I was so confused. I thought for a second that I had done something wrong.

"Before you go and get any ideas that you just did something wrong, or that I don't want this, or some bullshit thing about me being too much of a pussy to take you right now, let me set the record straight. If I'm going to fuck you, sweetheart, or rather, try and make love to you and last more than one fucking nanosecond, then I need to go rub one out in the shower."

I was actually grateful that he had just allayed my fears.

"So go lie down on the bed and give me ten minutes. Then your sweet, sexy, body is mine. Got it?" he asked with just the right edge of aggressiveness.

I was so damn turned on, I couldn't even come back with anything snarky or cute. All I could do was nod my head. He nodded his in return, and grunted. I practically ran to my bedroom. I could hear my shower running in the bathroom. I was shaking in anticipation. I imagined the water cascading down his body, much like I wanted a shower of his cum to cascade down on me.

Oh shit, that's probably TMI!

I told myself to be a good girl and lie down on the bed, adhere to his command. I hoped I survived this powerhouse of a man—he was once again acting like the unstoppable force I needed him to be. There was only one thing I wondered at that point: in preparation for our lovemaking, should I rub one out too?

Chapter 14: Shedding the Layers

Everly

I decided not to, actually. It isn't a big deal for a female to come a million times; in fact, it is preferred. I knew he'd love how fast I would get off— and the number of times I could get off. I didn't have too much experience with multiple orgasms, but I figured they were clearly on the menu tonight. After all, he *was* Brent.

I did the armpit-sniff check to make sure I still smelled good. I thought about sneaking into the bathroom to brush my teeth really quickly, but I knew I'd end up hopping in the shower with him if I did that. So I pulled a mint from my bedside drawer and popped it in my mouth instead; that would have to do. I also pulled out the box of condoms I had purchased specifically for our encounter. I set them on the top of the nightstand. I was proud that, once again, I carefully had thought, planned, and prepared for this operation. Now to execute it! I laughed to myself, thinking his military ways were rubbing off on me already.

I couldn't wait for other things of his to rub off on me either.

I wasn't under any illusions about getting pregnant or getting some disease, so condoms were a must. I suspected Brent was clean, though— and I had obviously been willing to sleep with him last time. We'd never even bothered with "that" conversation. But since I had had time to think, things were different.

I wasn't very worried, because I assumed the military ran panels of blood work to ensure their troops were healthy. And I sure knew *I* was healthy. For fuck's sake, he'd just returned from the desert! I was pretty confident nothing would have happened over there, and I sure knew I hadn't gotten any action while he was away. But fuck me . . . if neither of us had brought rubbers tonight, I would have used cellophane if I had to. I'm a resourceful girl. Yeah, I was that desperate for him.

I was still clothed except for my shoes, which I kicked off by the side of the bed. I decided to dispense with the top and bottoms, though, and just to wait for him in my undergarments. I had even managed to make a trip to a swanky lingerie store to surprise him. I overpaid, of course, but I knew our first full night together would be worth it. I'd just cut back on my coffee or make some other sacrifice in my finances to be able to afford it. You know how much the night meant to me if I was willing to sacrifice my coffee! I spritzed on some cucumber-melon spray, making sure I hit the targets. The necessary areas any girl needs to spray are the neck, the mandatory crotch shot, and then into the air in front of you so you can walk through the scent cloud to coat yourself.

I also applied some lip tint. I read somewhere that men are driven wild if the color of the lips on your face matches the lips of your pussy. Yes, ladies, this requires you to actually study your petals. There was no shame or embarrassment in doing so on my end—I just imagined my research paying off. I, for one, wanted to use all the weapons in my arsenal to seduce a man. Correction! To seduce *this* man, even if he was an easy target. Brent was the most special man I had ever met. He was worth it, and I wanted to please him. I also decided to dim the lighting in my room. I wanted it slightly dark to make it sensual, but not pitch black. I needed to see my man.

I'm testing out that term of endearment a lot . . .

I heard the shower turn off, so I quickly scrambled into bed, anxiously waiting for him to appear. I was panting so hard that I felt sure he must have been able to hear me through the wall. I was just so keyed up. I was already soaking wet, and my pussy was screaming for attention. I dug my nails into my palms; the bite of pain helped stave off the hunger brewing inside my starved body. I was definitely HFTS—hurting for the squirting—by that point, and I was afraid I'd end up coming before he even entered the room. I couldn't keep my legs still. I tried to squeeze my knees together as the throbbing intensified and the aching in my cunt became overwhelming.

I heard the bathroom door open, so I sat up to take a peek. He walked the two steps out of the bathroom and was quickly standing in my bedroom doorway with hungry eyes. I guess I had expected to see Brent either in a towel that would've been too incredibly small to house all his masculinity, or in some state of dress. But he wasn't. He was naked as could be. I moaned so loudly, it was probably disturbing. I threw myself back on the bed. Even looking at him was overwhelming. He was too much! All those months of hoping, wishing, dreaming, praying, and driving myself crazy—it all came down to that moment.

I didn't hear him walk into my room, let alone come over to the bed, so I didn't know where he was. I finally worked up the courage to look. I was being such a coward about this whole situation!

What, am I some high school virgin? I'm being ridiculous.

I had to scold myself! I peeked. He was still standing in my doorway with a stare that could only be described as "the Brent look." It was predatory, sexy, all-consuming, and hot, hot, hot! I was surprised I didn't incinerate on the spot. Clenching my thighs together again did not help—it only made me more aware of the absolute need to conquer him and come.

I can do this. I can take him.

***

Brenneth

I summoned all the willpower I had not to ejaculate again so soon. *Fuck me.* I'd just gotten off in the shower, and already my dick was harder than before and ready to go again. It had never been like this. It was because of Everly. *She* did this to me. I had been thinking about this moment and dreaming about it since before I even left for the desert. Now there she was, staring me in the face. I felt like it was my first time taking a woman all over again.

I always found myself just gawking at her. I think her beauty and sexiness shocked my system. That was something I didn't think I'd ever get used to. She did it for me in every way, and I was beyond taken with her.

I was in love.

That may seem crazy to some people, but from the moment she practically ran me down at the graduation, I had fallen for her—literally and figuratively. When I fell, I never stopped falling. I could admit it to myself. I wasn't going to scare her for now by revealing that, though. The fact that she had shown up at the party meant so fucking much to me. It solidified what I already knew.

I just found it funny that I was supposed to be the one to sweep her off her feet, and yet she had managed to do this role-reversal thing. It didn't bother me in the slightest that she kept surprising me—I was man enough to accept her need for control. I had plenty of testosterone, and she had plenty of estrogen. So at the end of the day, we both knew the gender score even if the line blurred a little sometimes. I could handle it. I could handle *her*, and she could certainly handle me. I just adored how powerful she was one minute, and then the next almost shy. We could both choose to be in control sometimes, and to give up control other times. We could both just be . . . together.

"Ev . . ." I rasped out.

Her head snapped up. I had caught her staring eagerly at my cock. She looked at me in the eyes intently. I think she had registered the use of a nickname. Her beautiful face was suffused with that luscious pink color again. I was so drawn to her pouty lips. Their color drew me in, but I couldn't figure out exactly why. This woman was a walking wet dream for me.

We both needed a few moments to collect ourselves. I knew I would catch her off guard by walking out of the bathroom naked. Hell, I surprised myself. There was simply no point in putting on any more layers when they were finally going to come off.

The need to be with her was pulsing through my veins. Desire was radiating off our bodies, and the humming down below, urging me to conquer, was a deep, ravenous sensation. I knew the hammering in my heart would not subside until she was mine completely and fully. I was *cunt*centrating so hard on her glorious figure lying there. And, fuck yeah, I was thinking all kinds of dirty things. She brought a wild, uninhibited creature side out of me. The need to drive into her was palpable; I was lost to lust.

She was wearing a sexy, ice-blue, lace bra-and-panty set. It looked amazing on her. In the dim light, her skin beamed and beckoned to me. The blue lingerie gave off a beautiful, alluring glow. Her eyes were electric—and transfixed on me. I looked her up and down, and down and back up again and again. Her bare feet were even fucking sexy and dainty, just like in my dream. Never mind that that dream had turned into a nightmare later. This sure wouldn't. She was the real deal, in the flesh, and I couldn't wait to taste, touch, and discover everything. The tiny snippet of her essence I had tasted back in February was nothing compared to what I'd feast on next.

I didn't know where I wanted to start first on her. Sex had always been about pleasure and the ultimate goal of getting off, just because it felt so good. This was so different, though. It was still about pleasure—of course I would take the opportunity to blow my load—but it was more about the culmination of two people becoming one. It wasn't a race to the finish. When I came, it would be inside her. Releasing into her would help me connect to her in a primal way.

I could see the box of condoms on the bedside table. I was fine with using one. I made a mental note to inform her later that there would be no more barriers between us going forward, though. She would also soon find out that tonight would be a turning point in our fledgling relationship. Once I had her, I wasn't letting her go. If she or I weren't ready to say the words, I'd show her how I felt with the joining of our bodies and by the movements we'd make. I'd have her limbs singing a fucking glorious tune after I played and strummed her most intimate parts.

I inhaled deeply, savoring the flavors and scents swirling in the air. It was a heady combination of her feminine juices mixed with her fruity perfume. My mouth watered as I took everything in, and I could feel my balls tighten while my dick pulsed. It was unnerving how much I desired her.

All the nights of lying in my bed alone in the sandbox were about to be rewarded. I was thriving as a person because of her—and the pulsating head of my cock was finally coming home. Her silky entrance would be like the stairs to a temple, and I would drop to my knees in honor of the power she had over me. A switch had flipped in me a long time ago, and she was the one who could turn the power on or off.

How do I tell her what she means to me, what she does to me, what she is to me?

There was only *one* way at that point.

As my cock jutted forward, tall and proud, and a drop of pre-cum leaked from the tip, I walked around to the side of the bed. She laid there, completely still, with eyes wide open. My big hands caressed her cheek, and she closed her eyes for a moment as if cherishing the touch. She was so striking when she let me see this soft side of her. I was in awe of her strength, but I was paralyzed by her softness. I gently sat on the bed, and she kept her eyes closed. I kissed each eyelid as she smiled shyly. I planted a kiss on her forehead, then added a chaste one to her lips. I was going to go slow, sweet, and gentle. My passion was all-consuming, but for her, I would fight the need to drill inside immediately. She needed finesse and care at first.

I kissed her neck, then licked the spot I had just kissed. I blew on the wet area, and she sighed in contentment. I saw gooseflesh pop up on her skin. I knew she was feeling it everywhere. I wanted her to feel *me* everywhere. I wanted to reach the heart of her with the riot of sensations I was causing. I flicked her earlobe with the tip of my tongue, and then sucked it into my mouth. She began moaning uncontrollably. She released her hands' grip on the bedspread and arranged them on my head to hold me in place. Inwardly, I was so elated that I could affect her so easily and that she responded in the most divine way. Her desires spurred my desires. I never wanted it to end.

I kissed her shoulders and the sides of her ribs, ignoring her breasts for a minute. I kissed across her stomach and licked her belly button, tugging on the hoop she wore this time. She squirmed, and her breathing was heavy. Her legs were starting to thrash. She had let go of my head to once again grab the bedspread. I positioned myself to be over her instead of sitting to the side. Even though she wasn't looking at me, it was so sexy and more intimate somehow. I didn't think she kept her eyes shut because she was shy or embarrassed—I thought it was because she needed to feel things on her terms.

I placed a kiss at the apex of her thighs, right on her pretty, blue, lacy panties. I smelled her deliciousness since I was so close to her tight hole. I couldn't help myself. I had to lick her right on the nub, through her underwear. She gasped in surprise, and I could smell and see a gush of liquid seep out as she coated those pretty panties. I knew her velvety lips needed to be sucked, tasted, stroked, and cared for. All in good time, though. She was ripe and ready for the taking, but I would be patient—tonight. I didn't trust myself not to blow my own plan to shit, though, so the panties had to stay on for a little longer.

I moved my way back up her stomach and cupped her tits in my hands. She arched her back for me as if presenting them on a platter. This was the best kind of gift. I would certainly oblige by accepting them.

"Sweetheart, you're so fucking gorgeous. God, I have never wanted anyone or anything more in my life. I need to be inside you, but I also need to touch you, and taste you, and feel you everywhere. I will never be able to get enough of this." I was overcome with emotion.

Whether she realized it or not, I saw a tear leak out from each eye and fall to the bed. I didn't think anything was wrong; in fact, I thought everything was perfect. Maybe it was just as powerful and moving for her as it was for me. I kissed her eyelids again and then took her lips, sweetly nibbling on their plumpness. I swirled my tongue inside. She opened to me easily, granting me full access. She moaned into my mouth, and I moaned right back, matching her fervor. She grabbed my head again and held on tightly. I pulled back after a few minutes, and she released me.

She finally opened her eyes.

I gasped at what I saw. It was trust, it was acceptance, and it was . . . love.

I wanted to fucking tell her that I loved her too, but I kept quiet. No more words. Just action. I slid my hands under her shoulders and unclasped her bra. I pulled the fabric away and threw it behind me. Her tits stood up, the points puckering under my gaze and admiration. I sucked each nipple into my mouth and gave them little bites. The tips were so pink and delectable, I couldn't stop myself from indulging. She closed her eyes again, lost in what I was doing to her. Her body was quaking a little, and I imagined she was getting close to orgasm. I desperately wanted to give her one before I entered her in order to ensure she was slick, juicy, and beyond ready to receive my large cock.

I kept sucking one nipple while rolling the other with my fingers. Then I alternated. I stayed on those beauties for quite some time, all while she managed to flail about. Finally, she hugged me perfectly around the waist with her long legs, and I was nestled right in between them. Right where I wanted to be. My dick was rubbing and rocking against her heat—the panties would have a hole in them soon if we kept at it. The beast raging inside me was starting to come unleashed. I knew I couldn't stop it this time.

I reached my hand down to her pussy and pushed the panties to the side. I lightly touched her folds. Ah, so feminine and intoxicating. She was fucking soaked and needy. I growled against her breasts. I needed to feel the delicateness inside her. I tentatively swirled my pointer finger around the entrance to coat everything further, and then dipped it into her channel. She clenched down immediately on my finger, gripping it so perfectly. I made the in-and-out motion, and then added a second digit.

"Oh my God, Brent. I need you so badly. I'm on fucking fire here. Please!" she cried out.

I knew she was begging for release, and it was so good to hear. I would give it to her. I would give *anything* to her.

"Fuck, I love it when you say my name," I succeeded in responding.

I added a third finger, stretching her further. When I did, she was stuffed full. I had to really work to get in and out. I knew my cock was obviously wider than three fingers, so I knew I would have to take my time getting her ready to accommodate me. Her insides gripped me like my love for her gripped my heart. My love and lust were undeniable. I removed my hand. When I entered her again with my fingers, I only used two. But this time I stroked her walls and hooked them just so, right where I knew her G-spot was. As I did that, I used the pad of my thumb to rub her engorged clit.

Her bundle of nerves protected by that sexy hood was protruding, begging for my touch. I knew everything was concentrated in that one, small, monumental spot. She went off like a dam had burst and the levies broke apart. Wave after wave of sweet liquid flowed from her center. I pulled my hand away again, but only so I could lap up the rest of her release with my lips and tongue. She screamed and screamed, and I ate and ate. She was succulent. The musk of her cream made my libido ignite like it contained the fuel of all the oil reserves in the world.

After she rode out the vestiges of her wild orgasm, I knew she was ready to finally take me to the absolute depths her pussy would allow. The time had finally come. I moved to grab a condom, and I thought once more about how many layers I'd shed so far.

This would be the last time a layer would be put between us.

Chapter 15: Rigid Digits

Everly

Brent rolled the condom down his long, thick, delicious shaft, and I licked my lips at the sight. I wasn't big on dirty talk, but he brought out a side of me that was even new to my ears.

For fuck's sake, we all know I'm no prude or saint by any means, but this man made me want to be a filthy, even more foul-speaking, slutty girl.

I wanted him to push so hard and deep into me that I could taste him in my mouth. I wanted to be backdoored and worked over. I wanted to be his cum dumpster. I wanted his rigid digit to keep sliding in and out of me and make me scream and cream until my bed was ruined.

Who am I?

I was fucking Everly Reynolds, that's who. And I was Brent's bitch. Okay, I realize I may have taken the language a little too far, but the feelings were indescribable. He was with me in body, mind, and spirit. I had already had one orgasm, and I was poised for another. This multiple-orgasm thing was going to be addictive; I could see that happening *for sure*. I definitely regretted not sleeping with Brent all those months ago; tonight there would be no room for regrets, apologies, or dwelling on the past. I wanted to move forward. And we would. Together.

Once he had sheathed himself, he moved from the side of the bed to position himself on top of me once more. I could feel the weight of him pressing me into the mattress. It was the most sinful feeling, knowing I would be completely and fully taken by him. He lined his long, thick rod up with my entrance, and I gasped before he even pushed in. I was eager and impatient. I never knew I could feel like that about someone. After all those years of being lonely, I didn't even know I wanted something like him. He made me want everything.

Just the tip pushed into me, and my slick opening greedily held him there as I shuddered and quivered from his hardness. He was steel. He was perfect.

He closed his eyes, and I couldn't help but stare at him. I knew he was trying to go slow. I didn't want slow, though. I knew this was something more than just a fuck, but I needed it hard and fast, to feel him lodged within my body. I spread my legs wide in welcome so he could get in as far as possible as soon as he felt ready to push on through. I wanted him to ram into me with the force I knew he could bring.

His eyelids opened, and the smokiest, most smoldering look greeted me. I gave him what I'd like to think of as a signature sultry smile, to let him know to proceed. It was like we were both in tune. He knew what I needed, because the next thing he did was shove his cock forward through my tight passage—he did it so hard, in fact, that it would have hurt if I weren't already prepared. I cried out in pleasure. He held himself there for a moment so I could adjust to the thickness and length of him. He was by far the biggest man I'd ever been with. I know some girls say size doesn't matter . . . but my God, it *does* matter! Now that I knew what heaven was like, how would I ever move on from those Pearly Gates? I realized I had been kidding myself all these years. Everything else was just a lay, a fuck. This was transcendent.

I wrapped my arms tightly around his neck and held on as he slowly moved in and out of me. He had his face buried in my neck, so I moved my mouth to his ears and went to town. Nibbling the lobes produced the sexiest sounds from his lips. He was breathing hard into my neck, and I'm sure my hair was in wild tangles. His breath was frantic. I loved that mussed look, though, that I knew we'd both be wearing afterward. And even though his hair was short, he'd have that "just fucked" appearance when I got through with him. Our bodies were already slick with sweat—another reminder of what we were doing. I caressed his back with my hands. He was moving so slowly, it was almost unnerving. I knew he could be gentle and sweet, but I had expected raunchy, dirty, and fast this first time. Mostly because I knew we were both deprived, desperate, and starved.

The way he moved me, literally and metaphorically, made it all the more apparent to me that I was falling harder and deeper for him. Tears came to my eyes knowing he was touching me in every way possible—deep, so very deep. The way we were joined told me everything I needed to know. I didn't want to be one of those chicks who depended on another person, but I felt like I needed him as much as he needed me.

It was utterly clear that I was faced with the unknown. My future had a big question mark hanging over it. That's probably why I never let anyone truly "in." Once they're in, that means they become a part of you.

But too late in this case. Brent was a part of me already. Question mark be damned and cursed to the pits of hell.

I loved him.

That realization was an eye-opener that was both freeing and terrifying.

I locked my legs around his midsection and dug my heels into his buttocks so I could draw him deeper into me. I was getting good leverage, and I could kind of set the pace too. I arched my back as he sucked on my neck. I licked and sucked his ear again, and this time, I could taste the saltiness of his skin. The perspiration from our lovemaking and the soap from the shower were intoxicating. Pheromones were definitely swirling all around us. It was delicious to experience this. It spoke volumes about the lust I had developed for him.

He started to move a little faster, and I was becoming more and more wet. My pussy was hugging his cock more and more firmly too. As he moved in and out, it was getting harder and harder to let go. I wanted him to stay in me—permanently. Together, in this position, we were safe. No one could touch us!

I loved his taste, his smell, his sounds, his beauty. Brent was a beautiful man. I know he had a beautiful body and mind, but the biggest, most beautiful heart accompanied all that. I was so glad I had never married. I was so glad I went through all those losers to get to the prize at the end. I kept reaffirming to myself and the world that he had been worth the wait.

I think his self-control had considerably waned, because he began moving like a piston in and out of me, at a rapid speed. I could not keep up. My heels were even getting sweaty from his skin, and they were slipping off his scrumptious cheeks. The overwhelming jackhammering of his dick jolted my senses, and brought me back to the moment. I was in complete and total ecstasy.

"Sweetheart, how do you want me to come? Or really I should be asking, which position do you want to be in when I come?" he asked with barely contained urgency.

I wanted to tell him to stay just where he was. But I suddenly felt like trying another position too, because it wasn't one I normally tried. Doggy-style wasn't usually my thing. With most of the guys I'd been with, it wasn't an option; I didn't like them feeling like they had the upper hand. I knew with Brent, it wouldn't be that way. We'd also have plenty of time to do cowgirl, reverse cowgirl, sixty-nine, and every other conceivable position again and again after tonight—or whenever we both recovered from this round.

"Brent. Oh God! I want you to take me from behind. I want you to ram into me and slap my ass. Make it red, Brent," I begged.

He groaned almost as if he were in pain. I knew the statement I had just delivered hit him right between the eyes; well, the fly's eyes, that is. The time had long since passed for any sweet, gentle lovemaking. This was the ride I needed and wanted so desperately. I wanted to feel wild, vibrant, on fire, and like a live wire. I knew he could give that to me. He could do anything.

We could do anything. We could be everything to each other. He brought out the side of me that made me want to be his dirty girl. He pulled out quickly from my cunt, and we both groaned and agonized over the loss of our connection. I knew it was only temporary, but it was still torture not to have him in me.

I sat up, then turned over so I was on all fours. I took a deep breath. I was in such a vulnerable position. I knew full well Brent would be kind—and that I was the one who wanted him to take me that way. I breathed in through my nose and out through my mouth. I could feel his big, strong hands on my hips. He moved them down to rub the globes of my ass. I was on full display for him, and I enjoyed that he was admiring his view. I knew this had to be an erotic scene for him; most guys loved a spread pussy on display.

"Mmm, mmm, mmm. You have the prettiest and tightest little ass—to match your pretty pussy. Fuck, Ev, I'm going to lose my mind here," he groaned out in that sex-dripped voice.

I continued to breathe. I let him continue to take in the view and rub me back there while he got ready to finish the round. I expected him to ram into me any second, but instead he delivered a smack on my left side that had to have left his palm stinging. I felt it everywhere. I yelped, and my pussy clenched along with my cheeks. Oh my God, it was glorious! I was sure a nice red handprint was evident already, but I moaned knowing he had done what I asked.

"Fuck yeah, I'm your dirty girl. Smack me again," I moaned out.

I didn't even know what the hell I was saying. I dropped my head to the bed and bit the comforter when he smacked my cheek again, but on the right side. I know it was unintelligible, garbled verbiage I kept repeating as he caressed the globes and gave me two more smacks on each side. My ass was on fire, but in a good way. I knew it would be smarting the next day, but I would deal with it then. All I knew now was that I felt alive, just like I wanted to be. He could make me feel a million different things—no one else had ever come close.

My cunt was probably glistening and overflowing with honey. I had never been so turned on in my life. I cannot believe I managed to hold myself off, but I know it's because I wanted to come around Brent's cock the next time. He ran his fingers up my slit and kept going all the way to my back door. He continued his exploration right up the seam of my ass, lightly touching the forbidden rosette. I had never had anal sex. I was game, but I wasn't stupid. I knew it wouldn't be tonight. I'd have a lot of preparation to do before that experience could happen, otherwise he'd rip me apart. I think he was just trying to give me pleasure and test me in the moment. I heard him growl as he rubbed the tight ring of muscle around my asshole.

"Have you ever been fucked back here, Ev?" he questioned.

I was shaking and quaking because of the intensity of how and where he was touching me.

"I asked you a question, Ev," he stated.

Wow. This was the side of him I knew was there, just simmering below the surface: the true alpha male. I didn't by any means think he was a dom, but I could tell if he ever ventured down that path, he would skip the rudimentary beginner's class and go straight to advanced placement. I didn't know if it was because he was a military man, or if it just came naturally to him, but he was so hot when he talked that way!

Why *hadn't* I ever want to be taken like that before? I already knew my answer. Because it was never Brent before.

"I'm waiting, Ev. And I'm getting impatient back here—on all counts," he spit out.

I knew he wasn't mad; it was more that he was impatient, like he said.

Why am I in such a stupor?

I breathed in shakily and finally replied, "No, I haven't. I've never wanted to before. Well . . . I never wanted to before with anyone else, that is. I do want to, though. With you."

He didn't say anything for a few moments. We were both paralyzed in place. I assumed he was thinking.

Finally, I felt him lean down to my ass. He kissed me on my left buttock. I jumped a bit because I was so confused by what he was doing.

"God, you're so fucking perfect. I don't think I can tell you in words how lucky I feel to be with you. You're everything, Ev. I want to take your ass. But it won't be tonight. I can tell you, though, when we work up to it and finally get to do it, it will be one of the most pleasurable sensations of your life. And I can't wait to share that with you. But for now, I need that pretty pussy so badly. I need to come in you and have you spray your juices all over my cock. If I don't have you soon, I may fucking go postal. Oh no! I didn't mean to make a bad joke!" He laughed.

I felt some more liquid flow out of my channel. His words were wicked, naughty, and lethal. He had made me come with his tongue—without ever actually touching me because of that incredible mouth. He was a talented son of a bitch, and all mine! I moaned in response to him. He placed his hands back on my hips in order to effectively position me. I tossed my head from side to side in anticipation. This was going to be the wildest ride yet. He inhaled deeply, probably to center himself before he plowed forward—and probably because he could smell my arousal permeating the room.

I put my face to the mattress to brace for him. He once again lined up our sexes and, without a warm-up of any sort, just shoved his full length right into my pussy. He was ramming in and out so hard, I figured I'd have to go on a search-and-rescue mission for my nose ring in the morning from my face mashed into the bed. But the beast was unleashed, and I lost it. I screamed and orgasmed more intensely than I thought was humanly possible. I wanted to tear down the walls. It was completely overwhelming. He had claimed my body.

I didn't feel powerless in that position; I felt invigorated and on top of the world. I screamed and cried out for so long, I didn't realize he had come too until he slumped over my body and started kissing my back. I definitely felt the weight of him, given the way our bodies were pressed together, but I couldn't even voice a complaint. Somewhere in the barely conscious state I was hovering in, I was taking in everything. On a conscious level, well, this girl still needed recovery time.

We both literally fell over sideways onto the bed.

Goddamn, this man is a machine!

He had to be some kind of military experiment. There was no way a man like him could exist and just be walking the earth freely, able to fuck like that.

How the hell has he not been kidnapped and held prisoner by some obsessed woman?

I would consider turning to a life of crime if it meant I got to be with his cock each and every day. My DSLs—ahem, dick-sucking lips— would never leave his cock to even come up for air. He could beast-mode it and make me a wet mess of ecstasy anytime I needed it.

Okay, I blame him completely for my current lack of rational thought.

I finally turned over to face him. We kissed softly on the lips. It was the sweetest of gestures, and confirmed that I had met my perfect match. The last thing I remember before dozing off was that I was warm, safe, and happy. I couldn't imagine not feeling the same way with him whenever we were together. As I said, I couldn't survive being apart now that he was in my heart. There, with him, I found my happy place: the home I had been searching for and didn't even know it.

I had found *him*—and he had given me the royal treatment.

Chapter 16: Concoction

Brenneth

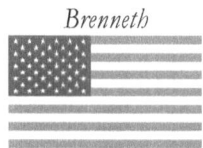

During our first encounter, Ev and I collectively orgasmed more times than I could count. We finally passed out from our lovemaking. It was the most magnificent feeling to be sated, happy, and content. I woke up the next morning—well, hell, after glancing at my watch, I realized it was the afternoon, actually. Anyway, I woke up the next afternoon with Ev still wrapped around my body. Our legs were tangled together, and it was the most amazing feeling to recognize that she was pressed to me in a possessive way. The air smelled like pussy and dick, and I breathed in the cucumber-melon fragrance on her sweet skin. I moved my lips back and forth across the crown of her head, enjoying the feeling of having her snuggled up to me.

I didn't want to move. I was quite comfortable. Her bed had the softest sheets and comforter I ever slept between.

Damn, I have to get a set of this shit for my own bed.

I don't think I'd ever slept so well in my life. No nightmares, no restless sleeping, just absolute fucking peace for once. I don't think it was just the bed, though. I think it was Ev. She calmed me. Well, shit, of course she could rile me up easier than a rattlesnake being shaken in a bag, but she could also soothe me on a level I couldn't comprehend. I needed her, plain and simple.

I really did want to talk to her about important things, but so far I hadn't been able to see past my lust. Of course she was the most important, precious thing to me. But when you've been on a deployment and deprived of basic things like sex for months on end, well, your mind teeters on a dangerous tightrope—you're literally on the verge of madness. In the end, lust will always win out—for me, there was no hope so long as I was

97

around that particular woman.

There were so many questions on the table, I didn't even know where to begin with her. She hadn't stirred yet, so I was left thinking about all that needed to be addressed. I was trying to figure out how to casually bring up the text message she had received, since she seemed distressed about it. It may have been nothing, but nevertheless, I was going to be a protective bastard now that she was mine. I also wanted to get to know her better. If we were ever going to do that, then we'd have to talk about actually having a relationship, one that hinged on us working things out and coming clean with each other about our faults.

I didn't need—or want—every damn detail about her past, but I needed enough to get an idea of what she had been through. In return, she deserved to know why I was so fucked up; I owed her that. After we'd shown our respective hands and played our cards strategically, I would certainly tell her that I wanted her to get on birth control, if she wasn't already. I would also tell her that we wouldn't use condoms going forward. I had vowed last night that we would never let them come between us again; the box was practically empty anyway—and riding bareback was a must. Additionally, I had to find out how bad her panic attacks were. I was afraid I'd send her into one if I brought up painful subjects, but I also wanted to be there to catch her if she fell. I had never forgotten the one she had the night before I left. But she couldn't hide from me forever. It was quite evident we both had shit going on in our heads, and I was more than willing to navigate through it together—if she was.

We needed to figure out how our relationship could be ops-normal. I didn't know anything outside of the military, and she had mentioned her overall history with the military was brief. So, we would both have a lot to work on in terms of adjusting to each other's lives. I was a newbie, or FNG—fucking new guy—at relationships. I suspected Everly wasn't much more advanced in that department than myself. There was other shit to talk about too. Just thinking about contemplating all the topics I knew we *should* discuss made my head pound.

Fuck, I still needed to find a place to live.

Just then, Ev stirred against me.

She lifted her beautiful blonde head and looked around as if just finally realizing where she was. I grinned when she discovered I was lying next to her. I could see the wheels spinning as she replayed the escapades of the night before. She bit her lip—I imagined in response to the images. I could get used to waking up next to her every morning. Her softness always took me by surprise; seeing it made her seem all the sweeter. She stretched, and I suspected she was sore . . . everywhere. Hell, I was even sore myself—but I was ready to go for more rounds whenever she felt up to it. I had lots of lost time to make up. Her curls were wild and sticking out everywhere. It was the sexiest bedhead I had ever witnessed.

"Good morning, sweetheart," I said in a sleep-roughened voice.

She smiled sweetly at me, then threw a pillow in my face. I chuckled, and she laughed back.

God, I fucking love this woman.

She never did anything or said anything I thought she would. Life with her would surely never be dull for one damn moment.

Her stomach grumbled, and mine answered back. We had slept through breakfast. I would gladly have made her lunch. I was shit at cooking, but I got by fine with my meager skills because I'd been taking care of myself and on my own since I joined the military. She made a face when our stomachs became overly vocal. I couldn't tell if it was embarrassment or what, but I didn't give a shit about stuff like that. I knew women's bodies did all manner of things. I wasn't one of those guys whose fantasies were ruined once a girl took a shit or something. Other men needed to grow the hell up if they thought that way. I mean, Christ, we were all human!

I brought her hand to my lips and kissed the top of it. I knew small gestures like that meant a lot to Ev. She always seemed so surprised by the little things. I even surprised myself at times when I was with her. I didn't think she was one of those women who expected chivalrous guys, but I hoped on some level she'd let me spoil her. I considered her my equal, of course, and would never make her feel like a "little woman" who thought she was supposed to be barefoot and pregnant in the kitchen. I couldn't even conjure up that image. Ev would have my balls served up on a rusty platter if I was ever that way toward her. Although the barefoot-and-pregnant scenario sounded pretty friggin' hot.

Fuck, that's premature.

"Tell you what. Let me make you lunch. Then we'll shower. I'll have my parents pick me up so I can get my truck out of storage. Later tonight, I'll come back for you and take you out for a real date. Then we'll talk about—everything. I'm sure you have things to say that are probably burning a hole through that pretty fucking mind of yours, but you're going to have to wait until then," I informed her.

She tilted her head as if trying to gauge my mood or motive. Then she gave me that saucy smile of hers and bent down to kiss me on the lips. I still couldn't believe she hadn't spoken yet, but I was too busy with her lips to think more about it.

Then the minx suddenly twisted my nipple, giving me a goddamn purple-nurple.

What the ever-loving fuck?

In turn, I swatted her ass. She giggled and buried her head in my neck. She mumbled something, but her response was muffled by my skin.

"What?" I asked.

She laughed again and replied, "I said you're adorable in the morning, Tech Sergeant Peters. I may have to keep you around just for my amusement. I don't really eat that much for breakfast—or even lunch, for that matter. Coffee is what I run on, but I'm sure we can scrounge up something in my kitchen. You seem like a guy who needs to eat, given your body and appetite . . . for everything." She waggled her brows and went on. "I'd love to go to dinner with you. A date sounds perfect. And yes, I agree that we need to talk . . . about a lot of things, actually."

The way she said the last part made me a little nervous, but I wasn't going to worry too much about it. We could get to it later. We both got up from the bed, and I threw on my boxers. She put on my T-shirt from the previous night—sans panties. That helped my dick get wide awake. Forget morning wood, I was having afternoon tree trunk.

We both took turns doing our business in the bathroom. I swished some mouthwash I found by her sink around in my mouth. When I walked out to the kitchen, I couldn't help but admire the view. She reached up in the cabinet to grab mugs, and the shirt rose up her backside, giving me the sexiest view of her naked cheeks. She had the most perfect ass. I couldn't wait to take it and make mine again. I didn't care if I was caught gawking at her like a purse whore in a handbag store. I could have watched her all day, even though she was just doing the most mundane tasks.

She set out two steaming mugs of that fucking heavenly smelling brew. I was grateful to get something in my stomach. I was a coffee guy, even though I usually opted for iced coffee no matter the season. Hot coffee would do just fine, though. I was not a complainer. I could certainly go with the flow; you had to be adaptable in my profession. Half the time, on deployments, I was deprived of something I would have normally considered essential anyway. Even the smallest comforts weren't always easily accommodated over there—that could be something as simple as not having your favorite body wash stocked at the military store.

"How do you take your coffee?" she asked.

"Believe it or not . . . I take it in a way that probably sounds like a pussy drink. Eh, fuck it! I take four spoonfuls of creamer and two packets of Splenda," I told her bravely.

She laughed so hard I thought she was going to drop her mug. Tears streamed down her face. Well, I guess I was there "for her amusement," like she said. I made an annoyed face, but I had expected that reaction. Besides, her laugh was infectious. I couldn't *not* laugh at myself because of her response. She was so beautiful.

What a puss I am. Fuck, my drink is probably more of a chick blend than hers.

After she collected herself, wiped her eyes, and set down her mug, she sauntered up to me. She placed my mug on the counter next to hers and proceeded to sensually wrap her arms around my neck. She smiled as she kissed my lips softly. I groaned at the contact. God, she was so hot. I loved each and every side of her. I didn't know how to pick just one; well, I guessed they were all equal because they were all *her*.

"I'm glad I amuse you so much," I chided.

She gave a *harrumph* and kissed me chastely again. She slid her hands down my neck and to the front of my chest. She didn't stop until she had cupped my manhood with her long fingers. I almost stumbled backward when I felt her—I didn't expect that!

"You don't always amuse me. Most of the time you drive me . . . nuts," she said saucily. She applied a slight pressure to my groin area to emphasize the word "nuts." Then she went on to say, "That is definitely a bitch drink, but I adore you for owning it. You're always surprising me. And by the way, I take mine black—or with just a little sugar and creamer. I guess it depends on my mood. I'll surely never forget your con*coc*tion though." She squeezed me again when she emphasized the syllable "cock."

Fuck me. This woman will be the absolute death of me!

***

Everly

Brent had left just a little while ago to retrieve his truck. His parents picked him up. They were the sweetest people. Brent's entire group of family and friends was really growing on me. I was glad to have a little alone time, though, because I needed to process everything. We had the hottest sex of my life. But obviously, it was more than that. There was something so deep and pure between us, it left my heart aching when he wasn't near. It's like my *heart* recognized his absence. Of course, I could totally function without him; I just felt a loss when he wasn't close by.

God, did that sound pathetic? I hope not. Well, fuck it. If it did, it was too late.

I was too deep into this now, with him. Last night had only confirmed that I was hopelessly and irrevocably in love with the sexiest, sweetest, most amazing man.

I would tell him about the letter. In fact, I would try and tell him about *everything*. Some of it was going to gut me, but I was willing to divulge bits and pieces if it meant we could forge a future together. I wasn't naive in thinking it wouldn't be painful. It might even send me into a tailspin, having to relive some parts of my rather unpleasant past. But for him, I would make the effort. Tonight would be really important. I knew it would be a pivotal turning point in the road leading to "us" as a couple.

I also really wanted to look good for him.

On the rare occasion when I decided I needed a fellow female opinion, I'd invite my neighbor over. I've mentioned Dawn before. I couldn't very well call Caylan for this situation, so I figured Dawn would help sort me out. As I've said, we'd maybe see each other a handful of times a year, but we were still friendly enough. It wouldn't be awkward for me to call her over randomly for such instances. Dawn was forty-five, divorced, no kids. She opted for pet goldfish since she told me she wasn't going to be "that cat lady." Well, I wasn't going to be that cat lady either, if I had my way.

I needed her to help me decide what to wear for the big date. She causally laid across my bed, reading a magazine. She was waiting for me to make my appearance and do the fashion-show thing that we women like to do. I thought maybe leggings would work. I stepped out of the bathroom and did a twirl in front of her. I didn't want to have camel toe, and I told her as much. See, I like Dawn because she doesn't sugarcoat anything. She's blunt, just like me. I needed an honest opinion.

"Girl, that's not camel toe . . . that's more like a moose knuckle!" She laughed so hard she had a river of tears sloshing onto her T-shirt.

I maturely gave her the middle finger. Then I huffed and puffed while stomping back into the bathroom. She continued to laugh her ass off. I heard the cackling of giggles through the damn closed door.

What a brat!

I wanted to smack her!

I obviously decided to change. Clothes were strewn all over the bathroom. They were hanging over the edge of the tub, hanging from the shower curtain rod, and stuffed on top of the sink in twisted piles. I should have just stayed in my bedroom. I wasn't so modest that I couldn't change in front of her. I wanted that "wow factor" moment when I came out, though, so she'd get the overall look and effect. Clearly, I was failing at this.

I was overthinking it. I knew it, yet I couldn't stop myself from obsessing over what to wear. *Damn nerves!* I had already tried about ten different hairstyles and finally settled on straightening my curls with a flat iron to sport a new look. I guessed that Brent liked my feisty curls, but the dinner would call for a different look—one that would make me stand out. I was becoming one of those girls dressing for her man, not for herself.

Okay, for *one night* I could try and dress how I thought he'd like to see me.

I decided that I would forgo panties, no matter what I ultimately decided to wear; they would just get in the way. The bra was necessary to give my tits the cleavage and full roundness I wanted to achieve—I loved that about bras. At least I was lucky in that department, though—my tits were perky enough that I could have gone without a bra, but I always worried about my nipples being too hard and noticeable. With some women, I knew that was the point—pun intended—but it wasn't my thing.

I came out next wearing a long, fitted black skirt. It was made of a clingy-but-stretchy material that hugged my torso and lower half perfectly. I thought it was just casual enough, but yet had that flirty appeal. I matched it with a pair of tan wedge sandals, a black tank top, and a tan knit shrug. It almost looked like the tank and skirt were one piece, if you just happened to glance. I thought I looked tall, lean, and sexy. I wore dangly gold earrings and put a gold, star-shaped stud in my nose. I felt like a star in the outfit, so I'd definitely deck Dawn if she thought otherwise.

"Well?" I asked her as I spun around.

I rolled my eyes, thinking she couldn't snag me on camel toe, moose knuckle, or some kind of elephantiasis remark about my twat this time. Dawn didn't say anything at first—I was hoping it was a good sign. Maybe I'd rendered her speechless, which could only mean winner winner, chicken dinner.

She finally said in a sing-song, "Nailed it."

I blew out the breath I didn't realize I had been holding. I couldn't wait until Brent got back, because I was dressed to impress. I thought to myself, "Toe-be-gone." I wouldn't make the mistake of putting my swollen pussy lips on display again . . . well, not until we were back in the comforts of my place and I was underneath him!

But as I said, we had a lot to talk about, so I would have to wait and see where we'd end up after dinner. I meant that literally and figuratively, by the way.

Chapter 17: Go Fork Yourself

Everly

We were sitting at dinner at a really nice steakhouse in Rittenhouse Square. The place was modern, clean, and had these really interesting glass fountains everywhere. I liked the sleek look and contemporary atmosphere. The lighting was just right. Restaurants that were so dark you couldn't even read the menu were a pet peeve of mine, but this place was just perfect. The soft music was on point, and the grilled-steak smell all around us made my mouth water.

Brent loved my outfit. He couldn't stop staring at me and complimenting me throughout our meal. He even said my hair was beautiful straightened; I was so surprised he noticed little things like that but I very much appreciated it. I was *not* used to the kind of attention he was giving me—it was genuine and from a place of unconditional adoration on his end. He accepted me, and it was a hard concept to grasp.

I had actually eaten a big meal, and we were waiting on our dessert. I never usually did sweets, but I was also trying to prolong our evening since I was not ready to have "the talk." I was nervous, a sensation I was not accustomed to feeling given the fact that I grilled people for a living and always got to the story. I wondered if I often made others feel equally uncomfortable with my probing. It wasn't like Brent had even asked me anything yet. I didn't dare question him on many subjects either. But somehow I was still uneasy. I reached for my necklace for comfort.

"Relax," he said, then gave me that megawatt smile.

I nodded in response. *Crap, I wish I could share his calm demeanor.* But I couldn't do it. I kept sipping my wine and fidgeting incessantly. I took a deep breath to steady myself. I felt so introspective suddenly. I couldn't even look him in the eye for the time being. Instead, I decided to focus on his body. That was always a very welcome distraction, and I knew it would overtake my other thoughts.

He was dressed in dark khaki pants, black boots, a black belt, and a button-down, striped gray shirt tucked into his pants. I wondered what the leather would feel like against my skin—not necessarily with him using it to whip me or restrain me, more like just caressing my naked body with it. Suddenly, I wished I could purr like Pussy. He had the first few buttons undone, and what shone through at the neck was a plain black T-shirt. He looked so damn sexy and edible. I'd definitely take *him* for dessert . . . to go.

Even dressed in this more-sophisticated style of clothes, his undertone of pure male ruggedness still stood out. He just exuded masculinity and sex appeal. The magnetism of his presence always sucked me right in. He didn't even have to be doing or saying anything—I was just drawn to him by some invisible field. I hadn't ever seen him with stubble before, so it was arresting to witness the sexy appeal of his unshaven chin and jaw. I imagined he had purposely refrained from shaving since returning home, especially since he didn't have to be in uniform again until Monday. He told me that he would still have to in-process back into his squadron, and he'd informed me he'd be busy all week at the base but afterward would get to take leave for a few weeks.

I was so lost in my thoughts that I hadn't even realized the scrumptious last course had been delivered to our table until Brent held up a forkful of chocolate lava cake, clearly suggesting I taste it from his fork. I snapped my head up and stared into his smoldering eyes. His look was a sinful one that conveyed feeding me was something he considered erotic. He could make the simplest tasks hot as hell. I parted my lips with a small gasp. I was totally rethinking the whole no-panties thing. At first, I had wanted to go commando because I thought he'd go wild when he discovered I was bare underneath, but now there was no barrier between my most, delicate lips and the fabric of my skirt.

His eyes were half-lidded and stormy as he placed the tip of the utensil to my waiting mouth. I opened and accepted the decadent bite. I closed my eyes and groaned as soon as the sweet taste overloaded my tongue. I was savoring the confectionary goodness, and he growled in return. He always answered my noise with a noise—whether it was a conscious response or not, I didn't know. I loved that I could do things to him just as easily. I must admit, I was grateful we were going through this sensual act at the table instead of talking seriously. It was, in fact, making me relax, which I figured was his ultimate goal. My tissues were becoming swollen, and I suspected his cock was becoming engorged, if it hadn't been already. I licked my chocolaty lips and finished swallowing the bite in my mouth.

When I opened my eyes again, I was enthralled by the hulk of a man I saw gazing back at me. I picked up the other fork on the table and fed him a taste in return. It was so sexy to feed another person and watch him enjoy the flavors. He looked at me the entire time, not breaking eye contact once. I couldn't sit still. I was trying so hard to shift back and forth, as if that would alleviate the needy, burning feelings I was wrestling with. *Yeah, good luck with that,* I told myself.

It was his turn to feed me another bite when my freaking phone went off with that goddamn alien ringtone again. I dropped the fork by accident while reaching for my phone to silence it. *Go fork yourself, Stuart!* I yelled in my head. *Ugh.* The loud clang of the metal hitting the surface of the floor echoed loudly enough to be heard by the other nearby patrons, and the spell I was under was broken. Brent did not look pleased, but I didn't know if it was because of the interruption or because of something else. I ground my teeth, turned my phone to silent mode, and stuffed it back in my purse.

Crap, how am I supposed to relax again?

***

Brenneth

Dammit, something is up. I was pissed because I had just gotten Ev right where I wanted her, and then I got fucking cock-blocked by her phone. I knew she was nervous and freaking out because she was worried about our impending talk, hence my need to calm her down. Then that piercing ringtone broke through the progress I was making. I would damn sure get answers tonight because, once again, she did not seem happy about whoever was on the other end, texting.

I wiped my palms on a napkin and reached for her hand. Her fingers grasped mine willingly. I always needed to touch her. I could be patient and try to start all over again with the feeding, but I think both of us lost our appetite when that text came through. It was time to do this, before I lost my nerve.

"Listen, Ev, we need to talk about some things. The very gritty, hard shit I'll save for when we're alone—either in the car or at your apartment. But the minor shit we're going to get out of the way now," I began. Then I sighed.

I turned my head to make sure we wouldn't be overheard. Thankfully, we were far enough away from other tables that we would have privacy if we kept our voices down.

"I'll kick it off by telling you that the fucking condoms need to go. That's not the most important thing on this topic train, but it's an easy one to start with. I hope to hell you can get on birth control soon, because I want to feel you and be inside you—bare. I haven't slept with anyone since before I left. I get tested often because of the military, so there is nothing you need to worry about from me," I conveyed honestly.

She blew out a breath and then told me words that were music to my ears. "I'm already on the pill, so no worries there. I haven't been with anyone either—in a long time, actually. I want you to be in me too, with nothing between us."

She said it with a little hesitancy, and I had a feeling it was because there was an underlying second meaning to her statement.

"Thank fucking God. Okay then, that's settled. Moving on. Next order of business. You need to understand something. You're. Fucking. Mine! Normally I'm not a possessive bastard, but I can't help myself when it comes to you. You make me crazy at times, and other times I need you like I need my next goddamn breath of air. I may not always know if I'm coming or going with you . . ." I winked at her to make sure she got the double entendre of "coming."

She just stared at me, not knowing what to do, so I continued. "I don't know where we'll end up or what you want to happen between us, but I'm going to put this out there: I want to be with you. I've wanted you since you fucking ran me down at the graduation. I haven't stopped thinking about you from the moment I met you. You overtook my thoughts the whole time I was deployed. Now if that makes me a giant pussy or pussy-whipped, then so be it. I need you, Ev."

She was breathing heavily, and I saw a visible tremor work its way through her body. I felt it, because I still had her hand clasped in mine. She trembled at my words. I didn't know if that was a good or bad thing. She looked down. I would give her all the time she needed to either arrange her thoughts or take a breather before responding.

"I got your letter," she admitted as she bit her lip.

At first I was quite confused. I didn't know what she was talking about. Then my eyes probably widened to the size of saucers, and I fired back with, "What the fuck?"

***

Everly

Well, what did I expect, really? Of course I knew he'd be pissed. If he had *wanted* to send the letter, he would have. I knew that going into this. I didn't expect to lead with that, but I didn't know how else to respond to his profession of commitment. And now it was too late to call back the words. I wanted to tell him so badly about the letter because I didn't want to start our relationship off with secrets or omissions pertaining to important matters. *How the hell do you react when someone tells you "you're fucking mine?"* I wanted to tell him I had been his from the moment he ran into me. But I couldn't do that, and my mouth once again got me into a predicament.

He started sweating. *Oh no.* I recognized the symptoms. I remembered how, when I first met him, he was sweating. He came bolting from that entrance and tore down the corridor in the auditorium like a madman. If I suspected he had PTSD before, well, this only confirmed it. I knew he was going someplace else in his mind; I couldn't figure out what the trigger could have just been, though. Maybe the letter reminded him of something that happened over there?

I began to worry about the frequency of his mental retreats. He dropped my hand. Losing that contact stung my body and wounded my heart. I wasn't going to let him have an episode alone, though. He had helped me through my panic attack before—I could help him through this. I reached for his hand again and squeezed it hard. He looked at me as if desperately trying to stay in the here and now.

"Talk to me," I implored him.

He didn't respond, so I tried again.

"I'm sorry to blurt it out like that. I know you probably have a lot of questions as to how and why I have it in my possession. I realize that letter was private, that you probably had no intention of sending it, but I'm *glad* it came to me. It couldn't have come at a better time. I *needed* that letter. That's why I reached out to your sister to find out when you were coming home. Brent . . . I need you too. I want to be with *you.* I don't know where we'll end up either, but I want to try."

That was probably the closest thing he would get to an "I love you" tonight. It would hopefully be enough for now, especially since he hadn't said it either, even though I knew it was there on the tip of his tongue.

He still hadn't snapped out of his attack. I figured he heard me and could probably process my words, but he was lost. The sweating persisted too. I wished he would come back to me.

Okay, time for more confessions. I downed the remainder of my wine in one gulp. I needed the alcohol to be flowing through my bloodstream for the next part. I bet it was going to get his attention.

I bit my lip and forged ahead. "So, I'm an orphan."

Chapter 18: Tripped Up

Everly

And just like that, he was back. He shook his head to clear it, used the back of his hand to swipe across his brow and remove the sweat, then he squeezed my fingers using the hand I still held. I was so relieved to see him come back to the moment, even though it had gutted me to reveal a piece of my history I had no intention of ever imparting to anyone. No one knew I was orphaned in infancy. When I left that shitty, parentless life behind me fourteen years ago, I never fucking looked back, and hopefully never would have to. I hadn't told a single soul about my past. Brent was definitely my future, and I knew it would be necessary for him to have a glimpse of my history in order for us to move forward.

"What just happened there? Where did you go? Tell me," I begged him. The "please" I should have said stayed silently in my mind.

God, I can't stop being a harsh bitch even for one second.

"I know you probably still need a minute to process everything. I also realize I just dropped a big surprise in your lap, but you looked like you needed something to pull you back. I guess it's no secret that we both get too deep into our own heads sometimes. I know you said to save the hard shit for later, but you know me. I can never seem to follow the rules . . ." I tried to add a little humor to lighten the somber mood.

He let go of my hand and sat back in his chair. His mouth was hanging open as if he was in a state of shock. Then he moved his hands to his head and grabbed his scalp. I felt terrible, because I didn't like to see him so unhinged. It was also very disturbing to watch because I felt so helpless. I knew I had pulled him back from wherever he went, but I had also been the one to send him there in the first place.

God, we're quite the pair. Matching fucked-up head shit.

I was done talking for the moment. I would wait him out.

He let go of his head and slowly dragged his hands down his face, rubbing at his eyes as he went. A very tired, exasperated sigh escaped his lips. I didn't think he was frustrated or upset with me, just the situation. I don't know how long we sat there in silence, staring off in different directions. Finally the waiter came by and dropped off the check.

Brent pulled out his wallet and dropped cash inside the check holder, then placed it back on the table. I didn't know if that signaled we were done and should stand up, or not.

Fuck this shit.

I was getting more pissed off with each second that passed by.

I realized this was hard for him, but it was hard for me too. Baring my soul had not been on the menu for the night. I folded my arms across my chest to let him know clearly how huffy and pissy I was getting; this was my favorite universal sign of indifference. The scowl on my face was probably not the most attractive expression, but suddenly I didn't give a rat's ass.

He finally looked me in the eyes. I had to swallow hard to get rid of the knot in my throat. His eyes spoke volumes about the torture he was going through. I knew he was agonizing over what to say when it was right there, deep in his orbs. I felt like an ass again. My temper always got the best of me. It's difficult. You don't understand what it's like.

I didn't *want* to give a crap about *anyone*—that's how you get hurt. But he, along with his family, had to go and win me over with their ways, and in such a short time too. With caring comes painful shit that's sometimes hard to deal with. That was why I needed to remind myself that he was worth it.

All this was new and foreign to me. I was struggling.

"I know you probably don't want to discuss your parents putting you in the system, and that's fine. That was completely unexpected to hear, and it caught me off guard. But I guess it snapped me out of whatever *that* was." He groaned and shook his head.

"Look, Ev, I'm sorry. I'm sure there's a lot more to your childhood than I ever thought. I suspected something was complicated, since you were so reluctant to talk about it. Believe me, there are some things I don't like to talk about either. I'm sure you've figured out by now that I probably have a case of post-traumatic stress disorder. I have never been diagnosed, nor do I plan to ever *be* diagnosed. The military claims it won't mess up your future career, but I don't want to take the chance anyway. Once you're labeled, it's game over. I can't jeopardize everything I've worked for. I've been doing my best to deal and cope, but I realize I probably can't do it on my own. I just feel fucking weak and pathetic. I mean, I'm a dude, for Christ's sake. I'm not supposed to be fucked up like this."

He seemed so defeated by his admission. I admired his strength and determination, though. He kept going in his come-to-Jesus moment, only taking a slight pause in between his confessions long enough to formulate what he wanted to say next. I choked back the knot because I knew this was difficult and painful for him. Sharing yourself is not easy; obviously, I knew that better than anyone. You feel naked, exposed, and vulnerable. I didn't want that for him per se, but I knew he needed to get it out. It was like a wound that needed to be lanced; you have to let all the junk seep out in order to rid yourself of the harmful bacteria.

"I'm sorry about that," he said solemnly.

I nodded in acknowledgment.

He went on to say, "I don't think you realize this, but usually *you're* the one who calms me. I know that sounds weird given the fact that we were just reunited, but it's true. That letter was my . . ." He broke off.

He looked off to the side for a moment before continuing. "God . . . the letter. It's certainly true that I never meant to send it. It doesn't matter how it got to you. Half of me wants to be happy you did get it, but the other half doesn't. I needed that letter too. It probably sounds fucked up, but it was like having a small piece of you over there with me. The letter kept me sane, and I went nuts when I thought I lost it. Thinking about what I did when I couldn't find it sends me back to places I don't want to revisit. I don't want to venture down that path anymore."

He returned his gaze to me and looked me straight in the eyes, unblinking.

"But I have you now. You can truly give me comfort. You're all I need," he croaked.

Tears probably glistened in my eyes, but I didn't want to wipe them away and call attention to the little traitors. *Damn, I don't like doing this. I don't like this emotion thing.* I hated this part of opening up to someone. There's a host of feelings that accompany love, because love simply isn't enough. If you signed on for one piece of somebody, well, you agreed to it all. *Am I ready?* I kept telling myself I was. I couldn't keep torturing myself by second-guessing—that wasn't fair to him or me. I needed to put my big-girl panties on, a laughable thought considering I wasn't wearing any, and suck it up. *Deep breath, Ev!*

"Brent, you're far from weak. Don't you think I also feel like shit at times? And I'm not trying to add more stress to your already-full plate, but I haven't had a panic attack in years. Yet for some reason, that night, I did with you. Crap, I'm messing this up. What I'm trying to say is, I think we both bring out the good *and* the ugly in each other. I'm scared of letting this happen between us, but I'm also scared of *not* letting this happen. I'm not running from you. Would it probably be easier to just walk away from each other? Of course it would, but I can't. This is just so complicated." I said the last part mostly to myself.

I shifted in my chair, but not to adjust for the lack of covering between my legs this time. I needed to fidget so I would have something to do besides rub my necklace. We really needed to get out of there. I didn't want the walls to close in on us any more than they already had. We both needed some air, and I needed to be somewhere I could get truly calm.

With the bill already settled, I excused myself and made my way to the ladies' room. After doing my business in the stall, I stood at the sink and washed my hands. I looked into the mirror and didn't like what I saw. It's a hard truth when you can't make heads or tails of what is staring back with absolute clarity—pure irony at its best.

Was I worthy of Brent, truly and fully?

I had to believe Brent and I were good for each other. Sure, neither one of us *wanted* to dredge up all this horrific shit, but maybe that was part of the healing process. I also had to believe we could heal each other. I had to believe we were meant to be together. I was not a rainbows, leprechauns, and hokey shit kind of girl; nevertheless, I believed there was a reason we had found each other. I dried my hands and made my way out to the vestibule.

He was waiting for me. As I was passing by the crowd of people waiting to be seated, the hostess turned from her station and inadvertently bumped me, causing me to trip. That bump sent me flying right into the back of a man dressed in a suit.

Ugh, why do I always have to be running into someone these days?

I made a mental note not to ever tell Brent I admitted that *I* had run into *him* that day! I could see the hostess in my peripheral vision, continuing to walk off; clearly, she hadn't noticed the chaos she caused. I practically bounced off the man. Thankfully, I managed to avoid falling on my ass. He didn't stumble in the least because of my mishap.

Anyway, as I was actually about to apologize, for once, to the gentleman I had run into, he turned around.

I sucked in my breath.

Holy shit, it's Stuart!

***

Brenneth

Ev excused herself to go to the restroom as I headed for the door. I think she needed a break from me for a minute, and in theory I got that. But being apart from her didn't make me happy, because it meant she was trying to distance herself in some way. I didn't like that. I didn't like the idea that she was seeking out space away from me. I didn't want to give her any opportunity to run. She was already skittish, but I knew trying to corner her or going all alpha was probably not the way to convince her to stick around. Going forward, I knew I would have to approach her carefully.

I thought standing by the front entrance would somehow make me feel better, since I could catch a breeze as people came and went. I hoped the fresh air would relax me.

It did not help. I still found myself jittery from our conversation. The people milling about and acting lost had formed a crowd, making it impossible to even breathe. I don't do crowds. I don't like crowds. Crowds remind you of things you don't want to remember. Crowds remind you that you would be helpless to react in a situation because there would be too much going on, too many people in your way. No one in the military really talks about it, but I think it's an unspoken thing that crowds are a trigger for some of us, if not most of us.

I had to admit to myself that I suffer sometimes. I just hoped and prayed those around me didn't notice. Small things bothered me. For instance, I especially didn't like movie theaters. They annoyed the shit out of me. Usually there's only a few exits, and they're dark. The element of surprise would be on the enemy's side; you're a sitting duck basically. I also hated having people behind me. If I couldn't find a seat in the very top row, then forget it. Out.

Restaurants are okay; I just prefer not having my back to a plate-glass front window or something like that. I prefer to be able to see out and around, to gauge the atmosphere. My eyes darted around every room—it's not that I'm disinterested in what someone might be saying, or that I'm not paying attention. I was just constantly on high alert and observing the perimeter. These behaviors came with the territory.

It just is what it fucking is.

I needed Ev to understand me. I needed to hope we could make this work, despite how messed up I was. She centered me. She righted me on my feet when I felt like I was falling and plunging deep into the earth with no way to stop myself before heading into an abyss.

How do you even make a person understand the enormity of all that?

I was worried I'd scare her off if she knew I needed her so badly. Maybe by her getting the letter, she already understood in some way. She was right about one thing, though—this was a complicated situation we found ourselves in.

I figured my roommate in Afghanistan, Jefferson, was the one who sent her the letter. It didn't really matter who it was, though. I was done thinking about it. We were going to move on. Everything would be out in the open, and I didn't need the letter anymore since I had her.

I was very much anticipating her return to me. It felt like she had been gone a while, even though she had gone to the restroom only moments before.

I wanted to take her back to her place and show her with my body how much I needed her. I wanted to possess her. I wanted to drive into her so she knew she was mine in every way. My skin itched to feel her up against me.

I sighed in relief when I saw her finally start to make her way from the restrooms at the back of the restaurant to where I stood by the doors. I couldn't wait to get the fuck out of there. She hadn't locked eyes with me yet, since there were so many people in the way. She was doing her best to maneuver through, and she made it as far as the hostess stand.

It all happened quickly, but the hostess turned abruptly and caught Ev at just the wrong angle, causing her to run into the man in front of her. His back was to her, but I could clearly see what he looked like. Before he even turned around to face her, I hated to admit that I got a case of jealousy. As far as dudes go, he wasn't bad looking at all. I couldn't help wondering what Ev would think of him.

As the guy turned around, I could see a spark of recognition—and appreciation—gleam in Everly's eyes. I couldn't tell if she knew him or not, or if she was in fact friggin' ogling him or not. I was damn sure going to find out what the deal was, though, because I didn't like the feeling I was getting in the pit of my stomach. My gut usually told the truth. It guided me when I needed it, so it was doubtful it was failing me at that moment. There was another man standing to the guy's right, also dressed in a suit; he appeared to be an older version of the fucknut. Maybe it was his dad or uncle.

Since she'd run into him, Ev hadn't looked my way once to even see if I was near. That pissed me off. She started chatting with said fucknut, and he had put his hand on her upper arm as if he to steady her. All three were laughing it up. It was an odd scene since I felt like such an outsider. The ache in my chest was almost as painful as the ache in my groin. Goddamn, I needed her . . . immediately.

I sidled up next to Ev and slid my hand around her waist to anchor her to me. I proceeded to nuzzle her neck and ear, making it damn well known that she was mine and I was her man. I ignored the two men in front of me, even though they had previously held Ev's rapt attention and introductions were warranted.

"I missed you, sweetheart," I said as I kissed her neck and groaned in her ear.

She cleared her throat rather obnoxiously, probably annoyed by my obvious stunt. She had every right to be pissed, but I didn't give a damn.

She could take it out on me later—and I'd give it right back. I refused to acknowledge the two men in front of me, and I didn't plan to until she made an attempt to introduce us.

I could play a dangerous game when I wanted to, and I was determined to win whatever the fuck game we were playing.

Chapter 19: "Everneth"

What the hell is wrong with Brent? What does he think he's doing? What kind of game does he think he's playing? I so wanted to knee him in the balls for pulling that stunt. He was being absolutely bratty. I will admit that when I saw Stuart, a million thoughts flooded into my head at once. First, I had never seen him in a suit, so that threw me.

Okay, so I looked him up and down and was very pleased by the ensemble. I am a female, for Christ's sake. I could certainly appreciate a handsome male standing in front of me.

Second, what also struck me as different about Stuart was the fact he didn't look like the frat boy I knew him to be. It was like seeing him for the first time, and in a different light. I heard myself apologizing for running right into his back, which is surprising since, as I've said before, I didn't normally do that sort of thing. He tried to right me on my feet and even cracked a joke about how I finally tripped up for once—he's told me before he sees me as "little Miss Perfect." We all laughed about my reaction to his comment, because I was floored. I'm a hardass and take no prisoners in my line of work, but I didn't realize colleagues viewed me such an overachiever. It was actually a nice compliment, although unnecessary.

If Stuart only knew how far I really was from perfect, he wouldn't be constantly chasing after me. I hadn't realized he carried such a torch for me—until that moment. Despite all the text messages, I just attributed the attention to more of a lust or crush; curiosity on his part. Then another pertinent thought occurred to me . . . Stuart had just texted me about twenty minutes earlier. Of course I had ignored it, but he had magically appeared and was there carrying on a conversation with me. How bizarre and stalkerlike and weird! I had been about to ask him whether he had actually known where I was when Brent came worming his way in.

I wouldn't let Brent know that when he kissed and nuzzled into me he made me squirmy and wet between my legs. He was being a total jackass, all because he was probably jealous. There was nothing to be jealous about, and I thought I had made myself clear as being on "Team Brent." But apparently, in boy language, that didn't mean dick. I swear, as soon as men feel threatened, they're ready to whip out the ol' ruler.

I cleared my throat to indicate my distaste for his behavior. I even rolled my eyes at his immaturity. Maybe I'd squash "Everneth" before it even got off the ground. Yup, see what I did there? Hey, if celebrities could have their fucktard combined names, then I could have mine.

Brent was still sticking his tongue in my ear spitefully. I continued to let him make an ass of himself. Finally, Stuart jumped in there.

"Umm, hi. I'm Stuart Davenport. This is my father, Herbert Davenport of Davenport Enterprises," Stuart said to Brent.

I noticed that he kept his eyes on me even as he introduced his father.

Brent's head popped up for a second. Maybe he remembered his duty as a member of the armed forces—and a gentleman—to project some semblance of good manners. He straightened up to his full height.

Jesus, he's so easily riled up and provoked.

He gripped Stuart's hand very firmly. I could see the tension and strain in Brent's face; I guess he was trying to refrain from crushing Stuart's bones. Stuart did a good job of holding his own. He didn't even bat an eyelash at Brent's action. The tic in Brent's jaw made his frustration evident. Then Brent roughly dropped Stuart's hand and quickly shook Mr. Davenport's, exchanging pleasantries with him.

When Brent grabbed me around the waist again he announced, "I'm Master Sergeant-Select Brenneth Peters, Everly's boyfriend."

He stared Stuart down as he said the words. Stuart faltered slightly at the term "boyfriend," but he recovered quickly.

"Why, Everly . . . I've never heard you mention a boyfriend," Stuart replied in challenge.

Oh boy, he's totally goading Brent, and he damn well knows it.

I narrowed my eyes into piercing slits. *Ugh, maybe some girls think this type of banter is hot, or get worked up watching two males piss over them.* To me, was just ridiculous.

I wasn't the least bit flattered. In fact, I was insulted by the whole display. How could grown men act that way?

And for Brent to throw out the military title like he had could only mean he needed to feel important. I could understand it, but it wasn't necessary. Then again, Stuart had thrown his dad's name around for notoriety, so I couldn't very well begrudge my "boyfriend" replying in kind.

Brent technically *was* my boyfriend, I supposed, even though we hadn't yet officially said it. And Brent couldn't very well have expected me to mention him to anyone since we just reunited. *This is all just so infuriating and ridiculous! Ahh!*

"So what brings you here this evening, Stuart?" I asked, coyly playing the game. I couldn't wait to hear his answer.

Stuart's eyes shimmered with playfulness as a sly grin spread over his lips.

Crap, does he think I'm flirting? Damn, that was not my intention at all.

My game was to find out why he kept stalking me. I could feel Brent's grip on my side tighten slightly, as if trying to hold himself in check. You poke the lion with the stick . . . well, you're going to end up getting your hand bitten off.

"Father and I were going to have a nice dinner and discuss some business developments. That's why I texted you—to see if you wanted to join us to celebrate," he said, looking right at Brent. He continued, staring me down, "As you know, Davenport Enterprises owns the building in which we work. But as of late, I've convinced my father of the merits of acquiring our small publication. We're still ironing out the final details, but by all accounts, it's a done deal. You know there will be plenty of beneficial opportunities for employees when this venture goes through. And I will be named CEO."

I gasped and paled at the announcement. *How in the world could I have found Stuart attractive just a few minutes ago?* Brent dropped his hand from around my waist, probably because he was afraid he would hurt me if his grip got any tighter. I knew Brent was going to be pissed about the text message; clearly, he had put two and two together and realized it was Stuart those times it chimed. Now was not the time or place to get into it, though.

I took my hand and ran it up Brent's back as a sign of reassurance. I needed him to know I was there, that I was his. I didn't want him to think I welcomed Stuart's advances. I also thought touching Brent would somehow calm me down too. I was doing my best not to make a fool of myself and hyperventilate in front of my new boss. *My new boss? Fuck!*

Mr. Davenport smiled at Brent and me in a predatory way. "My wife and I are quite proud of Stu. His Princeton education has surely paid off. He's following in my footsteps. The internship at the newspaper was just the beginning. We have no doubt he'll take the publication to new heights while making the necessary changes to ensure profitability and amenability—on the whole."

Mr. Davenport looked right at me as he said the last part, as if he had only added it for me. I felt like I was missing the big picture, and it was the worst feeling given my usually innate ability for astute observation. Had Brent finally clouded my vision and ability to do my job going forward?

I closed my eyes for a second and bit my lip, trying to understand or at least grapple with what he was insinuating. The two men had thrown so much information at me, and yet they had hardly said anything. Their words weighed a ton. I had underestimated Stuart all along. He was calculating, he was cunning, he was highly intelligent, and he was lethal. I was usually so good at reading people, yet I misjudged him; that bothered me the most. *Shit, there's a ruthless side to Stuart I never noticed before.* I had thought the persona he played at work—surfer boy, didn't-give-a-fuck intern—was something else entirely. All the time, his true nature was there, simmering under the surface.

Stuart would do just fine in the newspaper industry, better than me even. He had probably been in training for schemes like this coup his whole life. His daddy surely groomed him well to do his dirty work: infiltrate a business and make a move. Maybe Stuart and his father had been playing our publication from the beginning. What I thought was a carefree-but-eager intern, turned out to be a . . . what? A plant? A spy? The wheels were turning and spinning in my head; I was burning so much rubber in there. I wanted to massage away the headache that was forming at my temples.

I could see the matching gleam in his father's eyes as he saw me starting to piece everything together. Clearly Davenport Enterprises hadn't become a successful conglomerate without savvy businessmen at the helm. And what the hell was up with the phrase "beneficial opportunities?" Was that supposed to be a damn hint that I should be on my knees? Did they think I was going to be threatened and blackmailed into being his bedroom—and boardroom—bitch to keep my job? *Not on your life, buddy!*

I was so mad at myself for the times I had mentioned to Stuart that working for the *Philly Timez* was my dream job. I'd also told him numerous times that his unwanted flirting wouldn't screw anything up for me. The whole time, he was probably laughing at me. *But what is his damn endgame here?* I had to believe there was still a master plan in the works. It seemed like we were only scratching the surface. I was also struck with fear about my own job security and my colleagues'. Would Steve even remain our managing editor?

The room began to spin as I thought about all the scenarios and possibilities. I was shocked Brent hadn't jumped in there to say some choice words yet, but thank God for that. He most likely was thinking of me and not wanting to fudge things up even more for my career. I didn't even know what I wanted to do. I loved my job. But how much would things change? What would my future there look like? I was not a quitter. Dammit, Stuart knew that about me too!

"Why, Everly, I don't believe I've *ever* seen you speechless," Stuart teased.

I dropped my hand from Brent's back, put my arms at my sides, and squared my shoulders. I took in a deep breath before speaking to smooth the tremble I was afraid would come out in my voice. I would never let my countenance betray me. The polarity of my feelings and emotions pulled me in different directions, and I was helpless to stop them.

"Well, I'll see you on Monday then, Stuart. Brent and I have celebration plans of our own. It was nice to meet you, Mr. Davenport. You gentlemen have a good evening. I can't wait to hear the *full story* behind how all this came about," I said with a little bit of sarcasm in my tone at the end. I wanted them to know I would be investigating their bullshit deal.

Brent took that as our cue to leave. He placed his hand on the small of my back and steered me out of the restaurant, but not before nodding his head at both father and son as we exited. When we got outside, I sucked in a grateful breath of crisp, cool evening air. Brent rounded on me, despite the press of people hanging out near the entrance and walking on the sidewalks nearby.

"What the fuck was *that?*" he bellowed.

I had already asked myself the same question. I was not ready or prepared to explain just yet, though. Especially not to him. I was trying to make sense of everything. I knew he needed answers, but dammit, I did too.

I turned my steely gaze on him. He knew when he got fired up—well, I was just as fired up, mimicking his behavior—this is what we did. I would not back down or be submissive to his anger.

"Not here!" I clipped out.

I turned and stomped off. He followed, falling in step with me. We were both walking toward his truck in the parking lot behind the restaurant. He tried to grab my hand. I didn't know what for, but I was not having it. I didn't want to be touched just then. It was unfair of me, but I didn't care. He grunted and let out an exasperated sigh.

I didn't give a damn about his frustration. I was reeling from all that had just happened myself. I needed a second to think. I didn't want him to overwhelm me or overcrowd me with his needs and wants. *Does he not understand that not only has my personal life taken a hit tonight, but that my professional life is also in jeopardy? This can't be happening.*

We reached his truck, and he, being the ever-surprising, chivalrous man, opened my door. I couldn't even muster a thank-you. He walked around to his side and got in. I was still seething from all that had happened. I didn't want to regret getting together with Brent for one second, but my life had not been at all complicated until he showed up. *God, I sound like such an ungrateful, cruel bitch.* You need to understand that *I* suddenly felt like the lion being poked by the stick. Except I wanted to take that stick and stab someone in the face with it. Biting an arm off simply wouldn't do.

Brent gripped the steering wheel, white-knuckling the damn thing.

His jaw was set again in the tightest, firmest clench. I turned my face to the front and stared straight ahead, not even looking Brent's way. Even my peripheral vision seemed to have tunnel vision; all I could see was red, anger, and frustration. I wanted to cry, but I wouldn't do that. Especially not in front of him.

I was not too *proud* to show emotion, because Brent had already seen me at my best and worst. But I would not cry over what just happened. I had been through harder, tougher, and more fucked-up shit in my life. That was not going to be the moment that broke me. But the door Brent opened in my life, and in my heart, left me vulnerable and exposed; *that* frightened me more than anything. My defenses were down—anyone could charge the gate and storm the castle. Reality was a capricious hag that could go to hell.

I was still lost in my self-condemnation and self-loathing party when Brent grabbed my face and kissed everything away. At first I felt like resisting his warm, wet lips. But then I yielded, let him sweep in and take over. I melted against his body, becoming overheated in an instant.

I would use him. I knew I was horrible for doing it, but I would take from him what I needed—and I suspected he was doing the same. I needed to feel in control, and I know he recognized that. Luckily, I didn't have to undo my seatbelt since I had never fastened it. I hiked up my skirt to midthigh, threw my leg across the console, and climbed onto his lap. I was straddling him perfectly, locking my thighs to his sides so his lower half was nestled perfectly at my center.

He lowered one hand from where it had been clutching my face and moved it under my skirt. He ran his hand across my mound, finding I was bare. He growled with absolute abandon at his discovery. I was grinding on his clothed cock, moaning heavily into his mouth. We were so starved for breath, but I needed to attack his mouth even more with my tongue. The fierceness and ferociousness of our attacks on each other spoke volumes about the way we both ached and craved to connect. For the time being, he'd drawn me out of my funk, and for that I would reward him immensely.

I stopped sucking his mouth and whispered in his ear, "Start the car, put it in drive, and hang on tight. This ride is going to get even more wild."

Chapter 20: Full Speed Ahead

Brenneth

Before I let Ev climb back over into her own seat, I took advantage of the handful of woman I had in front of me. *Fuck, she's so damn sexy.* I felt like an asshole because the night hadn't gone as planned at all, not after what she revealed.

I think kissing her when she was upset might have been a dick move; no, really, it was. But I had bet that she maybe felt like I did about needing an escape. There's no better stress reliever than going at it. You get out all that frustration, pent-up anxiety and emotion, and work it out physically in the hottest way possible. Still . . . a selfish, dick move, though!

I gripped her ass cheeks as she was moving up and down on my pants-covered crotch. I couldn't believe she hadn't worn wear panties. No woman ever went commando for me—just another reason Everly got to me. It's like she always knew what I needed and wanted without me having to voice it. We still had a lot to talk about and work out, of course, but for now . . . I'd take it. It would take both our minds off the heavy, hard shit. I could definitely use the breather. I sucked at her lips for another minute or two, then reluctantly released the grip on her fine hiney.

"Sweetheart, we need to get moving. As much as I'd love to fuck you in public, you're right. Let's get out of here and continue this wild ride at your home, where I can properly worship you," I said with a devilish look.

She slid back farther on my lap and slowly moved off me. Then she slid back into her seat. Once she was strapped in, I turned on the ignition, put the car in gear, and exited the parking lot. We drove for a few minutes in silence, maneuvering down one-way streets. We were both content just sitting there. Then, I finally made it to the on-ramp, and we were on I-76 and heading back to her apartment. She flipped up the truck's middle console, which divided her seat from mine. At first I was confused, but then she stretched her seatbelt until it was all the way extended and made her way toward me. *Oh fuck, her intensions are becoming perfectly clear. How am I going to drive if she's driving me crazy?*

I growled, either in warning or by way of invitation—not sure which. Maybe both. Safety first at least, because I was happy she still had the damn seatbelt on. She took her beautiful, long fingers and undid my belt and then the button and zipper of my fly. I swallowed hard in anticipation. I also adjusted my position in my seat, preparing myself to pay attention to the road as best as I could. This was the worst type of distracted driving—and the ultimate test for a man to not fucking crash. It is also the hottest thing of your life to have a woman's lips wrapped around your dick when there's no escape for either of you. We both were in control of a big engine, and that made it even hotter.

She reached inside my fly and shimmied my cock out of my boxers. She really had to work my dick out of the tangled fabric because it was so engorged from all of her teasing. Once free, it jutted out like a solid, granite statue. I had been dreaming of a moment just like this since we first met. Any guy can attest to the fact that women size up a man in a second and deem them hubby material or not. Well, ladies, we dudes do the same thing—except we're sizing up your oral skills.

The moment she leaned down and put her mouth on me, I about came flying out of the seat. I gripped the wheel and let loose a slew of obscenities. I just looked straight ahead and kept focusing on keeping on the road. *I have to concentrate on the lines; they'll guide me through this.* That was my one, singular goal: to stay within the lines. *I can totally do this. I have to do this.* Not only was she playing with my manhood, she was playing with my sanity too. Her lips hugged my cock like a warm blanket. Her mouth was smooth, silky, and so very wet. The sucking sounds she made while her head bobbed up and down had me sweating bullets.

I shifted every few seconds, practically squirming like a newbie getting his first blow job. Road head, though, is something indescribable. You can't put into words what it does to a man. Conveying what it feels like is pretty much trying to describe where you go during your takeoff from an orgasm. Some things were just a mystery—and would always remain a mystery.

"Fuck!" I yelled. I needed to try again. *Must not lose consciousness,* I repeated to myself like a mantra.

"Fuck! You feel so good. I'm not going to be able to last that long," I murmured.

It was almost comical, the welcome torture and pain that was being delivered to my dick. Her velvety tongue just kept lapping at my sensitive tip. I was sure semen was already starting to leak out. She didn't even need to use her other hand to move up and down my shaft. Her mouth was enough.

She succeeded in giving me a bonus by softly cupping my balls and caressing them while she serviced my cock. It was amazing that she managed to get her hand through the small opening of my fly, but somehow she did. I didn't want to be one of those guys who moved my pants down to my knees—it would be my luck to get pulled over like that. I was not going to be caught with my pants literally down.

She practically purred. Maybe she had been spending a little too much time with Pussy these days. *Aw, fuck.* My mind was going to mush. I wasn't making sense. I was going to that place you had to go in order to refrain from spilling your seed early. I thought of everything I could that was unsexy. It was a difficult task given that fact Ev was moaning. She even removed her hand from my balls and moved it under her skirt to pleasure herself. Her moans grew louder and harsher, and then she bit down lightly on my cock, which made her come by her own hand from the finger-fucking she was administering to herself. No amount of thinking unsexy things was going to get me out of this one now. *Too late!*

I moaned and white-knuckled the wheel as I thrust up into her mouth. My hips moved of their own volition as I pumped her throat. Fuck, it felt like it would never end. She kept swallowing and sucking all the while. She was a damn dream. Every man's fantasy. I'd said it more times than I could count—she was perfect!

I rode out the storm until finally my dick was done throbbing and I could feel the blood starting to retreat; consequently, my cock softened. Usually chicks can't wait to be done and spit out your spunk, but Ev didn't seem bothered by it one bit. She had taken everything I had given her, and she even licked her lips when I glanced down at her.

Fuck! Again, it was a miracle I didn't crash. I had just experienced the biggest high of my life. It was earth-shattering and moving in so many ways. She kissed the tip one last time, tucked me back into my pants, and buttoned and zipped me up. God, she took such good care of me. Even simple gestures like that surprised me. Well, I would definitely reciprocate when we got back to her place. I was completely undone and at her mercy. I could and would never let her go, and she would really learn that later. I had already told her that she was mine, but I needed to spell everything else out for her.

She straightened back in her seat and pulled the passenger visor mirror down to fluff her hair and reapply the lip gloss that she had pulled out from her purse. That action was sexy too. I liked to think about how she had rubbed off her gloss in the process of rubbing out cum from my cock. I let out a shuddering sigh. I was still coming down from the mountain, but this was the time to remind her of important things.

"As I told you before: you are mine, Everly. We are going to make this fucking work. I need you, and I'm not letting you go," I explained.

"It was really that good, huh?" she teased.

"This is no joking matter. Of course it was mind-blowing. You damn well know that! But *we* are happening. We're going to talk once and for all when we get back to your place. Then after that, I'm taking you to bed. We're not coming up for air until you're close to passing out," I threatened.

She licked her lips again. *Damn, I guess she'll have to reapply her pout with another coat of gloss.*

***

Everly

Shit, there was no getting out of this one. Okay, I'd be a big girl, suck it up, and take one for the team. I guess it was better to get it over with. We arrived back at my place. We greeted Pussy, who couldn't have been any more disinterested, and I made us some coffee. We didn't dare go near the bedroom because we knew we'd never talk if a bed was near us. Even though we had made use of the couch before, I would muster the strength to behave myself.

Crap, where to start? Okay, I'll take the lead and go with this. I owed him an explanation about Stuart anyway. So I guess it was only fair that I be the one to run up the white flag.

"So Stuart's been texting me for several months. They've been flirty in nature. I, of course, ignored them and told him to back off. I said that it was unprofessional. I tried to be diplomatic, given the fact that his dad owns the building. Thank God I didn't do what I really wanted to do, which was knee him in the balls. But I guess he's my new boss, so there will be no knee-balling now *or* in the future." I shuddered with the willies just thinking about that prospect.

I sipped at my coffee lightly, needing to occupy my hands. Brent didn't interrupt; he was being a good listener and letting me pace myself. I held my mug in one hand and reached for my necklace with the other, moving the pendant back and forth along the chain. You could hear the metal-on-metal sound of the pendant sliding. But Brent, being the good military boy he is, just continued to sit and wait. I looked at his beautiful face. I was so grateful for his patience and understanding.

"Anyway, I don't want to talk about work. Just know that I *didn't* welcome his advances. Hopefully, there will be no more of it going forward. I'm assuming it was all a game to him anyway. I don't know if he was just buttering me up for the takeover, or if he wanted some office slut, or what. It doesn't matter. I'll figure it out another day. I'll be damned if he runs me off, though. I will leave on my *own* terms—that's for damn sure. No man gets to decide my future for me." I winced when I realized how my choice of words there at the end probably sounded to Brent.

Brent frowned and took a sip of his coffee. Probably mulling over my last statement. He remained silent, in his reticent way.

"Okay, so next subject will be short, simple, and not so sweet. As far as me being an orphan, there's not much to tell there. I had a very shitty childhood. I was abandoned at birth and I grew up in the system, right outside of Pittsburgh. I was shuffled from foster home to foster home. It went on for years. You never develop a sense of belonging, or home, when that shuffling happens. You never get comfortable because you know you'll be moving on again sooner or later. All the horror stories you hear about foster kids are pretty much true," I said with a sad sigh.

Brent paled and looked sick, probably realizing our childhoods couldn't have been more different. He was about to say something, or ask me something, but I held up my hand, halting his speech.

"Before you ask or say anything, I want you to know I was never sexually assaulted or anything like that. They tried. Fuck. Did the men and boys in those homes ever try as I got older. But I was a smart girl, and I was very resourceful. I never made myself pretty. I just tried to blend in. I purposely made myself look like a mousy little thing, made my appearance as unattractive as possible. You might think they would prey on ones like that *more*, but they actually didn't. I was like the tomboy no one messed with. When I started developing boobs, that was a little harder to deal with. I eventually resorted to taping them down and wearing baggy clothes. I don't have big boobs anyway, as you know. But I did whatever I could to not draw attention to them. And you damn well know how hard it is for me to not stand up for myself," I admitted in a sad tone.

Brent shifted in his seat. I knew he wanted to hold me, but I scooted back to rest against the frame of the couch. He inched closer and put his hand on my knee. That was fine. I let go of my necklace and patted his hand. I know he wanted to comfort me, but *he* needed the comforting more than I did, hearing this for the first time. I puffed out my cheeks and held back the biting tears that wanted to flow. I was braver than that. I would not break. Again, it wasn't because I was afraid to have Brent to see me like that, it was because I was not going to let the bastards from my past win.

My brows knit together in consternation as I went on. "There was all manner of shit that went on in those homes. Sex, drugs, no food, no love. There were even those *Mommie Dearest* moments of 'no wire hangers' or everyone asking at school how Billy managed to fall down the stairs *again*. I was grateful I made myself small—a wallflower and a dirtbag that no one gave a shit about."

I shook my head and ran my fingers through my hair to smooth the nonexistent tangles, suddenly feeling dirty. I also worked my hands up and down my arms, feeling suddenly chilled to the bone. Fuck, I hoped some of those other kids were as lucky as I had been. I managed to make it out practically unscathed. I don't know how any of us survived.

"So as you can imagine, when I finally was considered a legal adult, I made a vow that I would always be in control. The panic attacks are a byproduct of me having to hold it all in for all those years. There was no one to tell. No one to cry to. No one to listen to me. So I decided I would never feel small again. I would never be taken advantage of, and I would be sure to say what I wanted. That does get me into trouble sometimes, but it also saves me. It reminds me that I am a survivor of sorts. That I will not let my childhood define me. That I can be strong," I breathed out and closed my eyes.

"Brent, I have never told a living soul about what my necklace means. It means everything to me. It may sound corny or cheesy to someone else's ears, but I don't give a shit. I'm sure you've wondered what the letters mean. They're not the initials of a former crush, or something scandalous like that. It's simply an acronym. The *N-G-U* stands for 'never give up.' It's my daily reminder that I will persevere. I will be a success, and I will overcome anything. I will not be that mousy, tomboy girl who hid behind layers of clothes, dirt, and *Little Orphan Annie* crazy curls. I will be a fierce woman, a warrior, and an advocate for females. Above all, I'll call it like I see it. If that makes other people see me as a bitter, spiteful bitch, then so be it. I've been called a lot worse before, so 'bring it the fuck on' is what I say to them," I declared.

Brent couldn't resist. He took the mug out of my other hand, placed it on the coffee table, and pulled me to his chest in the tightest bear hug. I felt cherished, safe, and loved. I hugged him back, infusing myself with his love. *It is love, isn't it?* I swallowed hard and then gently extricated myself from his embrace.

"Well, anyway, that's my sob story. And no, I don't want to try and find my birth parents, if you were going to ask. I don't give a damn. Even if they had their own sob story to explain how I came to be or why they ended up giving me away, it is what it is, and that's that. I wish them well if they're alive, and if they're not, then I'm sorry they're dead. Actually, your sister said something to me that got me thinking about them recently. She said something about roots and wings, but it still doesn't compel me to want to find them. I don't know them. They are strangers to me, and I'd rather remain blissfully unaware." I was adamant about this.

"Ev, of course I'm curious—but I wasn't going to ask. If I've learned anything so far about you, it's that I have to let you tell me things in your own way, and in your own time," he clarified as he ran his fingers through some stubborn pieces of my hair that wanted to curl up again.

He sat back and propped his ankle on his knee, as if he was getting comfortable and settling in for something. I assumed his body language alluded to the unpleasant nature of what he was about to share.

"Well, I suppose it's my turn to tell my story. And I think I may need to borrow your necklace for this one," he said half-jokingly.

Chapter 21: Front-Page News

Brenneth

Well, this is going to suck. But if Everly could be brave, then I needed to match her attitude and determination by being brave myself. Some wounds were better left covered up by a bandage. The covering let the cut heal, and the bonus was that at least it stayed covered. But when you rip off a bandage and force the wound to be exposed to the air? Well, you're just inviting a whole host of things to happen, aren't you? I was actually serious about rubbing the necklace. It would be nice to have a fidget spinner, talisman, or stress ball for a change, to help keep me in the here and now.

After all, the nightmare that haunted me was the fear of letting myself retreat elsewhere. I was afraid I'd go off again to some faraway place in my mind. I needed to keep repeating a mantra to myself: *I will remain here, with Ev, in body, mind, and spirit.* I sighed heavily after taking a sip of the now-almost-cold coffee. It wasn't the temperature that bothered me; it was just bad and left a bitter aftertaste in my mouth that stuck to my tongue. I swallowed and began my tale of woe.

"I joined up before –9/11. Before our world was forever changed. Before the days of constant deployments and absolute terror heard 'round the world. Each attack or terrorist threat reopens these wounds for me. It's a gripping horror that keeps me up at night or pulls me back into a place I can't describe. The thing is, I'm not afraid of meeting my maker; it's more that I worry I won't be here to protect my family. Of course I don't *want* to die; I'll fight like hell to stay in this world. I fight for what I believe in and fight for those I love," I conveyed as I looked deeply into Everly's sparkling eyes.

I think she really *heard* the words. She could see into my soul, see what I was so desperately trying to proclaim. I nodded my head without her even having to ask the question, though. For the first time, I saw the woman I loved actually cry. A small tear fell from the corner, and she hastily wiped it away. We were opening each other up the more time we spent together, and it was truly a beautiful thing. The words needed to be out there, projected far and wide. I swallowed hard. I was part nerves, part overwhelmed with love, lust, and an earth-shattering, all-consuming passion for the woman.

"I love you, Everly. You are the most amazing woman I have ever met. I know we haven't known each other long, but it doesn't matter. As long as neither you nor I care about that, then fuck anyone who'd judge us," I said.

A delicate shiver worked over her body, apparently due to my words. I was hoping she had needed and wanted to hear them. Saying them was a salve to my fragile psyche. I didn't realize how badly I had needed to get the feelings off my chest. She annihilated me, and she didn't even know it. I had never been so totally and completely affected like this by any woman, and, of course, never would be again. She surprised me when she placed each of her soft hands on my face and cupped my cheeks affectionately. She was so close to my mouth that her breath puffed out onto my lips.

"I love you too, Brent. So very much. I agree. Fuck anyone who judges us. Your sister seems to think we can make it, and by all accounts I'm inclined to believe in that and trust in it. I never had a family, so being accepted into the fold of yours is also something that terrifies me. You truly are a hero, though. You need to know that and believe it," she explained.

I wanted to disagree with her on the last point, but she shushed my lips by pecking at them with tiny kisses.

"Don't argue with me and ruin this. You may paint yourself in a different light, but don't discount the way we all view you. If it's hard to accept on your end, then that's just tough shit. You're the one out there doing what you do every day. I don't know how you do it or why you do it, but I want to learn. Whatever or whenever you want to tell me and are willing to share, I'll be all ears, in every way," she explained as she bit down on her juicy, perfectly pink bottom lip.

I knew our conversation was far from over, but I couldn't help grabbing her and hugging her to me again with an iron grip. She had just made me the happiest man in the world by returning my profession of love and affection. I had never been in love, never expected to be in love—I was going to have to work at it. I had never wanted something, or someone, so much before in my life. I could not fail her. I wanted to be the man she needed.

I had plenty of friends who had successful marriages, as well as lots of friends who didn't. Military careers made for a hard life, but I suppose any occupation that entails long hours, risky work, constant movement, and unpredictable conditions would make things difficult for all involved. Christ, I couldn't even think about what it would mean regarding children, especially with four years left to go in my career before retirement. *Yeah, that conversation will have to wait for another time.*

She held on to me just as intensely, and we stayed like that for a little bit. But I felt like I had to finish my story in order for her to get the full picture. She and I always seemed to be on the same page, so it was no surprise that because of her *newsiness*—yeah, not nosiness, though there was that too, but I was trying to be witty, even if it was just in my own head—I knew she would want to have the whole story. That was just her way, and I understood it. I never wanted to be old news to her or ultimately be put out to pasture. I needed to be front-page news, the lead story in her life.

"I appreciate you sharing these things. It's just, I want to understand you even more. I want to know about *you*. I want to know everything. Like, why did you join? Why have you stayed?" my inquisitive girl asked.

"Hmm, you don't ask the hard questions, do you?" I teased.

Her face fell a little. I knew this rattled her as much as it did me. She probably felt bad for asking, but she had every right to.

"I'm just playing," I explained.

She relaxed, marginally. I slid her onto my lap and readjusted us both so we were sitting back, comfortably positioned against the couch. She tucked her head under my chin, and I was happy I didn't have to look in her eyes; it would make it easier for me to begin story time. I stroked her back. We just sat there for a few minutes, breathing rhythmically. I said to myself *I am not going to lose my shit when I start recounting the past* one more time. *Okay, here goes.*

"So I'm going to end up kinda starting backward. With that beautiful brain of yours, I know you'll be able to keep up and make sense of this shit. So . . . I had surgery last year, and I forced myself to recover quickly by doing physical therapy and whatnot. I doubt Caylan has told you this, but she was attacked last summer by a deranged stalker. The short version is that he kidnapped her, but Alexi and I came to her rescue. The son of a bitch died at the scene. Before I scare the crap out of you, I'll just say *we* didn't kill him. I wanted to, but he ended up drowning. It's a long fucking story, and maybe one I'll tell you another time. But for now, it's part of *my* story, I guess. I can't help but thank God that I worked so hard at recovering quickly and doing physical therapy. I was only two months post-op at that point," I stated.

Ev popped her head up. Shock was written on her face, and she covered her mouth to stifle a gasp. "Oh shit. I had no idea," she said sadly as she shook her head back and forth in disbelief.

I moved her back to where she had been tucked under my chin. Yup, I was an asshole for making her look away again, but I needed to focus on the wall to keep forging ahead with this craziness.

"Yeah, it was a pretty fucked-up situation. Clearly, she's okay now. She probably didn't tell you this other part either, but that's actually how she and Alexi met. At the hospital, I mean. You see, at the time, I was recovering from surgery at the hospital where Alexi was working. When Caylan came to visit me, she met him in the break room. As they say, the rest is history," I conveyed.

"Jesus. Why did you need surgery?" she questioned.

"I was injured. My left leg had little bits of shrapnel in it that still needed to be removed because another civilian doctor had screwed up the previous surgery. I think that was my third or fourth surgery, actually. I don't know. I can't remember, and it doesn't matter. Anyway, Alexi's hospital was the best around, so I went ahead and had them correct everything. Luckily, I'm a quick healer, so it's all good now. Like I said, focusing on getting my strength back served me well the day of Caylan's attack," I recalled.

"Caylan always acted like my injury was a lot worse than it was. Believe me, it was bad, but obviously I am fine now. She's just a worrywart, but I adore her for it. Lots of physical therapy ensued, but it was well worth it. That's why I was able to go on this last deployment, because I had finally been cleared to do so," I clarified.

I ran my hand along her back again, comforting both of us. I could feel her spine through the fabric of her shirt. It reminded me of how fragile she was. Sure, she was strong in other ways, but physically, she was delicate. I loved that about her. I rolled my eyes at myself because I realized I was getting off topic once again, fucking trying to distract myself. It would only prolong this shit. *No, best to get it all out and in the open.* And, of course, I was leaving out the detail that I had *volunteered* for my last deployment. That was one piece of information that I would forever keep to myself. Really, no one would benefit from or understand my reasoning, and you couldn't convince me otherwise.

I licked my dry lips and went on. "So now to the gruesome part. I told you what my job entails when we went to the bar that day. Normally it's an easy job, no big deal. But when we're deployed, we're usually in harm's way because we're sitting ducks out on the flight line. So in 2014, I was deployed to Afghanistan."

I stopped for a beat to let that sink in before moving on. "I just happened to be walking back to my tent with a couple of guys who I didn't really know. They were walking a little ways ahead of me. Poor bastards stepped on an IED, and the damn thing went off. The explosion was instantaneous. The craziest shit I had ever seen. I was close enough to get hit in the leg by shrapnel, but lucky to be far enough away not to get killed. The other guys were blown to pieces. Fuck, it was horrifying. I was concussed, so I don't remember much, but obviously I remember enough. I was in and out of it for a few days. I just mostly remember waking up in Germany, in recovery after the first surgery, where they had apparently medevaced me."

After my slight pause, I went on. "Christ, no one likes to talk about this shit. I know it may seem like I'm a pussy for being so messed up over a leg injury, but it was terrifying, Ev. To watch those guys die right in front of me . . . it was enough to make me not want to close my eyes at night because it kept replaying on a loop in my mind," I said without even realizing I had my eyes squeezed shut. I was wincing—the images were *still* replaying in my head.

I stopped rubbing her back for a minute and rubbed my head instead—habit, of course. I opened my eyes and took a deep breath. "Fuck. I probably shouldn't tell you all this terrible shit. You don't need to be burdened by it or need it swimming around in your brain. But if you want to hear it, I'll tell it." I was hoping she would say she wouldn't want to hear it, but knowing her, I figured she probably did.

She caressed my thigh, trying to infuse me with courage, and said, "You need to tell it."

Damn! Okay. I resigned myself. "Being hit with that shrapnel was like . . . unimaginable pain. It's hard to describe. I've never talked to any combat vets about it, or really anyone for that matter. So I don't know if it's normal, what I felt. Not even the doctors talked about it with me; they just wanted to know my pain on a scale of one to ten so they could manage it. Going back to actually thinking about it is entirely different. Fuck, I don't know. It was like blunt trauma to my leg . . . as if there was heat radiating in that spot. Like someone took a bat and hit me repeatedly in the same area. There was no escaping. Even without the concussion, I think I would have passed out from the pain. I'm probably not making sense. I don't know how to articulate something of this nature."

I blew out a frustrated breath. I hope she understood my reluctance to talk about the topic and could understand that it was hard to put into words. But I was proud of myself for not going into a tailspin of panic and hysteria while recounting the details. I had mentioned before that I thought she brought the flashbacks out in me. But once again, it was reaffirmed that she also soothed me unlike anything else ever could. I didn't want to be this weak, though, and I needed someone, or something, to heal me. But Ev was truly my other half in life. I think I knew that all along. I think I knew that when I went over there in March. Half of my heart was back with her the whole time. The vast ocean that existed between us was symbolic of everything we had to wade through in order to reunite, so we could be one.

I hadn't finished the story, and I suddenly realized that. "So to answer your other questions . . . Why did I join? I joined because it's a calling. It's in my blood, despite all this horrible, screwed-up shit that it entails. Why did I stay? Because somebody has to do it, and I'd rather it be me out there protecting everyone than someone else I don't know or trust."

"I see it in you. I see it's something you *need* to do. I know trust is earned and not automatically gained in your book, Brent," she explained.

She had the uncanny ability to say things I was thinking, and that was also a revelation in itself. As if she was seeking comfort from me or trying her damnedest to bandage me up, she turned her face into my chest and hugged my midsection so fiercely, it was like she was trying to squeeze the breath out of me. She wasn't the most physically affectionate person, and I knew that. Fuck, she was a tigress in bed, but when it came to being romantic, affectionate, warm, and expressive, she didn't make sense. So this was an unbelievable gift she was giving me in showing me yet another facet of herself. I always knew she was perfectly *capable* of showcasing these types of emotions and actions, but until I heard her story, I hadn't quite understood where the hesitancy stemmed from.

Who had held her as a child? The stark clarity of having to accept that *no one* held her was heart-wrenching. No one taught her how to give affection. But nevertheless, she made the gesture on her own, for *me*. I kept thinking of how we were both changing each other more and more—and it was for the better.

She pulled away slightly from my chest so her response wouldn't be muffled. "You know me . . . I'm not one to be at a loss for words, but sometimes, you do that to me. I'm humbled by the fact you've shared all this with me. I'm so proud of you. I'm sorry about what happened to you, and I don't know what else to say—except that I hope I am worthy of being good enough for you," she admitted.

I was taken aback by her comments. For a second, I was almost pissed. How could she *ever* think she wasn't good enough for me? It was a punch to the gut, but I would remedy that. She was my warrior, my confident woman, my no-holds-barred, unattainable mountain. However, I was sure that all this talk of pasts and hurts and nightmares riddled her mind with insecurities and let them plague her again. That's why I often sensed that she needed protection—from herself. I could feel it all along. Underneath the surface simmered a demon of self-doubt and harshness, just waiting to rip out Ev's throat. That's why I knew she needed to keep the demon at bay. Each time it was given an inch, it wanted a bloody mile. It was capable of shredding her from the inside out.

I could almost taste the salt of her unshed tears. I was so hyperaware of her every move, and both the verbal and nonverbal judgments she was making about herself. I could tell she was also contemplating my confession.

I didn't want to be a bastard and take advantage of a situation where she was vulnerable, but I think we both needed a release—and that could only come in the form of being physical and intimate with our bodies. When we joined, it was like our souls crying out to each other. I needed it then, and I sensed she did too. We had said all we needed to say anyway, by that point.

The truth I knew was this: she loved me, and I loved her. I knew we'd navigate the shoal that was just teasing us below the surface, but that hadn't quite broken the water yet. We weren't at that stage as a couple, but we had started a journey together. I'd begin it by worshiping her body like I promised.

Chapter 22: A Game of Dog and Cat

Everly

Brent swept me up in his arms and carried me into my bedroom, then set me down on shaky legs. I was so grateful that we didn't need to say anything else. Words were overrated and probably dangerous to my system at the moment. I would feel him, and only him, without words.

He undressed me quickly and gently laid me down on the bed. Then he undressed himself. I was a wet mess already. My pussy was quivering and greedy; I needed him more than I needed air. He settled his massive, sexy body on top of me. It was the best feeling, taking his full weight and having him up against me. He smelled divine. The sweat and soap scents on his skin mixed together, giving off a powerful aroma that I could almost sink my teeth into.

I was happy he wasn't trying to do the intimacy thing. It would always be intimate with him anyway, because I loved him. But just then, I wanted to use him to fuck. I just needed to fuck. Maybe some people can't understand that, but it doesn't matter; it was about *my* wants and needs at the moment. I would analyze later, in private, Brent's impassioned speech about why he did what he did for the country and for his family. I would also examine what we were to each other another time. I could only say it was stronger than even love . . . but what to call it, I didn't know.

We didn't do the whole foreplay thing, thankfully, because it wasn't necessary. He plunged to the hilt in one swift action, and I screamed so loud I worried for a moment that I blew out my own eardrum. This was what I was craving, though: raw, gritty, dirty, frenzied fucking. Ladies, if you haven't ever truly been fucked, I mean really *fucked*, then you don't know the uninhibited, liberating and freeing experience it can be. It washes over you in a fierce tidal wave. When Brent came unhinged, it signaled that he knew a side of me I didn't know another human could touch or reach. I needed the wild side. I needed the wicked side. I. Needed. Brent.

He cupped my ass cheeks and used his lower torso to press harder against my pelvic area, forcing my legs to open wider. He grunted, and I moaned in return. But it didn't seem good enough for him. He pulled out suddenly, and I mourned the loss of him so deep inside me. I didn't have time to think, pout, or protest, though, because he picked me up again and held me in the air. I couldn't believe he could hold my weight—he didn't even need the wall for leverage. No, that strong man could do anything. And he did. I was impaled on his cock at lightning speed. I held on with my arms tightly wrapped around his neck, and I heard myself breathing harshly in his ear.

I was clinging to him like I couldn't get close enough. Next, he moved us over to a chair in the corner of my room. He sat down on it, lodged inside me the entire time. The new angle caused him to go even farther into my tight, wet clasp. Even though I was so lost in the moment, I couldn't help but chuckle to myself in my head. I knew the joke that other branches of service called Air Force members the "Chair Force." It was sad that the stigma still existed, but I knew he was a hero—a far cry from *any* stereotype. Now, though, he was giving "Chair Force" a whole new meaning!

I could only imagine how sore I would be the next morning; hell, I was still sore from the night before. But it was worth everything. Opening myself up to him, in more ways than one, was worth it all. The feral, brutal, savage beast he had become inflamed my passion in a way that words could not convey. I knew my pussy had to be glistening with evidence of my impending orgasm. I was so close. On the edge. The myriad of emotions I was feeling had me in their clutches. I needed a release so badly.

He reached his hand down and rubbed at my clit in rhythmic, skilled circles. In an instant, I was *clit*erally a rub away from going off. The final confirmation came in the form of words, though. I didn't think we'd be communicating verbally at that steamy moment, but leave it to Brent to surprise me.

"I love you," he rasped out.

That did it. My brain short-circuited, and the most intense blast of radiating energy flashed over me. It was a quick and epic explosion. Next thing I knew, his cum was also spilling forth in hot, creamy spurts all over my stomach. It was a violent release that rivaled all others. I knew he was marking me with his cum—it was the sexiest thing to witness.

We would definitely need a shower, but I didn't care about being sticky in the moment because it meant we had fucked each other's brains out. We collapsed on each other as he slumped back in the chair. I didn't want to move for anything. I needed recovery time. My eyes drifted closed, and sleep came for me.

***

Eventually, we showered and had a late-night snack. We were also both more than ready for bed. I climbed in to the heavenliness of my mattress with just cotton panties on and face-planted on my pillow. Brent slid in on what had already become "his" side of the bed. *Wow, we both actually have our own sides of the bed.* I turned my head so my face was exposed, and he likewise laid down on his side so he could face me.

The light was out, but my vision had adjusted enough that I could see him. I recognized that what I was about to tell him was completely out of character for me. As I kept telling myself, he was changing me. Well, no, *change* wasn't the right word. He was helping me *grow.* Change implied I was no longer myself. I was still myself with him; I was just a better version of myself. I bit my lower lip before speaking, nervous as hell.

"I want you to move in with me. If it's too soon, I get it. But you need a place anyway. What better way to see if this will actually work than to jump right into shark-infested waters? I know it will be an adjustment for both of us, but I'm willing to try. Err, I don't know how Maverick will do with Pussy, but we can see how that goes too," I stammered.

He lifted his hand and tucked a wayward curl behind my ear. Then he traced the outline of my face and smiled at me. He had the most beautiful smile and I once again marveled at the straightest, whitest teeth on a man. He really was so handsome, it hurt to look at him sometimes. His heart, though, was what got me. The fact that he could open his life to someone like me made me believe there must be a guardian angel out there somewhere, watching over me. I didn't even believe in that shit—I blamed Caylan for making me such a sap. I was becoming a marshmallow inside. Jesus!

"I know you wouldn't have brought it up if you weren't sure. So I won't insult you by questioning it. I'd love to live with you. I'll admit this is a little farther away from the base than I'd prefer to drive, but I'll make it work. If this does go my way, we'll eventually find somewhere else to live. That's a promise you can take to the bank, Ev," he stated.

With the living-arrangements discussion out of the way, we fell asleep wrapped around each other in a sinful spooning position. He felt so good and strong. I snuggled down right into his body like I belonged, and, well, maybe I did. That night I dreamed of a happily ever after with my airman. I didn't think anything could dispel the high my heart was on.

***

Brenneth

On Sunday, Ev and I lounged around. She did a little work while I prepped to go to the base the next day. It was lazy and relaxing, just perfect.

Monday morning, I left Everly with fresh coffee, a kiss, and a pat on Pussy's head. I walked out of *our* apartment. It was *ours* now, which I couldn't believe. It floored me that Ev had suggested living together. I jumped at the chance, without hesitation.

I was heading into work to in-process back into my squadron. I also needed to remember to give my supervisors my new address. Then my plan was to pick up Maverick from my parents later in the afternoon, so we could see how it went with cat and dog. Ev had told me she was going into the office, and I couldn't help but feel uneasy that she'd see that dickhead Stuart. I wanted to kick his ass. But I knew I needed to remain calm and not lose my head over anything, or I'd end up doing something stupid that I'd regret.

I was busy all day, running around on the base and getting paperwork signed, going to the clinic, and going to briefings. By the end of the day, I was more than ready to get back to Ev. My resentment toward Stuart waned slightly as the day went on. I texted her off and on throughout the day, sending messages of a flirty and sexy nature. I would have loved to get some nudes from her, but it was for the best she didn't send me anything like that—I would have gone AWOL instantly.

By the time I got to my parents' place, it was around six o'clock. It was nice to see them again, of course. Maverick had apparently behaved himself—I didn't expect anything less since he's a great dog.

I stayed for a few minutes to chat with Mom and Dad before I rushed off. They didn't raise me to be rude. Plus, I genuinely missed them. Years apart never lessened the bond we had. Not just because they're my parents, but also because they're just great people in general. My heart ached for Everly, though, because we came from different worlds. I was just so lucky and grateful that Ev really took to my parents, and they had really seemed to take to her too.

Mom spoke first when we sat down on the couch. She patted my hand and said, "I really adore Everly. It is so nice to see you genuinely happy."

"Thanks, Mom. It's more than just affection and happiness, though. I love her," I stated while looking directly at both of my parents.

My dad nodded his head, and my mom beamed. They seemed to have already known and accepted this conclusion. Thank God for their unwavering support for everything I do.

"Oh sweetie, we knew that already. Don't you think everyone could see it at the party? I think you're a good fit. Not that you need my input, but you know I always have a sixth sense about these things. She's a good one; I just know it," Mom remarked with the deepest sincerity.

It wasn't that I felt I needed my parents' permission or approval, but it was still great to hear. My dad was a man of few words, but the fact that he smiled along with my mom meant I had their blessing.

My mom suddenly clapped her hands together, as if an idea had just occurred to her.

"I'm just so happy for you. You have no idea how much it warms my heart to see both my children happy and in love. I never thought Caylan would find someone before you, given how young she is, but I never gave up hope that one day you'd fall for someone too," Mom said, swiping at a silvery tear.

I was choked up and overcome by emotion because of my mom's reaction. It once again made me realize how sad it was that Ev had no one to turn to for parental advice or love and unconditional support. I could be that person for her, though. I rubbed my hands down the thighs of my uniform pants, removing excess sweat. I knew my parents were also probably over the fucking moon about the fact that I had found someone who would accept all my damage and baggage. Ev was truly a gift.

"Well, I know Everly really likes you guys, and she's becoming great friends with Caylan. Although if Ev's apartment turns into a pink palace, then I'm out." I chuckled along with my parents at that thought. Then I continued, "I never thought Caylan would find someone so soon either, but she did. I'm grateful to Alexi. But I promise you guys I never would have let anything happen to Caylan. I would have provided for her. I never told you this, but I've saved up money over the years from all my deployments and combat pay. I had every intention of putting a down payment on a house for you guys. But damn Alexi beat me to it."

"First, don't cuss, mister. Second, although you are the kindest, sweetest son a mother could ask for, we never would have let you do it. The money you've earned is for you and you alone. What you've gone through during your career means you deserve every good thing in this world. Brent, maybe we don't tell you enough. Just know how proud we are of you, and how much we love you and adore you. You really are a hero, son." Mom sniffled at the end and pulled a hankie from her pocket to dry her eyes.

Damn, I'm one lucky son of a bitch to have them.

"Thanks, guys. You know it's hard for me to hear. You know I don't look at myself like that. I'm just another dude going to work, doing his job every day. But I appreciate you always being in my corner. You know I love you. I don't want to share Ev's secrets, but believe me when I say it means more to me than anything that you're embracing her. She had a rough childhood, to say the least. She doesn't have any family . . . Well, anyway, I better get going. Thanks for watching Maverick." I stood as I said the last part.

My parents hugged me and said their goodbyes. I loaded up Maverick in my truck and away we went. As we were driving home to Ev, I thought about my savings. I could get a place for us. I didn't dare spring that on her yet, even though I'd hinted to her last night we'd eventually be moving. I was also crossing my fingers hoping Maverick and Pussy would get along; that feline was such a damn asshole at times, I suspected she wouldn't welcome him with open paws. I knew I should feel special that she had at least taken to me so quickly.

We arrived home and . . . things went swimmingly with the dog and cat! Ev and I looked at each other in bewilderment, thinking it was actually kind of an eerie scene. Maybe we should have been worried we were in some alternate universe. Ev and I eventually ate dinner, and I was just so happy to be near her. I told her about my day, and she told me about hers. It was crazy how domestic we both became—practically overnight, no less.

She said Steve was loving her new columns regarding the things women only say to their girlfriends. Not that I know what I am talking about, but it did sound funny and fresh for a newspaper piece. I hoped she'd be successful. She said Stuart had walked around all day with an air of superiority. Even though the announcement about his promotion wouldn't be made public for at least a few weeks, apparently he was already scoping out his new office and dictating changes. Ev made it clear he was already settling into the role the little prick felt he was entitled to. I couldn't help but hate him even more. I decided, though, that as long as he kept Everly on staff, and as long as he didn't make a move on my woman, we could maybe get along just fine. Maybe.

Chapter 23: The News Never Sleeps

Everly

October 17, 2017

It had been over four weeks since Brent moved in. Believe it or not, things were going well. He went back to work after spending two weeks on R & R, and then had another two weeks of leave. I could only afford to spend a day with him here and there, but any time was better than none. He moved a few things into our place, but most of his stuff stayed in storage. He kept insisting he didn't mind keeping things at his storage unit, so I didn't argue.

Pussy and Maverick were still getting along great, but I was beginning to realize it was quite crowded in our tiny apartment. I didn't know when Brent would broach the subject again about moving. I was thinking I'd have to be brave and mention it, but I hated that I really couldn't contribute anything financial to the relationship. I'd probably get my security deposit back on the apartment, but otherwise, I'd be a moocher if we wanted to have a bigger place. I didn't like the feeling of depending on someone else.

We had never really talked finances, so I continued to pay all the bills. Brent offered, but I wouldn't hear of it. Having him there really didn't tack on too many extra expenses; utilities were included anyway. I just hoped my landlord didn't find out about my "guest" who was having an extended visit, because then Brent would need to be added to the lease. Frankly, if we were going to eventually get out of there, then I didn't want to sign on for longer terms with a lease renewal. Brent always bought groceries, though, so I appreciated that. He spoiled me when we went out on dates, which again wasn't necessary, but I let him win some too. I was hoping there'd be a promotion in my future, but with things so up in the air now at my office, I didn't know when that goal might be realized—if ever.

Brent and I had settled into a comfortable routine. We really were a great fit, and he had become one of my best friends. Correction, he actually *was* my best friend. It didn't even seem like it had only been four weeks since we officially became a couple. I felt like I'd known him a lifetime. We liked to watch movies together, go bowling at the base, snuggle and talk, take Maverick out for walks and to the dog park on base, hang out with his family . . . the list goes on.

We had just gotten together with the whole gang of friends and family at one of the group's favorite restaurants, for example, called Thai-Phoon, and the place didn't disappoint.

The past weekend, we celebrated Alexi and Caylan's one-year wedding anniversary; their actual anniversary was on the twenty-second, but that would be a private celebration for them. It was great to see everyone and catch up. I really liked everyone I met. Those in attendance included Gil, Anthony and his fiancée Shanna, Caleb, Liz and her kids, Alexi's parents, Brent's cousin Meg, and of course Fred and Milly.

But back to Brent and me. The steamy nights together certainly helped to solidify our relationship. Of course, I got my period in there at one point, but I was very accommodating to his needs in the oral sense. We could certainly burn up the sheets with our lovemaking. Each day he'd tell me he loved me, and each day I'd ditto that. I felt like neither one of us could imagine our lives without the other. I'll be honest in saying it wasn't as scary as it was in the beginning—shocker, I know!

The day before, the official announcement was made in the office that Stuart had been named CEO. Thankfully, he didn't can me or Steve, but a few of my coworkers got the boot as part of their "reorganizing" and "retooling" vision for the publication. Their severance packages were confidential, so I have no idea how anyone made out. If my pink slip was coming too, I just hoped it would be decent enough. I'll admit, though, that I wasn't too sad to see some of the guys in the office go. They had always viewed me as inferior—when we all damn well knew I could write circles around them.

Stuart assured everyone who remained that he wouldn't interfere in the day-to-day operations. He promised to still let Steve run things as he saw fit, but I didn't know yet if I could believe that. My new . . . err . . . *boss* spent the entire day with an interior designer talking about a complete remodel to Steve's old office. Steve grumbled a little, but ended up taking a smaller one—it's not like he had a choice in the matter anyway. I was just happy Stuart had something to focus on besides me and further ideas of cleaning house. He stopped texting too, and that was probably wise on his end. At least for the moment things were calm and smooth. I prayed it stayed that way because for once, dare I say it, I was really happy.

Ten days later, I was sitting at my kitchen table typing away, when in walked Brent. He greeted the cat and dog first, then made his way over to me, dropping a kiss on the crown of my head. He headed to our bedroom to take off his uniform. Most times, I'd ambush him and make him keep it on—that uniform did something to me—but I wasn't really in the mood.

I was trying to come up with my next column idea, and it was driving me crazy. Unfortunately for anyone around me, when I can't write I get frustrated easily . . . look out! I know I'm impossible to deal with. So sue me. My coworkers know to leave me alone when I'm writing at work. They call it my "creative genius," and they understand you need to work through shit in your mind to get to the good stuff buried in the middle, under all the crap.

I had my fingers poised on the keys and was deep in thought when Brent asked me something. My head snapped up. I was very perturbed that he had disturbed me. He did get that work was important to me, but I don't know if he *really* got it. Writing is either flowing through the blood in your veins, or it isn't. You can't pick and choose whether you're a writer or not. It picks you. And when it does, you are bound to spend most of your time penning something—whether you like it or not.

I said rather too sharply, "What did you say?"

He tried not to let his annoyance with my attitude show through, but I could see it there, just under the surface. He didn't deserve my harshness, but I couldn't help it. I know that's no excuse, but when I get in the zone, God help anyone near me.

"I simply asked how your day was, but I can see this isn't a good time to talk," he stated as he walked off.

I closed my mouth and clenched my jaw at his retreating form, showing my obvious disinterest in talking—even if only to myself. I also did that whole head-move thing that is the universal sign for "oh no you didn't." I stalked after him, leaving my precious laptop sitting on the kitchen table. I didn't have much on the screen, but I at least had enough to really start formulating a column. I could get back to it as soon as I argued it out with my man.

I followed him down to our bedroom. There he was in the corner, on my chair, leaning forward with his arms rested on his thighs and his hands clasped together. I guess he knew what was coming next. I decided I would not be distracted by the fact he was in *that* chair.

"You have my undivided attention now. Well, here I am, sweetheart," I tried to impersonate Jack Nicholson's famous line at the end and failed miserably, I might add. It was good enough—and effective. Although truthfully I felt more like it was a "heeeere's Johnny" delivery instead of an *As Good as It Gets* reference.

"I'm not doing this with you, Everly," he replied.

"Oh, so we're using full names now? Okay then, *Brenneth*, let's not do this. But you're the one who came at me," I fired back.

"You're not making any sense. Asking you how your day was and being interested in the woman I love is what? A crime? Fuck, sometimes I don't get how you can be the way you are. You don't have to go all psychotic on me," he barked.

That did it! Men should *never* call a woman psychotic. That just pisses us off even more and amps us up like you wouldn't believe. He thought I was psycho—I'd *show* him psycho! But he'd definitely delivered his mark, hitting me right where it bothered me the most. He took me back to my childhood full of abuse, making me feel like I was out of control or had no control at all. I hated feeling like I was crazy, worthless, or unwanted.

"Well, maybe you never understood me at all then. Maybe the honeymoon phase is over," I said, then swiftly turned because there was no way I was going to let the tears pricking my eyes be made visible to Brent.

On some level, I knew I wasn't really mad at him. I was just pissy with myself over work and how everything in my life overwhelmed me. Also, on some level, I knew I was being irrational. But when you're in that moment, you can't stop yourself or take a step back. I practically ran off to the kitchen to get back to work, wanting to disappear into my column and ignore Brent for a little bit. I figured he'd get the hint and keep to himself for the rest of the night, until I finally came to bed.

When I got to the kitchen, though, I froze at what I saw. Just as I was entering, Maverick jumped up onto the table to get to my uneaten bagel, sitting there on a paper plate. Consequently, he bumped my coffee mug. It was still full of steaming joe. I watched it all happen in slow motion, and I couldn't do a damn thing to stop it. The hot, steaming goodness I usually adore became my worst enemy in an instant. The mug tipped over onto my laptop. I just stood there, horrified.

Maverick ran off with the bagel; I think he knew I was about to explode. If fire wasn't coming out of my laptop, I'm sure it was coming out of my mouth, nose, and ears. But nothing happened to my computer like I thought it would. There was no exploding battery. Thankfully, I didn't have the damn thing plugged into an outlet, so there was no smoke. The screen simply went black. I heard a weird sound like the motherboard arcing and frying, and then that was it. I just knew instantly that it was dead. Dead, like my story. Dead, like my heart.

Okay, I'm being dramatic, but motherfucking hell!

I finally started ranting and raving like a lunatic, saying, "No, no, no, no," over and over again. I paced back and forth in the kitchen. Maverick was hiding somewhere; he was wise to stay away. Brent must have heard the commotion, because he came out of the bedroom. He looked at me, then looked at the mess of coffee everywhere on the table and floor. He wore a matching shocked expression to mine.

"What happened?" he asked.

"You can't tell, genius? Your damn dog fried my computer!" My voice was shrill and my tongue was abusive. "You just don't *fucking care* because it wasn't *your* computer. And you don't care because it's *your* damn dog," I accused.

"Calm down. Jesus. We'll figure this out. You know he didn't mean to do it; he's just a dog. I'll buy you a new one. I'm sorry it happened. All right?" He was pleading with me.

I got real quiet. And when you get real quiet and are no longer at that yelling stage, you head into the scary stage. I put my hands on my hips and stared up at the ceiling. I so wanted to hurt him—or something—in some way. Maybe I did need to calm down, but it's hard when you're so fired up. It's hard to reason with someone when they're in the state I was currently in. I probably needed to get out of the apartment and go for a drive. But Brent didn't give me the chance or space. I knew I shouldn't blame him, but . . .

"I know you're upset. I get it, but put this into perspective. No one was hurt. The laptop can be replaced, and I can clean up the mess. If you get this upset over a simple accident, how are you going to be if we have kids and they make a mess?" he asked sincerely.

"Are you fucking kidding me with that question? I can't even talk to you right now. You are so out in left field! How the hell do you even think this is insignificant? My *work* was on there! I didn't back up what I was working on because I never thought your damn dog would do what he just did. As far as the kid comment—fuck you!"

I was seething by that point. And even though I didn't mean it, I figured it was go big or go home. So I broke the back of the camel with the final straw: "Well, we aren't having kids, so it doesn't matter. Because I'd never have them with you!"

You could have heard a pin drop. Brent just stood there, not even reacting. I could feel the hurt, anger, frustration, and surprise rolling off him, though. I knew saying I didn't want kids with him was not the best thing to say, but we had never talked about them, and I *didn't* want them anytime soon. I really had to believe he didn't want them anytime soon either. But that's not what I said, obviously.

"Everly, I think we need some time to cool off. I'm going to go crash somewhere else tonight. Let me know when you're ready to talk," he stated. He walked off to the bedroom.

A few minutes later, he came back out with a bag in hand. He grabbed Maverick's leash and yelled for him. Maverick slinked past me. I felt more than guilty. Brent didn't say anything as he walked out the door. I didn't say anything either, and I certainly didn't try to stop him.

I instantly knew I had been a fool. But it all happened so fast. I regretted what I said, but I didn't feel like telling him that yet. I ended up cleaning up the coffee mess while Pussy sat there giving me the evil eye and judging the hell out of me. I figured she was mad that both dog and man had left us. I told her to get over it and threw a dirty paper towel in her direction. She stretched and walked off, going at her own pace, showing me that no one was going to run *her* off. Message received, Pussy!

I put my laptop in the stainless-steel sink to let it drain. I'd take it to one of the tech guys at work the next day and see what they could do. Despite it being a Saturday, one or two of them would be milling around— the news does not sleep on the weekend. If it caught on fire during the night . . . well, at least it was in a metal enclosure.

I grabbed a notebook from my shelf and made myself a new cup of coffee. I trudged off to bed, alone. Alone. *Fuck, I'm alone again!* Temporarily, but it still felt wrong. I definitely had a case of self-loathing now. And okay, I admit I *was* a little psycho during that whole argument. I sighed loudly. I'd make it right with Brent somehow. I stayed up for a little bit, trying to jot down in my notebook some of the ideas I had on my computer. I finally laid the pen and paper down and settled into a restless sleep that gave me some awful nightmares about happily *never* afters.

***

Brenneth

I was lying on the bed in my parents' guestroom. Maverick was on the floor next to me, and he seemed to be sad too about what had transpired. My parents didn't ask what happened, and I told them it was just for one night. I appreciated that they didn't pry, speculate, or judge.

I get that Ev's work is her life. Now that I've had time to reflect, I understand that's all she's had and known over the years. I knew once she cooled off, things would be fine. I could recognize that she was under a lot of stress and pressure too. This relationship stuff was complicated, but I was more than willing to keep working at it. I shouldn't have expected things to be perfect anyway. We were going to have disagreements; we were going to have blowups.

The kid thing hurt, though. It's not as if I wanted them right away; it's just that she had closed a door on a future before we even discussed it.

She made a decision for *us* that was not hers to make. We'd have to revisit that subject for sure. The argument was also reminiscent of something Alexi and Caylan went through. So I was praying there was hope for us. They had been able to work it out—so could we.

I felt marginally better once I had those realizations, and then I tried to fall asleep. Before I drifted off, though, I couldn't help but feel how much it sucked to not be with her. I had gotten too used to it. Too used to spooning. Too used to her sounds, too used to her body heat, and too used to making love each night that we could.

Everly definitely needed protection—from herself. I would have to tell her that, but I knew reality often doesn't feel good going down, so she'd have to swallow it for "us" to work. She was her own worst enemy sometimes. Ev had said before that she thought she was too much work for me to take on because of her past, but I didn't believe that. We just needed to keep giving "us" a chance and continue to progress. I realized I didn't fare well without her.

Chapter 24: Falling Down the Stairs

Brenneth

It was Saturday afternoon, and I decided that since Ev hadn't called, texted, or come to find me, well, I'd go after her. I was a big boy. I could swallow the morning-after pill. Shit, that sounded creepy, fucked-up, and weird. I just meant swallow the *bitterness* pill the *morning* after a fight; ya know, about being the one to crack first. Well, anyways, I'd look at this like a victory for both of us. She was still a prize that I was getting, and I was doing the noble thing by making up with her first. I've had some friends tell me make-up sex is hot, so I was looking forward to that too.

I went to our apartment first. She wasn't there, which was no surprise. I figured she had work to do. I had left Maverick with my parents, just in case there was no make-up sex. Of course, I wasn't worried that we'd *never* make up, but I didn't have the warm-and-fuzzies yet. We still had to work through some shit. And, well, that had been a nasty fight. I didn't want to press my luck with the dog—it could make it look like I was coming back no matter what, when really I didn't yet know *what* was what.

I went over and greeted Pussy, who was sunbathing in the living room window. At first she ignored me, but eventually I got her to purr like a car engine revving up. It helped that I apologized profusely for my egregious misconduct of having left her without saying goodbye. She eventually forgave me, and all was well in Pussy world.

As I looked around, I realized Ev had cleaned up the mess from the spill. I felt a twinge of guilt assail me about what had happened. I didn't see her laptop anywhere, so I wondered if she had gone to try and get it fixed. Being the smart guy I am, I also deduced that she had probably gone into the office. I know how she gets when she's working on something, and she probably didn't feel comfortable being home, for obvious reasons.

After I assured the cat that I'd be back, I decided to head to a tech store and buy Ev a replacement laptop. Even if she was by some miracle able to salvage her other one, it was old anyway. Now that I had money free to use at my disposal, well, my first order of business was to spend a little on her. And then I'd spend a lot on *us*.

I was definitely going to talk to her about moving and buying a place as soon as we settled things. If she wasn't comfortable with buying it with me, then I wouldn't pressure her. Things were happening fast, but I didn't see the point in renting anymore when I could put that money toward equity in a home; it just made more sense, and it was time I made my homestead.

I didn't care if she wanted to buy in Pennsylvania or New Jersey; either would be fine. I also wasn't worried about getting stationed somewhere else; with just four years to go, it wasn't likely they'd move me again. The general consensus around the base, even though I don't agree with it, is that people were wanting to get out of Jersey, certainly not the other way around. I thought it was safe to say I'd be fine until retirement.

After visiting Best Buy, and with a new shiny laptop in hand, I headed over to her office. I must say I also had a confident walk about me, thinking how my future was set. I walked into Ev's building with a smile, hard on, and a sense of peace. My erection deflated just a few steps into the place, though. I cringed thinking about how it was Stuart's dad's building—whereby the dickhead would probably someday inherit it. I decided to use another military acronym to perfectly define the situation, which is FIDO—fuck it, drive on. I needed to FIDO just then, because nothing was going to stand in the way of our happiness.

***

Everly

I had taken my time getting into the office that morning because I was still sleep-deprived from the night before, and also in a sour mood because of what had happened. Dozens of times I had picked up my cell to call Brent, and dozens of times I had put the phone down rather roughly on my nightstand. I even thought of texting him, with the same result. I felt lucky I restrained myself from smashing the screen; I don't think even shatter-proof screen protectors could save me from my own temper. I guess I could have gone over to talk to him in person, but I wasn't sure where he was staying. I figured he was at his sister's place or with his parents. Either way, I'd decided to go talk to him after I finished up things at the office.

I felt slightly bad as I was leaving that morning, because Pussy was in an even fouler mood than I was. I had to get out of the place once I finally showered and packed up my soiled laptop. It never caught fire, thankfully, but it was still leaking coffee when I packed it up. One of the techies at work, named Kevin, said it was not salvageable. I expected that assessment, but it still sucked. He explained that I did in fact fry the motherboard. Well, that was that.

Luckily, he had a spare he could lend me until I got another. We weren't provided with laptops, but that was okay because I could write it off on my taxes anyway. I certainly couldn't spring for anything fancy, but I'd get something decent. Brent was sweet to offer to buy me a replacement, but I couldn't let him do that. Not only did I need to apologize to the man, but I also owed Maverick some belly rubs and sorries.

I pulled my notebook out of my bag, then transferred all my thoughts from the paper version and typed them into the loaner laptop. Kevin had also given me an external hard drive to use for the time being, so I could start backing everything up. He encouraged me to back up to a remote site as well, so that was yet another thing I would have to add to my to-do list once I got a new computer. I typed away for a while, finally finding my rhythm. As I've said, when I get lost in writing, I get lost in time. Before I knew it, it was early evening. It would be dark soon, and I was ready to get home to Brent—or to find him, I should say.

I put my hands behind my back to stretch its lower half. Of course, that move sent my breasts thrusting forward, but I didn't care because I was alone and not showing off for anyone. Kevin had been the last one to leave, and that was probably hours ago. At least I *thought* I was alone. I heard someone clear his throat. I jumped in my seat, startled, then stood up abruptly. I turned around. There, directly behind me, was my new boss. I placed my hand over my frantic, beating heart, willing it to calm and slow.

"Jesus, Stuart, you nearly had me jumping out of my skin. I had no idea anyone else was even here," I said while still pressing my hand against my chest.

That move turned out to be a bad idea, because it took Stuart's eyes right there. His attention was ensnared by the action. As soon as I noticed that, I quickly removed my hand and placed it at my side. I shook my head to clear it. He hadn't said anything yet.

He looked different somehow . . . then I put my finger on it. He was casually dressed. He had been wearing suits since the takeover. I liked the jeans look better, because it reminded me of the way he used to be. Although, I didn't want him to *completely* return to being the old Stuart, because that also came with stalker texting tendencies.

I too was casually dressed in skinny jeans, Converse sneakers, and a light sweater that had a sweetheart neckline. I loved that pink sweater. Okay, I said it. I like pink, but truthfully that was the only pink thing I owned. Caylan had better not get any ideas about borrowing it if she ever sees it. Anyway, I thought I looked okay, but it's not like I was trying to impress anybody. I was still bummed about the fight. And I definitely had *not* expected to run into my new boss.

"I'm sorry I scared you, Everly. I didn't mean to. I came in a few hours ago just as Kevin was leaving, but you were deep into it. I know better than to interrupt your flow. So I went into my office and did some work. I didn't feel comfortable leaving you here all alone. It will be dark soon. When I heard your fingers stop pecking away at the keyboard, I figured you were either taking a break or done for the night. So I thought I'd come say hi. And just so you know, I plan on doing a full security upgrade to the building to ensure the safety of my employees. Well, really I have lots of plans, Everly. And *you'll* be included in some of those plans," he explained while looking deeply into my eyes.

Many thoughts started swirling around in my head after I processed what had just come out of his mouth. First, I couldn't believe *he* got it about the way I liked to work, yet I felt last night that Brent hadn't. Second, I couldn't understand why he was going into protective mode on me. Third, I was shocked he had all these so-called plans for the newspaper. It made me think he really *was* the man for the job and was very much invested in the future of our publication. Lastly, I had no idea what to make of the "plans" he was referring to with regard to me. I didn't know if that was a creepy remark, a very genuine one in terms of my work, or some kind of innuendo. Me being the person I am . . . well, you know, I had to ask.

"What's that supposed to mean? What 'plans' do you have for me?" I questioned, using air quotes, even though I hated when girls did that.

He smiled one of those big, boyish, movie-star grins. I admit I melted a little bit. God, he could be so cute sometimes. But I was committed to Brent, so there was never a worry I'd succumb to Stuart's charm.

"That simply means I see big things happening for you here. You are by far the brightest, most real, most talented, and prettiest writer we have on staff. You have to know this about yourself. Don't get me wrong . . . Steve is a great guy and has been a great managing editor, but he's been holding you back since the minute you walked in the door and got the job. You are capable of so much more. I can see you filling his position one day. And if I have it my way, which I always do, that day will be sooner than later. You just need someone to push you in the right direction," he said sincerely as he took a slight step forward, letting his words, body heat, and eyes sear me in place.

Okay, point for Stuart for throwing me off. For once I stood riveted to the spot, rendered 100 percent speechless. I think my head was still all jumbled from lack of sleep. I couldn't even process the idea of Steve leaving or Stuart making him leave, so I wasn't going to touch that one right now. I rubbed at my forehead and closed my eyes. I needed a minute to think.

I also needed to get the hell out of there. I had to find Brent.

When I opened my eyes, there Stuart was, a breath away from my lips. And my next thought was, *Oh no! He's going to kiss me!*

***

Brenneth

I decided not to take the elevator up to Everly's floor, opting for the stairs instead since I'm a fit guy and not lazy—just another opportunity to get some PT in since the military is big on fitness. I was anxious to see my girl and give her the new laptop. I kept thinking about having office sex with her, but I assumed she wouldn't risk it. But then again, she's a kinky woman, so who knew? As I bounded up the last set of steps, my face immediately fell, and I saw red in my vision.

My heart was stabbed, and I was gutted in an instant. There, on the far side of the room, at one of the last desks in the row, stood Ev and the little prick. He was *kissing* her.

MOTHERFUCKER!

I saw all I needed to see. I had to get the hell out of there before I ended up going to prison. I wanted to tear Stuart's nuts off and shove them down his throat. I wanted to scream at Everly and call her every name in the book. My mom had raised me better than that, but it was sure hard to keep it all in.

I turned and hastily reached for the railing. I was having a hard time making it down the stairs. I was afraid I was going to fall. How ironic that I had been falling *up* the stairs last December when I met Ev, and now I was falling *down* at the end of "us."

I guessed she ran to Stuart and found someone to console her. Or she'd been lying to me and seeing him all along. It also could explain why she didn't want kids. Was she just using me? Was I an experiment for her column? Or the other possibility was that she was fucking her boss, trying for that goddamn promotion he'd hinted at.

No matter which reason it was, none was a good enough excuse.

I'd never forgive her for this.

The first woman I had actually loved, decided I wanted to finally spend the rest of my life with, and she'd just shit all over me and my heart. I felt sick to my stomach. Sweat was pouring down my face. I needed to get out into the night air and cool off.

Fuck. Some things you just can't un-see.

Before I exited the building, I smashed the new laptop into pieces right on the tiled lobby floor. It took a few tries, but it was destroyed enough. The broken bits seemed to reflect what was going on with me internally. I thought that action would be effective in making me feel better by getting out some anger, but it didn't. It was a poor substitute.

I walked outside, gasping for breath. I couldn't believe what had just happened. I also couldn't believe I was falling apart again. Things had just been made abundantly clear that Ev had the power to heal me or completely destroy me—and the latter option won out. All my time overseas and all the pain I went through with my leg could not equal the hurt in my chest. She completely broke me. I would definitely need professional help now.

Jesus, I hadn't expected to ever find love. And when I finally did, I thought I was the luckiest son of a bitch. But I guess not everybody gets their happy ending. Sometimes life is an unfair bitch. I knew that from my time in the military. I just thought that for once life was going to be kind to me in the love department. But how wrong I was. Love delivered me a five foot nine blonde bomb—bomb, not bombshell.

She obliterated me. That IED hurt less, now that I think about it. But she was going to get a dose of her own medicine. I'm normally not the vindictive type, but she had unleashed a storm in me the likes of which no one had ever seen. There would be no mercy for her feelings. I would move through this fucking place like a force of nature.

Get ready, Ev, because it's coming.

Chapter 25: Stranger Danger

Everly

For a split second, I *let* Stuart kiss me. More because I couldn't believe he was doing it, not so much because I wanted him to. Again, there was attraction there, I'm not going to lie, but I would never go there with him, and I would never do that to the man I love. I lurched back, practically giving myself whiplash. Then I slapped Stuart across the face. Damn him for doing that to me, and consequences be damned if it led to my firing. Hell, it would be worth it because it was not welcome, asked for, or reciprocated lust or desire.

Stuart rubbed at his cheek and jaw. The crack by my hand had made a satisfying echo through the empty office area. I was boiling with anger. I balled my hands into fists. This was the last thing I needed to deal with. Here just when I thought I could get to like Stuart, really started to think he was a genuine guy, he goes and pulls this crap on me. He didn't really seem surprised by my reaction, but I could also tell he was disappointed. *Well, too bad, buddy!* When I'd told him a while back that he shouldn't go sniffing around my bush, I should have pulled out my holiday nutcracker and made my point more clearly.

"How dare you! I have a boyfriend. We fucking *work* together, for God's sake! You have no right to touch me in any way. That was such a dickhead move. So was that all just a bunch of shit that you fed me a minute ago? Was the end goal all along to get me into bed? Huh, Stuart?" I goaded him.

I kept shaking my head. I crossed my arms protectively over my chest. He had about two seconds to explain himself. Now I wished the upgrades to security had already been installed because I'd have his ass on camera. I guess it would be pointless since he was the boss anyway, but I wondered how his daddy would feel about sexual harassment in the workplace. Not that I'd use that angle to advance my career; it would be more to expose Stuart for the snake he was. If his father condoned that type of behavior, then I think others would also need to know about it.

As I had vowed to do, I'd already looked into the deal about his father buying the publication. Everything was legit. I was partly disappointed there was no story to unearth, but I was also relieved that everything was kosher. I really wanted to believe the best about Stuart, to believe he wasn't a slimeball. I was still having a hard time figuring him out, evidently.

Stuart held his hands up in front of him in a gesture of surrender. He was trying to placate me, and I'm sure he was damn worried about my reaction and the potential consequences. Let him try and fire me—see what would happen. I shouldn't have slapped him, but technically he put his hands on me first, so that knee-jerk reaction was more than warranted.

"Okay, Everly. I'm sorry, all right?" he asked.

I was shooting daggers at him and clearly making it known that it was in fact *not* all right. He sighed and put his hands in his jeans pockets.

Wise move, asshole. That's right; keep your grubby hands to yourself.

"I was out of line," he admitted.

"Ya think?" I asked in a vicious tone.

"Yes, I was. I have no excuse. Well, yes, I do, actually. I'm not sorry I did it. I'm sorry about your reaction, but try and look at it from my end. Before you go kicking me in the nuts, just hear me out. Please . . ." Stuart asked, pleadingly and sincerely.

I nodded for him to go on. I wanted to hear this epic excuse.

He cleared his throat. "Look, I've liked you since I started working here. Well, more than liked you. I did mean all those things I said. And no, my goal was not to get you into bed. Of course I want you in that way, but you really are talented and an amazing woman. Don't you see? Haven't you ever wanted something so badly, but it was out of your reach? Haven't you wanted to be with someone so badly it hurt? Everly . . . I just had to know. I just had to know if I had a chance here. I thought I could eventually win you over, but then you got that boyfriend. I guess things are serious. I didn't realize that until just now."

He had a sad look on his face, and he seemed to be trying to accept the situation we now found ourselves in.

He took a deep breath and sighed in defeat. "Like I said, I'm not sorry I did it, but it was the wrong way to go about it. What I *am* sorry for, though, are the text messages. I hope I didn't interfere in your relationship. I realize now that was also the wrong way to go about approaching you. Whether you believe this or not, I was trying to sweep you off your feet, but I guess it backfired. I really do want to see you happy, even if that means you and I will never have a romantic relationship—only a professional one."

I felt slightly better. I think I actually felt sorry for the guy. My face changed from one of murderous to understanding. I *did* know how it felt to want something that badly. But then I finally got what I wanted: I finally got the family I'd always desired. I finally got the acceptance I'd always needed. And I finally got the love I'd always yearned for. I got that with Brent. It would take a while, but I would eventually forgive Stuart for this—as long as he never did it again.

"It doesn't make what you did okay, but I guess I do understand. And you're right—it is serious. He's the man I'm going to marry. I've never said that out loud to anyone, but there it is. But so help me, Stuart, if you ever put your hands on me again without my permission, I will gladly go to prison over what I'd do to you. Boss or no boss. Got it?" I gave him that scolding, motherly look and tone.

He smiled boyishly again, and I relaxed. I really believe I could chock this all up to him being young and stupid. He was such a conundrum. One second he was Mr. CEO in a suit and giving orders, and the next he was back to acting like a dumb kid.

But I couldn't think about Stuart any longer. I had to think about my man. Now that the words were out there about a serious future with *him*, I needed to find Brent. We needed to hash things out and make up. I missed him terribly. It goes to show that even with only one day apart, I felt empty, incomplete, and broken. I couldn't wait to find him.

I said a clipped goodbye to Stuart, and he walked off to his office. I figured he was going off in private to lick his wounds. I didn't waste any time packing up my borrowed laptop and notes and stuffing everything into my tote bag. Then I headed for the stairs. Brent was rubbing off on me with the health crap. Not only did he make me eat more veggies and fruits, but he also encouraged me to exercise. I chuckled at his persuasive ways as I went down the stairs instead of the elevator. Man, that airman had an effect on me.

When I made it to the lobby, I noticed there was some sort of a mess on the floor. As I got closer, I saw that it appeared to be pieces of electronics. No, it was pieces of a *laptop*. I could clearly read the brand, especially since the top and base were mostly intact. The top and bottom had come apart, but I could tell what it once had been. Basically, the keyboard keys and pieces of the screen had flown off. *Hmm. Well, it isn't my mess to clean up.* It made me concerned, though. *Why would there be a laptop broken down here?*

Then I got a sinking feeling in my stomach, and I prayed I was wrong. I scrambled to get my purse off my shoulder and quickly pulled out my cell phone. There were no missed calls and no texts, sadly. But I wouldn't be discouraged from reaching out to Brent. So I frantically pushed his name under my list of favorite contacts. It rang four times and then went to voice mail. I texted him just in case he couldn't talk—wherever he was.

Hey. I tried to call. Where are you? Can we please talk? I really want to see you.

There was no point in asking about the destroyed laptop if it had nothing to do with him or us. So it was a waiting game. If for some reason I didn't get a response, I'd go into panic mode and assume the worst. If I did get a response, that clearly meant he was still talking to me, so that would be a good sign.

I tapped my foot impatiently, wishing a reply would come. Suddenly my sweater felt a little too hot; it was making me perspire. I closed my eyes and bit my lip, hoping against hope that he hadn't come to my office at the exact moment when Stuart kissed me.

Finally, after pacing in the lobby for an hour, my phone buzzed in my hand and made the chime indicating I had a text. I opened my eyes and unlocked the screen. I let out a blessed sigh of relief.

Yes. I agree we need to talk. I'm at my parents' place. They went to Caylan's for a visit. If you can come here, we'll talk.

I hurriedly typed out my reply: *Yes.*

I added a kiss emoticon, so I hoped he would get the message that I was coming in peace. I never use emoticons, but in this case it felt necessary. I walked to my car and drove off toward his parents' condo, feeling like we would surely work everything out.

I truly meant what I said to Stuart. I really did want to marry Brent. The moment he asked me, even if it had been right that second, I'd say yes. There was no point in holding back—we knew we were it for each other. I knew last night had been petty and stupid, and in the grand scheme of things, such a small blip on the big radar of our love. I couldn't wait to fix things between us.

I arrived at his parents' place feeling optimistic. I parked and made my way up to their condo. The building was gorgeous. I was so happy Fred and Milly had such a nice place to live. They really were the nicest people and deserved the best. If I was lucky enough to get to be their daughter-in-law one day, well I'd certainly never take them for granted.

I knocked on the door and smiled, thinking I would ambush him first with kisses, and then we'd work everything out. Well, actually, scratch that. We'd fuck everything out. I missed him so damn much. Not only did my heart ache for him, my body did too. We could do the apologies later. I so desperately just wanted to be close to him again.

It took a minute, but he finally opened the door. I was grinning from ear to ear, so happy at the sight of him. He was buttoning up a flannel shirt as he stood there in the doorway. *Hmm, maybe he just showered or got out of bed.* I was surprised Maverick wasn't there to greet me, but it was quite possible he was hiding under the bed from the Big Bad Witch I was. God, I had to make it up to the poor fella.

"Did I catch you at a bad time?" I teased. I moved in to give him a kiss on the cheek, but he dodged away at the last second.

Odd. I was confused. I frowned, but walked past him on my way into the living room. I guess he wasn't ready to literally kiss and make up. I headed toward the couch, ready to sit down and get comfy so we could talk. But then I noticed there was a purse on the table. I looked up at him as if to ask whose it was. I was just about to ask him out loud when, from down the hall, I heard a feminine voice. As the sound got closer, I could make out what she said.

"Thanks again for letting me come over. I really needed that. You sure know how to make a girl feel better," the woman said in Brent's direction.

What the hell is going on?

It appeared she had either come from the bathroom or the guest bedroom. She was noticeably straightening her shirt as she made her entrance. My quick perusal of her made me realize she was pretty enough. She had short brown hair and seemed to be fit. I wondered if she was one of his old fuck buddies from the base. I kept looking back and forth, from her to Brent. Each of us just stayed silent and unmoving, all caught in the web of an awkward situation. But which one of us was the fly, the spider, or the toad?

Brent stood casually at the entryway, still holding the door open. I was so confused. And then it all became clear in an instant. What I was witnessing was the final end of "us." Pain and devastation rocketed through my body. My heart didn't even register it yet, but I knew any moment that it would crumble to dust like a dried leaf blowing in the desert sky. I doubled over in pain. I had to sit down on the couch.

"I . . . uh . . . err . . . I should get going, Brent. Thanks again. I'll talk to you later," the home-wrecker remarked.

I couldn't even watch her leave. She grabbed her purse off the table and made her escape. Hell, I couldn't even look at *him.* I just sat there holding my stomach, willing my insides not to fall out. I had to think for a minute. I had to not hyperventilate, for one thing. This all had to be some kind of a mistake—or a sick and twisted joke. Surely what just seemed to have happened did not *actually* happen. Surely they did not just fuck in a place *I* wouldn't even dare fuck him in. I wouldn't do that to his parents—and I would never do that to him.

I still hadn't looked up, but I heard him close the door at last. He hadn't said anything, and I wasn't brave enough to start the conversation.

Suddenly I was a little girl again. I retreated into my mind, back to a place where I cowered and made myself small. I wanted to be Strong Everly. Strong Everly would grip his nuts and twist them until they came off. Strong Everly would yell the place down, be able to stand up to him and put him in his place. Weak Everly couldn't do anything. Any second now, I knew I'd need a brown paper bag to breathe into to try and keep from losing consciousness.

"I guess there's nothing left to say," he said solemnly.

He was right: there was nothing to say. He'd just confirmed it. He didn't deny it or try to hide it. So I guess he really had fucked her. *What the absolute hell? He knew damn well I was coming over.* He was the one who invited *me* over, for Christ's sake.

Jesus, he *knew* he'd get caught. Shit. He *wanted* to get caught.

But why?

I swallowed hard and channeled all the bravery I could muster. I'd never had a problem in doing that before. It burned my tongue to ask, but I had to know.

My voice was small and rough, "Why? I just have to know why."

I continued to look down at the floor, staring at the country pattern on the throw rug. I needed something to focus on so I could keep myself in check. He was quiet. A few minutes must have gone by.

Then he finally spoke. "Let's just say we're even," he replied.

At that, my head came up. I finally looked at his face and into his eyes. Where once I thought his face was beautiful and trusting, with the kindest, most heroic eyes . . . what I saw now belonged to a stranger. Perhaps I never knew him at all.

So why had he spouted all that about being in love and needing me? Told me that I was the calm in the center of his storm?

It was nothing but a bunch of horseshit. He lied to me! He hurt me, and he cheated on me!

And what the hell was that supposed to mean about being even?

I'd never cheated on him and never would. I was dying on the inside. What did it matter at this point to try to argue with him and make him realize how wrong he was, though? I didn't know if he was referring to Stuart or someone else, but it didn't matter. None of it mattered. And to think this was the man I thought I was going to marry. This was the man I stupidly gave my whole self to?

I rose to my feet, surprising myself in my ability to get upright. I carefully walked to the closed door. He stood to the side of it with his arms crossed in a stance that showed no mercy. He wanted to do battle, but he had already won. I was defeated, not even a worthy opponent. There was no reason to run up the white flag in this war; there was no need to surrender.

I had lost, and he was the victor.

We weren't too close together, but we were close enough. And I could swear my brain was registering him sniffing the air as I walked by. Funny, I used to do that to him so I could commit his unique scent to memory. But this wasn't funny. None of it was. It was heartache and utter devastation.

Good job, world, you managed to find yet another way to fuck me. Not only did you give me a good stab to the heart, but you finished me off with one in the back.

I shakily turned the knob on the door and made my exit. He didn't try to stop me, and I wouldn't have let him anyway. The truth was out as to how he really felt about me. I guessed I'd never really know why he did what he did—and that was probably the cruelest part about it all. I don't know if it was fear of the unknown in our relationship, or if he got spooked, or if he just got drunk. Whatever the reason, the list of possibilities could go on forever.

I managed to make it out to my car and fasten my seatbelt before I fell apart. The tears were streaming down, and a broken sob came out of my mouth. I leaned on the steering wheel for support. I had to cry it all out before I could be in any condition to drive home to my empty apartment. How ironic that at that very moment it started to rain.

Maybe I shouldn't curse anyone up there, I thought. *Maybe they're tears for me because of what just happened.*

Chapter 26: Go Big or Go Home Alone

Brenneth

Well, I did it. I got my revenge on the woman I love. *Love, not loved. Fuck, I still love her.*

At first, I didn't know if that whole scenario would even do any damage or hurt her. I didn't know if she even cared about the scenario that had just played out before her. Until she broke apart in front of me, I couldn't discern if she was just using me. But it was there in her face and actions; what I set out to do was mission accomplished.

So why didn't I feel better? Why did hurting her gut me more? For a moment, the fact that I *could* hurt her made me feel good, but then shouldn't that have told me something? Why would she even give a fuck if she *didn't* love me? I was the worst kind of bastard. I was also incredibly confused. I had to sit down on the couch and gather my thoughts. I sat in the same place Ev had just occupied a few minutes before.

I replayed the scene in my head. Christ, she had doubled over as if she was in pain. Was she really in pain, or was it all an act? Was it a ploy or ruse? I really didn't think so, now that I examined everything. Did I hurt her so much that I crushed her?

I had just been so mad when I saw her kissing her boss that I couldn't see past anything. I couldn't see logic or reason. Maybe there had been another explanation for all this. I was surprised she hadn't mentioned the broken laptop, but I also really hadn't given her a chance to mention *anything*. It had all happened so fast, and I was still trying to figure out what it all meant.

I really didn't think I could love or live with a cheater, though. For fuck's sake, she was the woman I wanted to marry and have bear my children. But what kind of a man was I to have just done what I did? What kind of airman did that make me? Worse—what if I *did* have children one day and had a daughter? Would I want her to be treated by a man the way I had just annihilated Ev? I was gutted by the thought that the only woman I had ever wanted to have that daughter with was the one I had just destroyed.

God, I wanted Ev. I think I'd take her any way I could get her. I needed her. She was my everything. I shouldn't have assumed the worst until I had all the facts, but yet I jumped the gun and did exactly that before I even gave her a chance to explain what had happened at her office. And I should have stopped it in the first place. Again, I was just so afraid I'd punch Stuart's lights out and end up in jail.

I was still harboring so much anger and guilt over failing Caylan. I had a lot of pent-up aggression toward men who prey on women.

Oh fuck! Is that what had happened? Did Stuart come on to Ev, and it wasn't welcome?

Suddenly, I wanted to vomit. I was sick to my stomach thinking I had just made the biggest mistake of my life.

Why didn't I see these possibilities sooner?

I never would have hurt Ev for anything in the world. I *told* her I wouldn't ever hurt her. I lied, and I failed her. Thinking back to her face and tortured eyes only confirmed I had done all of that.

I wanted to wrap her in my arms, hold her, and soothe the hurts I had caused.

I should have known something was wrong when she didn't want to fight with me. She was lost. She had gone somewhere else. My feisty warrior was shattered. *I* did that. I was supposed to be the one who put her back together, and she was supposed to heal me too. Instead, I took a sledgehammer to us both.

May God forgive me for my sins!

You know, the biggest bitch of it all is that I didn't think I could ever put us back together after this.

Isn't that the cruel ending I deserved? She thinks I cheated on her . . . but I *didn't*. It was pure dumb luck that my friend, Lucy, was in the city and at a restaurant with her boyfriend that very afternoon. While they were there, he dumped her. She took to social media to vent about it, and I saw her post. Since she was close by, I invited her over—to "comfort" her. And being the bastard that I was, I used her.

When I got the text from Ev I was hoping to get, it set the dastardly plan in motion. The timing of Lucy's misfortune—my gain— couldn't have been more perfect. Not only was I a shit boyfriend, I was a shit friend. I'd have to apologize later to Lucy for what happened. We weren't in the same squadron or group, but we were in the same wing on base.

When I heard the knock on the door, I made sure Lucy went to the restroom to freshen up and dry her tears; I had been letting her cry on my shoulder. Before I opened the door, I had purposely unbuttoned my shirt. Now that I could see what it looked like from Everly's perspective, I realized what an absolutely awful person I was to have orchestrated the whole thing. I went to such great lengths to paint a picture of myself as some kind of vengeful beast. Oh, I was a beast all right—and the biggest douchebag to ever have walked the planet.

If I were Ev, I wouldn't take me back.

I had to find her. I had to talk to her. I had to clear the air and confess what I did. I had to hear her side of things and make sure she was okay.

If Stuart had put his hands on her without her consent, then I needed to know that too. I hadn't managed to save my sister from trauma, but I'd be damned if I failed Ev as well.

I loved her too much to let her go. I deserved to lose her, and she deserved better than me, but I was a selfish prick. I needed her. I fucking worshipped her. I would get down on my hands and knees if that's what it took.

I heard the rain hit the windows to the condo.

Well, I wanted a storm, and clearly I brought one on.

***

October 31, 2017

It had been three fucking days since that disastrous night. Three days of torture and torment. It was Halloween night, and I was sitting camped out in front of the TV in my parents' living room, just staring at the blank screen. When I wasn't at work, I had been planted right in the very spot on the couch where it all had gone down. It was like my self-flagellation cell. I needed to atone for my sins, so I held vigil.

My parents were really worried about me, but they tried to not be intrusive. Mom kept trying to spoon-feed me and ensure I was taking care of myself. I was shit for company, and I knew that. Alexi called at Caylan's insistence, trying to give me some guy pep talk, but I didn't want to hear it. He said something about knowing how it felt being in my shoes. *Blah blah fucking blah.* I didn't think anyone could understand how I felt.

I called and texted Everly constantly. She didn't pick up or respond—not even once. I went by her place, but she had literally changed the locks. How she got maintenance to do it that fast I didn't know, but I was threatened with trespassing charges by her neighbor Dawn. Obviously, I agreed to leave.

The final blow to my soul had come earlier that day, when a courier delivered all my stuff. It was sitting on the counter, waiting for me when I got in. I didn't have much at her apartment, but for all intents and purposes, we had been living together. I had kept most of my things in storage in anticipation of us buying a place and starting our lives together. *Fuck!*

I laughed a hysterical laugh that sounded awfully like the Joker in *Suicide Squad*. It was good my parents had left a little bit ago to see Emeline all dressed up as a princess for Halloween. My mom said she'd take lots of pictures to show me later. I was useless and worthless and couldn't even offer a smile for my most precious, beautiful baby niece. I was a mess. Thankfully, my mom put a bowl of candy outside the entrance so trick-or-treaters could help themselves. I was in no condition to receive visitors or act friendly. My face and mood probably would have given anyone a good fright that night, though!

The next day was the same. I did all the mundane tasks at work and tried to keep myself busy. When I got back to the condo, my parents weren't there, but one very pissed-off Caylan was. A light vanilla scent was hanging in the air, which was the telltale sign that my baby sister was around. It was usually a comforting scent, but just then I was afraid of being judged by the one person who always had my back. She was sitting on the loveseat with her legs crossed and hands folded in her lap, just waiting to jump me.

"Oh Brenty-boo, you look awful," she said, calling me by her playful nickname.

Her anger immediately melted away, though, when she got a load of my haggard appearance. Sure, I shaved and wore my uniform properly, but I could only assume my face and eyes showed that I was a dying man. I knew deep down it would only be a matter of time before my mom would sic Caylan on me. I couldn't blame either one, since they loved me so much. But I couldn't even function beyond basic tasks.

Caylan rose to her feet, came over, and threw her arms around me. She squeezed me as tightly as she could for such a little thing. I didn't deserve her love either. She was pure, beautiful, and everything that was right in the world. A sister like her deserved better than bastards like me. I had long ago condemned myself to the pits of hell.

"Where's Em?" I asked.

Caylan held my face in her hands and looked into my eyes. Her face fell at what she saw. Moisture gathered in her eyes. I knew I looked bad, but I didn't think it was *that* bad. I thought I was putting on a good enough front. After all, I had experience with masking my fucked-up shit.

But this time . . . well, this time was different.

"I've never seen you so wounded," she remarked sadly. Then she sighed and went on, "Alexi is with her and Mom and Dad. They wanted to give me time to talk to you. Sometimes I feel like I need to be a big sister instead of a little one. I love you more than life, but sometimes you do some stupid, foolish crap. I mean, what were you thinking? I finally had lunch with Everly yesterday and dragged it out of her. What the heck is actually going on? She didn't tell me every little detail, but I heard enough."

She smacked my chest in a rough attempt at a reprimand, even though it was barely a feather's touch. Then she stomped her foot and balled her fists like she meant business.

"How *could* you? How could you break Everly's heart like that and . . . and . . . cheat on her?" she bellowed.

I scrubbed my face with my hand. I needed a swig of beer if I was going to get into this. I also needed to get out of my damn uniform. I told Caylan to give me a minute while I changed. I assured her I'd explain the whole story.

I returned a few minutes later with a beer in hand and a coffee for my sister. I would have offered her alcohol for this, but she really didn't drink and was still breastfeeding anyway. I marveled at her. She was such an amazing woman, mother, and at that moment, a big sister. She had returned to sitting in the loveseat, and I sat in "the spot." I took a long pull from my beer and then placed it on the coffee table. I stared down at the area rug under my feet.

I proceeded to relay the entire sordid story. Caylan's face ran the gamut of emotions. But she let me tell her everything before she commented. Obviously, she knew Ev's version, but hearing mine allowed me to see that the whole situation depressed her. Even though she thought the worst of me, of course she still loved me and would support me. And somehow learning the truth . . . well, that seemed to disappoint her even more. I could read from her expressions that she was hurting for Ev—and me. Caylan loved happy endings, and she always wanted one for all those around her.

Then she told me Everly's version of the fateful day. The most difficult part was hearing how Everly had slapped Stuart for the kiss that I unluckily witnessed. I needed a minute to get over hearing about *that*. I was so mad at myself for jumping to conclusions. Caylan was reluctant to tell me what really happened at first because she didn't want to be disloyal to Everly, but she prefaced it by explaining she was genuinely trying to help us. She told me that, if I knew the truth, she could help fix things. Thank God I had a beer to help get me through this. I was not much of a drinker and obviously no lightweight, but it helped a little bit.

How could Everly ever forgive me?

I was also relieved that Ev hadn't actually been hurt by Stuart in all of this. I still wanted to kick the fucker's ass, but Caylan said Everly assured her that everything was fine at work. Ev also told my sister that what went down between her and Stuart was simply a misunderstanding of sorts; I was grateful nothing more had happened between them, consensual or not.

After both Caylan and I finished imparting our pieces and sides of the story, we both blew out an exhausted breath. We slumped back in our seats from the weight of the situation.

"Well, big bro, you're in quite the pickle," she expressed while pursing her lips.

That was putting it mildly. It wasn't a pickle; it was bigger than a clusterfuck. I didn't even have a name for a mess of this proportion. I could see the wheels turning in her head, and I just knew she was plotting something, as always—it was the Caylan way. As much as I didn't want her to get involved, I was desperate for help. I should have thought to call her. Why I was such a coward, I didn't know. But I wouldn't look a gift horse in the mouth if she was going to help me.

"I don't know what to do. But I need to do *something*. I can't lose her. I want to marry her, and I don't know how to make this up to her. I don't know if she would even believe me about what really happened," I admitted.

She licked her lips and got that expression like a big idea had just occurred to her. "Well, in my experience, you go big or go home alone. And what I mean by that is you need to grovel at her feet. You screwed up big-time. I'm not going to make it worse by harping on it. I just think it will take some time and planning, but we can fix this. You let me work on her, and in the meantime, you work on pulling out all the stops for the biggest apology you've ever delivered in your life. I mean, you have to come up with the biggest gesture. You need to show your love, regrets, and your commitment all at once. Might I even suggest a real proposal? I don't know what will happen, Brent, but you at least have to try. I'll work on her by laying the groundwork—if she'll hear me out. I will tell her what really happened. I think I have a way with people, and she might listen to me. Besides, I'll use Emeline as a shield of cuteness when I talk to her. I'll take her out to lunch again this week, and I'll start working my magic."

She was beaming, and she rubbed her hands together conspiratorially. I appreciated her enthusiasm and optimism, but I didn't want to get my hopes up. Caylan was right, though. I needed to do *something*. I had to at least try; if I didn't, then what good was I? What kind of a man was I if I didn't fight for what I wanted, believed in, and valued most in this world? I told Everly I fought for those I loved. Well, I'd fight the hardest for her. It was the least she deserved!

I pulled Caylan up from her seat. She yelped in surprise. I hugged her fiercely and whispered my thanks in her ear. God, she was the absolute best. Even if Everly never forgave me—and I couldn't blame her if she didn't—I would not give up on us. I'd carry a torch for her until my dying days. No other woman would ever do, and I had to believe in my heart that I'd find a way to win her back.

Chapter 27: Maverick and Goose

Brenneth

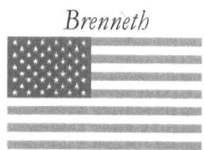

November 15, 2017

It took two weeks to plan my attack on her heart. I had the beautiful ring ready to go—and another surprise tucked inside the cargo pocket of my uniform. I took leave for the day—and the rest of the week—so if things went my way, I could celebrate with Ev.

I even bit the bullet and called Stuart to hash things out. We had quite the long, confidential talk. This talk was overdue, and I learned some enlightening things. He told me several times what a dumbass I was for doing what I did to Ev. At first, I didn't want to hear it from the fucker, but after he talked for a little bit, I realized he had a valid point. I even started to like him—slightly—after he apologized and explained his hand in what happened.

I actually felt bad for the dude. I didn't realize he was in love with her. Even though it made me madder than hell that he had feelings for her at all, I understood that love motivates you to do the best things *and* the very worst things. Not that I needed Stuart's blessing, but I did need his help. I needed him to come up with a story he could assign Ev to cover on the base.

Stuart happily went along with it and said he'd devise something. Plus, he said she could have the rest of the week off too so I could surprise her with an impromptu lovers' getaway—that is, if it worked and she took me back. Stuart promised me he would never lay a hand on Ev again, and I promised I wouldn't break his face. He certainly didn't have his feathers ruffled over it—and he let me know that he was actually more afraid of Everly than he was of me. Good point.

My plan was in place. It was set to begin in the late afternoon. It would be getting dark and colder soon, but the setting sun would be the perfect backdrop for the perfect proposal. Caylan texted me that she'd be there soon, with Everly. I had sent a friend to pick them up at the gate and to pose as their escort to get them on base. I think Caylan gave the excuse of wanting to come with Ev for the "interview," because she wanted more girl time with her. Caylan was a crafty one, and I owed her everything for helping me pull this off. Any minute, they'd be pulling up.

And I'd be pulling off what I hoped was the moment of a lifetime.

***

Everly

Stuart had given me a story to work on that I'd turned down at first because it involved going to the base, and I didn't want to be reminded of *him.* I was so scared I'd run into him like I had so many times before; it would be just my luck. I couldn't handle seeing him. It hurt too much. Caylan volunteered to come along for moral support and so we had girl time. She said she'd be my guard dog while I did the story. I was supposed to interview some officer about deployments and do a human-interest piece. My heart wasn't in it, but Stuart insisted that only I could write the story.

Caylan had taken me to lunch two weeks earlier and had bombarded me with an Emeline cuteness overload. I had a feeling she was buttering me up for something. She started out with pics of the baby in her Halloween costume, then quickly put Emeline in my arms, and made me feed her a meal. I was suspicious of her intentions—I had a keen sense about these things.

Finally, she hit me with it. I couldn't fall apart with Em in my arms. Damn Caylan knew that. I was proud of myself for remaining calm, even though I sucked in numerous gulps of air. I couldn't believe Brent had done all that to me.

Caylan told me what really happened, and I was speechless. A part of me felt better knowing Brent hadn't actually cheated, but another part of me was beyond pissed and hurt that he had *orchestrated* that whole scenario. How childish and ridiculous!

Caylan didn't try too hard to defend him, which I was grateful for.

She just kept reminding me that people make mistakes. She used her story of how she and Alexi got together as an example. She kept hinting that everyone deserves a happy ending. I had to hand it to the girl—she was good. But I wasn't ready yet to forgive and forget so easily. Brent constantly called and texted me, and even finally resorted to emailing me at work. I never answered him, but he still tried. Then yesterday, all communication had completely stopped. I wondered what was up, but I tried not to think too much about it.

The airman who escorted us from the gate pulled up to a large parking lot that looked like it could double as an airfield. My palms started sweating. I was getting nervous that we were either near Brent's workplace or actually *at* Brent's workplace. He'd never taken me there, but we'd driven by it before on our way to go bowling or to the dog park; that's when he had casually pointed it out. I had the feeling this was it, though. But a lot of the buildings on the base looked the same; I guess the dead giveaway was the flight line in the back.

I was dressed in a nice pair of slacks and a beautiful winter-white sweater. My necklace was on display since the sweater had a V-neck. I wore cute boots, and I had let my hair's bouncy curls run free for the first time in two weeks. I had been straightening it for days and days; it didn't feel right to do otherwise somehow. My nose piercing was a subtle silver ball stud. And not that anyone would see it, but I had matched my belly ring to my nose ring.

When the car stopped, I got out; Caylan didn't say anything, and neither did the airman. I noticed a group of airmen in front of the building, in formation. They were in three rows and standing at attention in uniform. The parking lot entryway was a big U shape, and they had managed to pack themselves in tightly between the curves.

Jeez, there must be at least fifty of them. Hmm, maybe they're doing drills?

Obviously our escort knew where he was going. We dutifully followed behind.

We got closer and closer to the airmen lined up, and I wondered if this was some sort of demonstration for my benefit. Were they performing, like, a mock deployment or something for the article? But then a crackle came across a loudspeaker, and a voice carried over the PA system.

My knees went weak at the sound.

It was Brent's voice. He was . . . what the hell? He was *singing*. He belted out, rather awkwardly, the Righteous Brothers' classic tune from *Top Gun*, "You've Lost that Lovin' Feelin'." I let the lyrics seep into my heart and soul. I closed my eyes as the tears streamed down. Caylan was crying too, dabbing her eyes. Hearing her brother's voice pledging his love and devotion to me affected her almost as much.

When the song got to the point where the lyrics said, "I'd get down on my knees for you," I opened my eyes. There was Brent just a few feet away, on his knees, in uniform. I hadn't even seen him approach. It had clearly been a recording of him singing, but it was amazing, and silly, and touching, and embarrassing—all at once. I was laughing and crying at the same time.

I would never have expected this man to make such a spectacle of himself. I could see the guys in formation cracking smiles at Brent's off-key notes and bad pitch. I imagined they had volunteered—all lining up to see this display go down at his expense. He was making a complete fool of himself, and I was loving every minute of it.

He whistled, and Maverick walked faithfully over. The dog proceeded to lick his face and shower him with love. I looked in the direction from where Maverick had come, and there was Alexi holding Emeline, along with Milly and Fred. I was so excited to see everyone. Brent got up and walked over to me. I swallowed so hard. I was breathing heavily, and my heart was fluttering so much I thought it might fly out of my chest. I couldn't believe everyone was there.

When Brent was only a few steps away, Maverick made his way over to me and nuzzled my hand with his nose. I bent down, threw my arms around him, and apologized. I rubbed his head and scratched behind his ears. There was something there. I looked at his collar. Hanging off it was a beautiful white-gold band with a sparkling round diamond. I gasped and looked up at Brent, who was again kneeling.

This time, he was on one knee. I shakily stood up. Maverick sat down beside me, at Brent's command.

"Everly. God, I'm so damn sorry about what happened. I don't deserve you. I know I don't. But I will spend each day making it all up to you. I swear on my life that I will never, ever, hurt you like that again. I want today with you. I want tomorrow with you. I want *forever* with you. I've loved you from the second I met you. Please marry me and be my wife. Put me out of my absolute misery, and give me the chance to show you I can be a man worthy of you. Let me be the Goose to your Maverick," he pleaded.

At that, I chuckled even though I was still crying. I couldn't believe everything he'd arranged to propose. I was overwhelmed. But the greatest emotion I felt was absolute, true love. I was so choked up.

But I managed to squeak out a reply.

"Yes," I said softly.

Hoots and hollers erupted from the guys and gals in formation, and . . . well, the formation pretty much broke up at that point. Caylan was jumping up and down and screaming to the side of us, and Brent's parents, niece, and Alexi all joined in with the clapping and cheering.

Brent stood up and wrapped me in the sweetest embrace, then dipped me back for a scorching kiss.

When our lips fused together, my heart bloomed and grew back like a dying flower that had finally gotten sprinkled with water. Tears formed at the corner of Brent's eyes, but I swiped them away.

I knew we still had some things to work out, but as I said before, in the grand scheme of things, was any of what had happened worth losing the love of my life over? No, it wasn't. What he did was wrong, but I could forgive him. He was truly a good and kind man. A brave man too, and a man who made mistakes. After all, we're only human.

Brent gave me the proposal of a lifetime, and in return I would give him my love and trust. I thought that was the end, but then he surprised me with one last thing. From the side pocket of his cargo pants, he pulled out a necklace-size box.

I took the curious box and opened the lid.

Nestled inside was a beautiful white-gold necklace to match the engagement ring he had slipped on my finger—once he removed it from Maverick's collar. I looked at the letters in confusion, not fully understanding at first whether it was a military acronym or someone's initials. I peered up at him. He chuckled, and Caylan giggled. Clearly, she was in on it. The letters were: TMBA.

"Well, my sister said 'go big or go home alone.' And maybe this is too over the top with the movie theme, but it only seemed fitting. You can either add this to the one already around your neck, or replace your other one. This new necklace marks our new beginning. It means 'Take My Breath Away.' And you definitely do that, Everly Reynolds," Brent said as he smiled.

I smiled right back. I had to rib him one last time: "Umm, you forgot to add, 'Your Highness.'"

Epilogue

Brenneth

December 2, 2017

It was Everly's birthday on December first, so I was taking her out tonight to celebrate. She had turned thirty-three but still told me to "suck it," since she'd always be a year younger than I was. I never expected her stop trying to one-up me—and I wouldn't have it any other way.

We had just closed on an amazing house. We couldn't afford to buy anything near Alexi and Caylan, but we were close enough to them, and still nestled in a great neighborhood. There were great schools with community activities, and even a community pool. Everly and I were both halfway in between our workplaces, so it was perfect. The house was a three-bedroom, one-and-a-half-bath colonial. It had a big backyard and plenty of room for Maverick to run and play.

There were so many great things going on in our lives, we had to keep pinching ourselves. I had sewed on M.Sgt. stripes back in October, so I was enjoying becoming the Noncommissioned Officer in Charge (NCOIC) of my section. Everly finally got a promotion at work, and was made assistant managing editor. She said Steve wasn't going anywhere for a few more years, but that they were grooming her to take over eventually. Stuart even managed to find a girlfriend and he seemed happy, which I was grateful for. I didn't want to invite him to our wedding, but begrudgingly, I knew I had to.

I let Ev plan everything for our nuptials. She wanted a small affair, and our wedding date was set for Saturday, March 3, 2018. I started taking some college courses—paid for by military benefits. I figured with four years to go, I could knock out a degree in teaching and do the Troops to

Teachers program. I thought teaching high school would be the best fit for me, and I thought I had a lot to offer kids.

Speaking of kids, Ev and I finally talked about that. We both agreed we did want them . . . eventually. First we wanted to get married and settle into our lives. So you can imagine our surprise when *three* pregnancies popped up unexpectedly. Ev and I kept joking about not drinking the water in the neighborhood, because we were in no way ready to take that on yet. Caylan was pregnant again, Shanna and Anthony were expecting, and even Pussy was pregnant. We had no idea how the last one had happened, but we were more than happy to welcome little fur babies soon.

I was thrilled when I heard about Shanna and Anthony's first child. Anthony would be a great dad, and he had lots of experience because of being a pediatrician; he was actually Em's pediatrician too. Shanna and Anthony hadn't gotten married yet, but they were talking about next summer, once she had the baby.

Ev and I were even seeing a therapist together. Not just to work through everything as a couple, but also because we knew it would be best to get help for our individual issues. My PTSD was much better and under control. And Ev's panic attacks had all but disappeared. We knew our issues would always be there, but we were taking the right steps in the right direction. I paid for the sessions out of pocket; that way, we didn't have to worry about insurance, or, consequently, the military being involved.

We had seen the whole gang just the night before, for a dinner party at Caylan's. She is the best hostess. It was a great evening with stories, laughs, and lots of fun. I did feel bad for Liz, though, because she seemed more down than usual. Her teenage kids pretty much kept to themselves by playing on their phones or interacting with Emeline. At one point, I noticed Caleb constantly staring at Liz from across the room. I didn't know what to make of it. I knew he had a thing for cougars, but I wasn't sure if that's what kept his attention and focus on her.

But I recognized that look. It was the look of a man on a mission. I kept my thoughts to myself, but I definitely had my suspicions. However, Liz was a married woman. I knew Caleb was an upstanding guy who wouldn't cross that line. I just wished Liz's marriage had been a happy one. She was a great, beautiful woman and deserved to be treated well. Maybe one day things would be different for her.

Everly was back to working on her column about raunchy things. This woman cracked me up with her wit. She thought I didn't read her stuff, but I always did because I was so proud of her. I thought back to one of her pieces that was published over the summer. She didn't think I even knew about it since I had been deployed at the time—I was the *Philly Timez*'s number-one subscriber, though.

We were about to leave the house for her birthday dinner, but I had one last trick up my sleeve. I dragged her through the house until we reached our bedroom. She was giggling about my eagerness to get her in bed, but it wasn't for the exact reasons she thought. I had a hidden agenda. Of course I'd pleasure the hell out of her, but I wanted to prove to her that I actually did read her column faithfully.

When we entered our bedroom, she saw a can of pineapple sitting there on the nightstand. She laughed so hard she fell over onto the bed.

Well, *I* couldn't wait to test her theory out on the taste.

The End

A Force of Nature—Playlist

"Believer" by Imagine Dragons

"Bitter Sweet Symphony" by The Verve

"How Do You Talk to an Angel" by The Heights

"Human" by Christina Perri

"Hurt" by Nine Inch Nails

"I Won't Give Up" by Jason Mraz

"My Songs Know What You Did in the Dark (Light Em Up)" by Fall Out Boy

"One More Light" by Linkin Park

"Say Something" by A Great Big World and Christina Aguilera

"Sign of the Times" by Harry Styles

"Take My Breath Away" by Berlin

"Wild Horses" by The Sundays

"You've Lost that Lovin' Feelin'" by The Righteous Brothers

Teaser: *Nursing Myself Back (A Tryst of Fate Series Novel—Book 3)*

Want to catch up with old friends and learn more about others? *Nursing Myself Back* will be the final book in *A Tryst of Fate Series*. All your favorite characters will make appearances, and you'll finally delve into the lives of Caleb and Liz. Enjoy this Chapter 1 sneak preview, my awesome-sauce readers!

Nursing Myself
Back

A Tryst of Fate Series Novel—Book 3

KARA LIANE

Synopsis

How does one escape the ghosts of the past and still find a way to heal the wounds left in their wake?

This is the third and final installment in *A Tryst of Fate Series,* from breakthrough writer Kara Liane. However, this steamy, contemporary romance book can also be read as a stand-alone novel.

Nursing Myself Back is an exciting and heartwarming story about finding love in the last place you'd look—right in front of you. Cardiology registered nurse, Liezel "Liz" Carter, is a recent widow. She has three teenage children and the untimely death of her alcoholic husband to contend with. Liz never thought she'd be a forty-four-year-old single mother with a broken spirit. She envisioned a different life for herself, but events from her past that could ultimately affect her future have surfaced. What she doesn't know is that the new companionship she's forged with her boss's best friend could be her saving grace.

Caleb Daniels is a thirty-four-year-old divorce lawyer who is definitely ready to settle down. He's been on the prowl for many years, searching for the right woman. His immense attraction to cougars makes things equally interesting and frustrating for him. Chance encounters with Liz have more than sparked his interest—and sparked his libido unlike anything he's ever experienced. Liz thinks she's gaining a friend in Caleb, but he's only biding his time until he can strike a deal with her heart, body, and mind. Will Liz let him nurse her back, or will she sentence Caleb to a broken heart? See what happens when court is in session for these two!

Chapter 1: Dead End

February 22, 2018

He's dead. My husband is dead. I know I'm supposed to feel something, but I don't. Maybe if I analyzed my feelings a little more, I could try to feel some sort of guilt, remorse, or sorrow. I would mourn the loss of the father my children no longer have, but he wasn't a good father, so that's a moot point. Come to think of it, he wasn't a good husband either. He was nothing. Just took up space in our house. I made it a home; he made it unbearable.

God, I probably sound like the most evil woman, but I swear I am not. I feel guilty for not missing him. I feel remorse for not trying to help him more, even though he dug that grave long before the end came for him. And the sorrow? Well, I'm sad that I'm lonely despite having my kids; I have been lonely for years. I don't remember what it's like to feel a man's touch—to feel a man's anything, for that matter.

I've watched a love that continues to grow and strengthen between my boss and his wife for the past few years, and I have been torn sitting on the sidelines. Torn because, on one hand, I am beyond thrilled that he found happiness with the most amazing woman and forged a life he deserves. But on the other hand, I am jealous of the life he has. For I could not—cannot—give that happy life to myself or my teenage children, and it's eating me alive.

I just attended my husband's funeral, and here I sit on my bed while I imagine everyone is downstairs snacking on the food I prepared for the reception. They probably think I came up here to my bedroom to collect myself because of the grief, but that's not really correct. I am a monster for not mourning the man himself. But William is not a man I will miss. He left me long ago, not the other way around. *He* is the monster.

The damn bottle became his mistress. The bottle became his only love. The bottle became his life. I was never anything to him. So why did we get married? Good question. I got pregnant, and years ago we thought it was the right thing to do. What I once thought was love was nothing more than infatuation. Our relationship was simply new and exciting. We both quickly realized it was ugly, wrong, and miserable. I coped with work and my kids, and he coped with his mistress.

Our children were nothing to him either. But they are great kids, and even though my self-esteem is in the shitter, I do take credit for their upbringing. All three are teens now, and I can't get over how the time has flown by. Tyler is seventeen and my brightest boy. I'm so in awe of him. Even with his autism, he makes me proud each and every day because of the way he excels in life and perseveres. Kurt is my fifteen-year-old, and he is one tough youngster; shit, does anyone say "youngster" these days? I'm so out of the loop with the youth, even though three teens live in my house. My daughter, Leah, is such an angel at thirteen. I don't feel I deserve to have such a patient, kind, caring, and witty girl. As she gets older, I can see us becoming best friends. However, right now, I have to be more "mom" than anything.

Yup, my kids still have a lot of growing up to do, but they're well on their way. They teach me a lot along the way too. I'm surprised William and I ended up with three kids, actually, considering he and I barely had a relationship—and that applied to sex or any other marital activity. I guess after I had my daughter, that pretty much was it for us. I can't ever remember making love after that. Well, it was never lovemaking anyway; it was always screwing. It was a way to blow off steam and stress, and we used each other. But one day, we stopped using each other for even that.

A knock on my bedroom door alerted me to the fact that I needed to get my ass moving and go downstairs. I still had to keep up appearances. The kids have had friends and family all day to occupy their attention, and they knew the inevitable was coming anyway. They are brave pillars of strength in all this. I mean, really, with me being a cardiology nurse, I've known for years what would happen to him—and I've made that fact known all along to prepare us. His liver could only take so much before cirrhosis would claim him, and claim him it did.

Good riddance! Shit! There I go again. I am *a monster.*

I swiped at my cheeks to clear off the tears, but my fingers came back dry. Oh, right. I didn't need to cry over William. There was nothing left inside for me to love. I could put on a brave front for my kids, but I had nothing left to offer anyone else. Sure, I wished someone could free me from the loss of love I'd been missing for years, but who the hell would take on a forty-four-year-old woman with three teenage kids? There was no one out there up to that task, and quite frankly, I didn't know if I could—or would—ever open myself up for a disaster of a relationship again. I had been burned before, and I wasn't about to go there again.

That quickly, I had forgotten about the visitor at the door. A second set of knocks echoed through the cold, dark, empty space of my room. I cleared my throat and steeled myself for whoever could be on the other side of that barrier.

"Come in," I said in a choked voice—again, minus the nonexistent tears.

"I just wanted to check on you, Liz," a very familiar, safe voice spoke to me as a man entered.

It was Dr. Alexi Graham, my boss. The familiar and constant man in my life—not like *that*, so don't get excited. I'd follow him anywhere, though. I had been with him for years. I started with working alongside him at the hospital, then I left to help him open and run his private cardiology practice. I was his favorite nurse, but that didn't make me egotistical. It's just that Alexi knew my checkered history. He knew all about my husband. He knew some of my secrets. But Lord, he didn't know them all—no one did, except for the ghosts of my past, and that is not something I'm willing to get into again.

I was always giving Alexi advice long before he met his wife, Caylan. I looked at Alexi like I was his big sister, and I wanted him to find his other half. When Caylan came into his life, it was like the sun shone on him for the first time, and it brightened his very existence. They have a stunning little girl named Emeline, and Caylan's currently in her second trimester of pregnancy with their second child. We're all hoping for a boy this time. They're the most beautiful family, and I do not begrudge them that. It is a sight to see and witness pure, absolute, and true love between two people.

I have been there for several monumental moments in Alexi's life. Just last week, for example, we celebrated his daughter's first birthday. I was there for important events in his wife's life too. They really embraced me as family, and my kids and I were grateful to extend ours to them as well. I was even lucky to have been one of Caylan's bridesmaids when they married in 2016. The girl sure loves pink—and I must admit I was fortunate I could pull off the pink-toned dress she put me in.

I knew I was nothing close to a classic beauty, but for my age, I thought I still looked good. It wasn't about looking good for William, though. No, I kept myself looking good for myself and my kids, and also for my job. I wanted Alexi to be proud that I was the epitome of health, a good example for our patients. Watching my late husband drink himself into an urn really made it abundantly clear that I would always eat healthy and exercise, and encourage my kids to do so too. They each were into sports, and I loved to go hiking and kayaking with them. It was the four of us, and we were content with that.

I could feel Alexi standing behind me, probably warring with himself over whether or not he should extend the hand I could feel hanging in the air and finally place it on my shoulder in a gesture of comfort. The phantom hand meant he cared. I didn't know if I even wanted that from him at the moment. The inner turmoil was about all I could handle.

I fidgeted on the bed, twisting the end of a lock of hair that had been hanging in my face. Today, I was using the hair like a veil or a mask of some sort. If I couldn't see out behind my hair, then they couldn't see in—or so I hoped. My stick-straight hair came down past my shoulders, and was a dirty blonde shade. I usually wore it up in a ponytail or twisted it into a bun; it's not like I had anyone waiting to run his fingers through it, so it never stayed down. But again, today I needed the veil.

I had a womanly figure, of course. Who wouldn't after having three kids? But as I said, I keep in shape and look and feel healthy. I was even told I didn't look my age and resembled someone in their thirties, so that was certainly the ultimate compliment. As long as no one called me a MILF, I was flattered. I just despised that term and thought it was such an insult to women.

Philadelphia, Pennsylvania, was our home. We would not leave it regardless of William's passing. He and I were both from a small town in Rhode Island, but I would never go back there. I never even went back to visit, and I certainly wasn't going to start now. I had no idea who all might be downstairs waiting for me from our families, and I didn't rightly care. At the funeral home, people made their rounds and gave me their condolences. I couldn't even remember who said what, or who was even present. It was still all a blur.

I sighed, but it didn't relax me. I also had to keep blinking due to the harsh light streaming in from the hallway. I wanted it pitch black in my bedroom; it went well with my mood and the color of dress I had donned for the occasion. The blackout curtains were more for me than they were for William when he was still alive. He didn't work, he just slept all day. He went on disability years ago, and I was only all too happy to get out of the house. I didn't have to worry about the kids because they went to school and had great sitters over the years; now, of course, they were old enough to do their own thing. William and I didn't sleep together because when I got home from work, he would already be gone, off to the bar. When I left for work in the morning, he would just be getting home and passing out on the bed in a drunken stupor.

William and I existed as ships passing each other in the night, and we both liked it that way. He didn't do anything family-oriented. We had a dead-end marriage. I guess I really was just waiting around for him to die. He was already dead to me anyway; he'd missed years and years of opportunities with his kids. So why didn't I kick him out or end it long ago? I couldn't even answer that one. I guess I was punishing myself for misdeeds; again, we're not going there. You don't need to be burdened by that sordid past.

"Thanks for checking on me. You know, you're my rock. You say you wouldn't know what to do without me, but I feel the same. Thanks for being here today. I know I'm not much for company, and I feel bad because the kids have to fend for themselves. I'll be down soon, though, I promise." I willed him to go away.

I could hear him breathing, and I knew he was running his hand through his hair, trying to judge whether he should really stay or go. In a difficult sign of acquiescence for an alpha male, he simply said, "Okay," and walked out.

The door shut quietly behind him, and I could hear his steps retreating down the hallway. I was in tune with my surroundings again. I listened to the sounds traveling up from the stairway for a little bit. I couldn't really make out anything, just inconsequential noise. It was comforting, though, and I found myself just sitting there, letting the minutes roll by.

***

Enough was enough. I had probably been sitting there for hours. I figured lots of people would have already left. It was time to check on my kids and come back to the land of the living. That didn't just refer to the fact that my husband's ashes were still sitting on my bedside table. I couldn't bring myself to leave "him" downstairs. This is the screwed-up part about me. I didn't want to spread his ashes, nor did I want to leave him on the mantle. I just didn't want to be near him. Jesus, I couldn't force myself to leave him anywhere else, though. It was only fitting that even at the end, he was a slave to a bottle of some sort.

I had really good night vision now, so I could see the urn clearly, resting lonely on my bedside table. My body was stiff from sitting rigidly for so long. I flexed my fingers and realized I had balled them into fists at my sides. I stretched my neck from side to side, desperately trying to work out the kinks. I dragged my sorry butt up from the bed and made my way down the stairs. There was no one in the living room. I didn't hear anything. Where were my kids?

I trudged through the living room and then headed into my kitchen. Still no one, so I decided to look out back. We had a nice patio area for hosting, and it was lined with patio heaters for chilly days like this one. I was just grateful it hadn't snowed recently. Sure enough, my daughter, sons, Alexi, Caylan, their daughter, and Caleb were out there, talking and watching Emeline play.

I sucked in my breath when I saw Caleb Daniels. It was a shock. I hadn't seen him in a few months—not since the last time we were all together for dinner one night at Caylan's house. I just stared through the screen door at him; luckily, no one had noticed me make my approach yet.

I was grateful I could admire him from afar for a moment. That's another screwed-up thing about me. My husband had just died, and there I was, able to appreciate the male form of another. Okay, this was where the rational part of me wouldn't take a back seat to the feelings I let lie dormant for far too long. Jesus, I was still a woman. I could at the very least admire. I was no longer married; I was a widow. Oh God, a widow, at forty-four. It was still so strange.

Besides, it's not like Caleb would ever be interested in *me*. I would be considered a cougar if I ever went for someone like him. He was what, like thirty-four? But my God, he was magnificent. He was successful, devilishly handsome, and so out of my league.

Caleb was a lawyer by profession, and he reminded me of Keanu Reeves in that movie *The Devil's Advocate*. His jaw was strong and confident. The dimple in his chin was sexy and alluring. His brown eyes were soulful, and the manicured brows above his lashes were captivating. He was a man who took great care with his appearance. But what I appreciated most was how humble he was. It didn't matter that he was successful, he treated you like a person and never flaunted his affluent background. Caleb was the type of man who would make an excellent father, lover, and companion.

Yup, he would one day make some girl very happy. He really was the ultimate catch. I felt something unfurling in my belly—and it wasn't because I hadn't eaten. It was because I was truly and utterly taken with that man. I had seen him at functions over the years, because he was one of Alexi's best friends. But I never looked at him besides being an acquaintance.

I was confused as to why he was even there tonight. We weren't close by any means. Then I realized he was just once again being a good friend to Alexi and showing support, which in turn was supporting me. I made a groaning kind of sighing noise, the kind you make when you look at something you can't have. Crap, I guess it came out louder than I intended, because all heads turned toward me. That was when Caleb locked gazes with my startled blue eyes.

***

Caleb

I would know her voice anywhere. I would know her sounds anywhere. I had been studying her for years. I've always been fascinated by Liezel "Liz" Carter. She was a breathtaking woman. She looked like she was thirty. I had a thing for cougars anyway, but she was hardly a cougar. Nevertheless, I was still drawn to her and could not fathom one good reason why I shouldn't be.

Her face was angelic, and her body was sinful. And fuck me for even being such a bastard in lusting after her when her husband had just died. But I couldn't help it. I plead temporary insanity. Fuck, no, it's *permanent* insanity when it comes to this woman. I have found myself over the last year finding any excuse to hang out with Alexi, just in the hopes of catching a moment with Liz.

I should feel really guilty about her deceased, selfish prick of a husband, but I knew enough about him to realize what he was. Alexi didn't ever betray her confidence, but he apprised me as to the gist of their situation. I knew Liz's marriage was a disaster. I never met her husband, and thankfully I never would have to. He threw away his wife, kids, and ultimately his life.

If Liz and the kids were mine, I'd treasure them. I'd never squander a second of our time. Liz was the kind of woman who deserved to be taken care of for once. She was the ultimate caregiver, but shit, she needed a man in her corner. She needed a man to touch her, caress every inch of her skin, and make her moan. I would gladly be that man for her. I would gladly sign on for a life sentence of being chained to her and giving her everything she needed; she just didn't know it yet. I was biding my time, but I'd make my move soon. I'd testify to that.

***

Acknowledgments

The story of Everly and Brent's romance is loosely based on my personal life experience. So needless to say, this novel was incredibly challenging to write and involved a lot of digging deep to get it just right. How could I do the story justice? Hopefully I nailed it! I wanted it to be authentic, genuine, gritty, and as always, from the heart.

I have to thank my family and friends once again for seeing me through another project, and therefore, another dream. Publishing this second book meant achieving a goal that has been long overdue. I consider myself a humble person, so please bear with me as I put these words out there. I have placed some of my dreams and goals on hold for the sake of my family; that's just what you do, and I am absolutely okay with that. You sacrifice for the ones you love, and that is quite all right. But there comes a time when it's finally your turn. This past year, I've said, "This is the year of *me*!"

I am more than just a wife. I am more than just a mother. I am more than just a woman. I can be anything and everything I want to be. I needed to prove it to myself first, though, before I could show it to the world.

My sons are far from being raised and launched, but I'm at the point where I can ease up a little bit and learn to let them shine when they need to and fall when they must. I always have a pillow in hand, just in case. You get my drift.

So, to my sons: you two drive me crazy, but you make my life fun, exciting, and worthwhile. Don't grow up too fast, kiddos!

Once again, thank you, Mom, for being my ever-faithful, loyal reading buddy! You're the best. Not only did you give me life but you also raised me well. Clearly I am a product of all of your hard work!

Dad, thanks for cheering me on. I know this genre really isn't your thing, but I know you're proud of me nonetheless.

To my in-laws: I can't tell you how much it means to me that you're always in my corner. You're the best!

Fran and John: I will continue to "pay it forward." You sparked something in us as a family, and I will be forever grateful for that.

I have to give a shout-out to all the military spouses out there. You have not only helped me professionally, but you've also helped me personally. I have forged so many amazing relationships over the years. I am indebted to this tight-knit group of warriors.

To my husband, Matthew: you inspired this! You gave me the story. You gave me the words. So, what I can give back to you in return is my whole self. You are absolutely, without a doubt, my real-life hero in uniform. I'd need another book's worth of pages to write my thank-yous just to you. Just know I love you and can't live without you. I don't know what else to say because the rest is private. I get too choked up trying to put it out there. But now that I've shared some of us with the world, I'm going to tell all what I've been saying to you for fifteen years: "Matthew . . . take my breath away!"

It's funny, because I used to be embarrassed to read books like this. I felt like I needed to be proper, demure, and put on this front that made it appear I was something I was not. I finally realized I'm a woman with needs. My husband never made me feel that I needed to be something I wasn't. I was the one who felt a need to project a certain image. I'm glad that one day I realized I could just simply be *me*. I love this genre. No one should have to apologize for loving it. We are women with needs, wants, desires, fantasies. They can be as dirty or as clean as we want them to be. I want to give to you something that you can sink your teeth into and not ever have to apologize for.

Thank you to my beta readers, proofreaders, and copyeditor. It means the world that you helped bring this story to its final stage. I'm truly grateful to each one of you!

So lastly, to my amazing, awesome-sauce readers . . . you keep me going. I began writing for myself, but when I quickly discovered there were people who actually liked what I wrote, it drove me to want to share this side of myself. I absolutely love steamy romance novels. It's not about the kink, though—even if that happens to be a perk. What it's about is the character development, the passion between the leads, the overall story, and the love that only humans can so deeply convey to one another. The human spirit is the most moving thing in this world, and if I've brought a little bit of that to all—or even to any—of my books, then I have succeeded as a writer. My advice is for you to go be you, go do you.

You haven't seen the last of me!

Hearts and smiles,

Kara Liane

About the Author

Kara Liane is a lover of all things romance. She holds several degrees, including a master's in management from Wayland Baptist University. Her husband of fifteen years proudly serves in the military. The family, which includes twin elementary-age sons and two adult dogs, resides in New Jersey.

Stay connected with Kara Liane by visiting her website: www.karaliane.com